TIMELESS *Regency* COLLECTION

the INNS of DEVONSHIRE

TIMELESS *Regency* COLLECTION

The INNS of DEVONSHIRE

SALLY BRITTON
ANNETTE LYON
DEBORAH M. HATHAWAY

Mirror Press

Copyright © 2021 Mirror Press
Print edition
All rights reserved

No part of this book may be reproduced in any form whatsoever without prior written permission of the publisher, except in the case of brief passages embodied in critical reviews and articles. These novels are works of fiction. The characters, names, incidents, places, and dialog are products of the authors' imaginations and are not to be construed as real.

Interior Design by Cora Johnson
Edited by Meghan Hoesch, Lisa Shepherd, and Lorie Humpherys
Cover design by Rachael Anderson
Cover Photo Credit: Servian Stock Images

Published by Mirror Press, LLC

The Inns of Devonshire is part of the Timeless Romance Anthology® brand which is a registered trademark of Mirror Press, LLC

ISBN: 978-1-952611-22-3

TIMELESS REGENCY COLLECTIONS

AUTUMN MASQUERADE
A MIDWINTER BALL
SPRING IN HYDE PARK
SUMMER HOUSE PARTY
A COUNTRY CHRISTMAS
A SEASON IN LONDON
FALLING FOR A DUKE
A NIGHT IN GROSVENOR SQUARE
ROAD TO GRETNA GREEN
WEDDING WAGERS
AN EVENING AT ALMACK'S
A WEEK IN BRIGHTON
TO LOVE A GOVERNESS
WIDOWS OF SOMERSET
A CHRISTMAS PROMISE
A SEASIDE SUMMER
THE INNS OF DEVONSHIRE
TO KISS A WALLFLOWER

TIMELESS VICTORIAN COLLECTIONS

SUMMER HOLIDAY
A GRAND TOUR
THE ORIENT EXPRESS
THE QUEEN'S BALL
A NOTE OF CHANGE
A GENTLEWOMAN SCHOLAR

The Seventh Star Inn

SALLY BRITTON

One

JULY 20, 1816

"Miss Baxter? Miss Baxter! Oh, I have news you simply must hear at once." The shout stopped Susan Baxter where she stood, though her hand rested on the door latch to her home. She turned, a smile already in place to greet her most talkative neighbor.

Mrs. Fanny Hatcher hurried across Fore Street, squashing her bonnet against her head when the wind picked up. For the first week of Summer, it was entirely too cold. But that would never stop Mrs. Hatcher from delivering the tidbits she overheard when serving customers at the inn she and her husband ran.

As she balanced a basket of fabric and notions on her hip, Susan couldn't help the quick comparison that ran through her mind when her neighbor stopped only a pace in front of her, chest heaving as she caught her breath.

Mrs. Hatcher looked every bit a respectable woman in her lovely pink dress, with an excellent figure and lustrous hair curling elegantly in a fringe beneath her bonnet. She and

Susan were only a few years apart in age, but where the innkeeper's wife had curves, Susan had angles. Where Mrs. Hatcher had rosy cheeks, Susan was freckled. Mrs. Hatcher was fashionably petite, while Susan felt like a weed who'd sprouted upward overnight.

"Are you all right, Mrs. Hatcher?" Susan asked when her friend took longer than usual to speak. The inn was only across the street, but the innkeeper's wife had likely run from the back door around the building.

"Fine, fine." She waved a dismissive hand before resting it on her slightly protruding middle. "This little one steals my breath away is all." Her sunny smile reappeared. "He has come at last. He is here *himself.* At the inn this very moment."

Most of the residents and business owners of Fore Street—the town's main thoroughfare from the River Dart—had anxiously awaited word from the new property owner. The Fairchild family had owned land and buildings in Totnes for nearly two hundred years, and when the last Mr. Fairchild passed without a wife or children, no one had known who might step forward to claim the properties.

That the man had come himself, unannounced and without warning, would cause a stir and speculation.

Susan hugged the basket closer to herself and looked up at the Seventh Star Inn across the street, a three-story building painted white with navy blue shutters and eaves.

"What is he like?" she asked her friend, whose usual excitable nature had thrown her into raptures.

"I haven't the faintest idea. Mr. Stonecroft went straight up to his rooms with Mr. Hatcher." Mrs. Hatcher clasped her hands together over her middle, her face glowing with enthusiasm. "I am going to put fresh flowers in all the rooms at once. That he is here at all must be a good thing—Mr. Fairchild never visited at all."

"A good thing," Susan murmured, a little knot of worry forming just below her heart. She tried to ignore it and hope for the best, just like her friend.

Susan put her hand on the door again, her eyes briefly noting a few chips in the mossy-green paint. Perhaps she ought to ready her own dwelling, in case the new landlord meant to look over all the properties he leased to others. "I look forward to meeting him. Mr. Stonecroft. Was that his name?"

"The very one he wrote in the register. I did take a peek at that." Mrs. Hatcher glimpsed the baker coming out of his shop a few doors down. "Oh, I must tell Mr. Giles. Perhaps he can bake us a cake for the occasion. Never tell him I said this, but his confections are at least a smidge better than mine." She winked at Susan, then hurried away with a wave. "Mr. Giles! You will never guess my news." They disappeared together into the bakery.

Susan stepped away from the little green door and looked upward at the old building that had been her home for a decade. The passing of her father had meant leaving behind the vicarage nestled between two hills and moving into town. Above a *shop*. At the time, she felt the world had ended. But Mother had made the best of things, their neighbors had proved kind, and now she could think of nowhere else as *home*.

"Pardon me, miss."

She jolted when she realized a stranger addressed her in the street and turned to see a man standing just behind her. He wore fine clothes and a tall black hat. He was taller than her but only by a few inches. That was the way of it for Susan, being taller than the average woman in Totnes.

She put her free hand to her chest, raising her eyebrows. She might be dressed humbly, but surely no gentleman would address a woman in the street without a proper introduction.

"Do you know anything about this building?" He nodded to the bookshop and her home above it, his blond eyebrows raised. He had blue eyes as cool as the river in winter. They sent a shiver through her.

She looked up at her home. "I believe this particular part of the street was built in the early part of last century. Farther up, there are a few houses dating back to Queen Elizabeth's reign."

"How interesting." He looked up again, then down Fore Street. He faced her again. "I am Collin Stonecroft. I have only just arrived."

"Mr. Stonecroft," she murmured, the earlier shiver now a full shock of cold. She curtsied, basket squeezed against her side. "A pleasure, sir. I am Miss Baxter."

"Baxter," he murmured, narrowing his eyes at her. "Baxter. You live above the bookshop."

She swallowed. Of course he knew her name. Her mother's name would be on the lease for their rooms. "Yes. With my mother, Mrs. Baxter."

He gave a sharp nod of understanding, then folded his arms and looked upward again. "Did you know this building is the newest property on the street?" He then shook his head as though it were some terrible piece of information rather than a mere fact. "Over a hundred years old."

"The inn is even older." She looked at the tall, white structure. "It has to be at least two hundred years old."

"I know." His nose wrinkled with obvious distaste, which was a shame given his otherwise handsome face. The man couldn't be more than half a dozen years her senior, yet he had the gravitas and unpleasantness of a man twice his age.

This is the new landlord? Susan experienced a horrid feeling, rather similar to putting her foot in a shoe only to discover it damp inside. Mr. Stonecroft, abrupt and unpleasant, was not what any of them had hoped for.

When Susan spoke, her words came out almost accusatory. "Everyone has looked forward to meeting you, Mr. Stonecroft."

"Have they?" he asked, as though distracted. The man couldn't even be bothered to give his attention to a conversation *he* had started with a stranger? "Excuse me, Miss Baxter. Pleasure to meet you."

She highly doubted it, given the way he hurried across the street back to the Seventh Star Inn. She watched him go, her perplexity bending mouth and forehead into a frown of confusion. He had sprung himself upon her only to vanish without a word of explanation.

Susan turned to study the building that housed two of her favorite places in the world. The bookshop and her home. She chewed her bottom lip as she studied the old, chipped paint, the ivy climbing one wall, and a barrel tipped on its side between the bookshop and the upstairs door. What did Mr. Stonecroft see when he looked at it for him to frown so disapprovingly and remark on its age?

Her eyes fell upon the loose paint on the door. Strictly speaking, the door's appearance ought to be tended to by the owner of the adjacent bookshop, but Mr. Tipperman was getting on in years and likely hadn't noticed both his shop door and the door leading to the rented rooms above needed attention.

"I do believe I know just the thing," she murmured to herself, tracing a swirling pattern over the chips. She wouldn't let Mr. Stonecroft sour her opinion of her home.

Stiffening her spine, Susan put her hand on the latch and opened the door, closed it, then slid the lock into place behind her. Some of their neighbors forgot to knock before coming up the narrow staircase to the rooms Susan and her mother shared. The bolted door ensured that no one else would surprise her today.

The stairs creaked beneath her feet, the sound as welcoming as the bark of a happy lapdog. She gained the small landing and pushed the next door open, entering the room that served as a parlor, sitting room, and dining hall for her mother and herself.

A fire burned in the hearth against the interior wall, flickering and dancing about gleefully in the coals and twigs. Though it was July, the year had turned unseasonably cold. In a worn velvet chair, her mother sat and worked on cloth tightly bound in an embroidery hoop. Mother looked up when Susan shut the door, peering over her wire-rimmed spectacles.

"There you are, Susan. How is the world outside our door today? As blustery and cold as the day before?" She clucked her tongue and put her work down on the arm of the chair. "Did you find enough scraps for the mending?"

"Yes, and in nearly all the right colors." Susan put her basket down on their small round table near the door. Three of the four chairs around the table matched, while the fourth was a close cousin in appearance.

Should she tell her mother about the strange meeting with the new landlord?

Susan hung her shawl on a decorative hook near the door, then untied her bonnet to do the same. She went to her mother and kissed her on the cheek. "Are you staying warm enough, Mama? Would you like a blanket for your lap?"

"No, dear. I'm well enough by the fire. This unseasonably cold weather is rather off-putting." Her mother tugged her shawl tighter about herself. "And I feel like a woman of eighty years."

"You do not look it," Susan said, lowering herself to the settee on the other side of the worn Persian rug. She studied her mother carefully, noting the grey hair at her mother's temples and the wrinkles around her eyes. At sixty-one years of age, her mother still appeared elegant in Susan's eyes. "I have news."

Her mother went back to her work. "Really? It does not sound like happy news, based on your tone."

Susan picked up a thin cushion from the corner of the furniture and hugged it to herself, tracing the embroidered roses her mother had added to brighten the dull fabric. "Mr. Stonecroft has come to Totnes at last."

Her mother's hand stilled, then lowered to her lap. She looked up at Susan, the twinkle in her eyes dimmed.

The solicitor handling the estate of their late landowner had spent six months searching out the man who'd inherited, and it had taken another three months to receive the news. All the while, everyone kept paying their monthly or annual rents to the estate as faithfully as ever. Including Susan and her mother. Every month, they tucked their banknotes into a wallet and went to the solicitor's office down the street, arm in arm and wearing their best dresses to pay their rent and hold their heads up high. Though their meager income after Susan's father died wasn't much, they never wanted for food, shelter, or medicine because they were careful. And cared for.

"I do hope he is a kind man," Mama said, her nose wrinkling as she thought the matter over. "I suppose he must be an attentive lessor to come and see for himself rather than send a representative."

Best not to tell her mother about her first impression of him then. "I am certain all will be well." Susan gestured to her mother's embroidery, eager to change the subject. "What are you finishing today?"

"Oh, Mrs. Prater brought over the christening gown for her granddaughter. It's the same one her own son wore, and she wanted to add a few little details to freshen it up. They named the little one Margaret, so I thought daisies would be best." Mama handed the hoop to her daughter. "What do you think? My eyes are not what they used to be at a distance, but I feel as sharp as ever when I do the close work."

Susan studied the tiny daisy petals formed from white thread. "Beautiful, Mama. I'm certain all the Praters will be in awe."

Mama laughed, accepting the return of her hoop and cloth. "Mrs. Prater invited us to dinner to express her thanks."

That was always the way of things in their community. The people of Totnes looked after one another. Susan had gathered scraps of fabric from the modiste that day, the seamstress claiming it as a repaid favor for Susan's mother embroidering a pair of gloves for a client.

Dinners, preserves, cloths, buttons, and even goose-down pillows had found their way into the Baxter women's lives. All of it charitable giving from their neighbors but given in a way that allowed Susan and Mrs. Baxter to keep their heads high, that allowed them to save their pennies for the unforeseen needs ahead of them.

Susan rose and went to the window, looking across the street to the inn. Windows upstairs were open, and white lace curtains danced in the breeze. Was her landlord in one of those rooms at that moment, scoffing at the old buildings and people in them now under his care?

They had been content enough without him coming.

Mrs. Hatcher appeared in the street below, a smile on her face and her hand on her round middle as though she longed to hold the child within so much she could not help herself.

Susan's heart gave a familiar twist of longing. Mostly content, she amended the earlier thought, then shook it away. Gratitude would keep her cheerful, as it always did. Wishing for something that would never be would only turn her bitter.

Worrying after Mr. Stonecroft's intentions would cause the same. And she would much rather remain a pleasant woman.

She left the window, a smile upon her face once more. "Let me make us some tea, Mama, and then we can read the book Mr. Tipperman loaned you." Books and tea, a cozy fire, and a comfortable chair—what more could any two women want?

~~~

Sitting at the window of the Seventh Star Inn looking out into the street, Collin puzzled over the woman he had met briefly only moments before. Window boxes full of flowers were beneath every window of the inn and the building across the street—not the most practical thing he had ever seen but eye-catching. Charming even. And the buildings appeared in good repair. No cracked glass or loose shutters caught his eye.

A hand tugged at his elbow. "Papa, can we go down to dinner now?"

Collin looked down into the blue eyes that matched his own, lifting both eyebrows at his impatient offspring. Elizabeth Maria Stonecroft, his only child and greatest joy, stared back with narrowed eyes. He managed not to laugh, schooling his features into an authoritative frown instead. "Beth, what have I said about patience?"

"That it is a virtue every young lady ought to possess," Beth answered without hesitation or conviction, sounding much older than her ten years. "You've also said a young lady ought not to gawk at things in the street, and that is precisely what you are doing, Papa."

He chuckled and held his hand out to her, and she put her slim fingers in his own. "This is very true. I suppose eating dinner would be better than gawking."

Though he had hoped to catch a glimpse of Miss Baxter

once more. He had left her abruptly when he'd spotted Beth waving to him urgently from the window of his room. He'd thought she needed him, but she had only wished to show him the view from her window to the river.

Mrs. Hatcher had appeared shortly after their arrival to welcome them both and tell them all about dinner that evening. She and her husband had been remarkably kind, despite his unannounced appearance. They were among many of his new tenants who likely found themselves curious about him and his intentions for their homes.

He pushed aside the squirming discomfort that came with the knowledge that the livelihoods of several families, even dozens of people, were now tied up in his ability to make sound business decisions.

Collin gave his arm to Beth to escort her down to dinner. As they left their suite of rooms, she looked up at a painting hung in the hall and a bouquet of flowers sitting in a bowl of water just beneath it.

"Papa, it's so lovely."

He nodded his agreement and took in the high ceiling and whitewashed walls of the inn with relief. Everything appeared perfectly clean, with modest-sized paintings and a handsome stag's head clear of dust. Windows high above let in the sunlight and warmed the atmosphere pleasantly. "Indeed, the inn is obviously in good repair."

Mr. and Mrs. Hatcher waited at a table to eat with them, a sign of hospitality, while their staff members served their table and another with two gentlemen who were staying at the inn as well.

Beth's most important question burst from her mouth after they were seated at a table in the main dining room, her eyes on Mrs. Hatcher. "Are there other children nearby?" She leaned forward in her chair, darting a quick glance at her father. "Or a garden or someplace where I might play?"

Collin put his hand on her shoulder, his smile trying to come out again. Instead, he cleared his throat, then met Mrs. Hatcher's curious expression. "We lived in London before this, and Beth did not have many opportunities to socialize with children her age."

They had lived in a poorer neighborhood with few children underfoot. Most were sent to the country, to boarding schools promising fresh air for a shockingly low monthly fee, or were expected to apprentice themselves or work with their parents.

Collin had visited a few of those country schools, and they only made him more loath to send Beth away than before. The low fees were as promised. The accommodations were not at all acceptable. He couldn't afford the more expensive schools in the country, and he wouldn't send his daughter away from him unless her circumstances would be better than at home.

"We have a few children always running about," Mrs. Hatcher answered, looking to her husband as she spoke. "But I cannot say which would be the most suitable companions for you, Miss Stonecroft."

Beth's shoulders slumped, and she looked to Collin with so much disappointment that he took the topic in hand. "Perhaps the vicar's wife would have some suggestions?"

"I'm afraid our vicar is a bachelor, Mr. Stonecroft." Mr. Hatcher exchanged a glance with his wife. "He will not be of much use for that, though his sermons are quite fine."

Mrs. Hatcher tapped her finger on the table a moment, then her expression brightened. "But perhaps I know someone who could help."

Collin watched his daughter's wistful expression change to one of hope. He needed to find her someone. She was too old for a nanny. Would a governess do? And would a governess help his Beth find friends when they finally settled in a house of their own?

He didn't know much about how a man of his station lived, or how to adapt to his new wealth, or how to staff a house. As an accountant for White's, he'd never interacted with the upper classes outside of noting their expenses and dues. If he were alone in the world, he could muddle through without worrying about the social implications of forming friendships.

But he had Beth. And she deserved the best that he could give her.

"We are eager to hear, Mrs. Hatcher."

Mrs. Hatcher's eyebrows drew together. "Well, there is a widow and her daughter. Their mister was the vicar over a decade ago, but when he passed, they moved into town. They still know most everyone."

He barely repressed a smile when Beth made a somewhat strangled sound of eagerness. "That sounds excellent. Where might I find these esteemed women?"

"The Baxters live across the street. They lease the rooms above the bookshop," Mr. Hatcher told them, pointing over his shoulder toward Fore Street. "If you opened your window, and they opened theirs, you could have a conversation over the heads of passersby." He chuckled to himself at the absurd idea. "We'd be pleased to introduce them to you."

Collin's throat tightened as he realized the late vicar's daughter was the woman he had so boldly addressed himself to on the street. A very pleasant looking woman who he had likely insulted with his quick coming and going.

He never had been particularly good at speaking to ladies. While he had approached, he had noted only her slim form and tall figure. When she turned to look at him, and he realized how young she was and met those lovely, dark eyes with his gaze, he'd barely been able to speak to her.

He cleared his throat and forced a smile for their hosts. "Thank you. If that becomes necessary, I will tell you at once."

"Of course, sir." Mr. Hatcher remained pleasant, not even guessing at Collin's discomfort. Dinner continued on with polite conversation, then Collin excused himself and Beth at the earliest opportunity to return to their rooms.

Collin went to the window of his bedchamber and looked out across the street to the bookshop, then the windows above it. The curtains were open, as was the window, and sitting within his sight was an elderly woman.

That must be the mother, Mrs. Baxter. A widow and an unmarried daughter. Would they be capable of helping Beth grow used to this new place?

To live above a business in town meant they lived in modest circumstances. He had seen his fair share of widows come and go from the boarding house where he and Beth had lived for the last eight years. They always seemed rather melancholy women. Downtrodden by life and helpless to better their circumstances. Several of them had acted as caretakers for Beth, feeding her meals and teaching her the most basic things a girl her age ought to know in exchange for whatever small sum Collin could afford at the time.

Beth, an energetic girl with a quick mind, had somehow stayed a cheerful child, despite their circumstances. Now she would never have to thrive *despite* their situation again.

He had money. He had all the time in the world too. Beth would have the very best he could give her—whether a home, her education, or her friends—with or without the help of a vicar's widow and daughter.

Two

Susan didn't particularly care for trout, but beggars couldn't be choosers. Neither could unmarried women in reduced circumstances. So with a glad heart, she handed over her coin to a fisherman's wife. Trout in the summer cost far less than mutton, and the fish was just as nourishing.

She tucked the cut of fish into her basket, along with the dried spices she needed to refill their stock and the once-used tea leaves, dried out again and sold for those who couldn't afford the fresher packets.

As she went about her business, she had to remind herself to put her concerns over Mr. Stonecroft's arrival out of her mind. The man's handsome visage had haunted her thoughts since the day previous, and she still hadn't mentioned their meeting to anyone else.

But today was market day.

Market day meant a lighthearted day of speaking with business owners and meeting unexpectedly with old friends. Friends such as Miss Carter and her devoted companion and former governess, Miss Fletcher.

"Miss Baxter, good afternoon," Miss Fletcher greeted. She was closer in age to Susan than her former charge. "What have you filled your basket with today?"

"Nothing terribly exciting." Susan fell into step beside the two, walking along the boardwalk and peering in windows. "I needed to find something for our dinner table. What about the two of you?"

"Ribbon shopping," Miss Fletcher said, looking at Miss Carter with a raise of her eyebrows.

"One can never have too many ribbons," Miss Carter said with an air of importance common in the youth of her station. At one and twenty, she ought to have perhaps concerned herself with more than adding to her ribbon supply. "Come to think of it, I should like to check at Yardley's to see their new hat designs. Perhaps we could purchase some feathers or silk flowers to complete my current masterpiece."

"I do love a well-festooned hat," Susan said, exchanging a smile with Miss Fletcher. "Especially those clever hunting caps with pheasant feathers. They are quite eye-catching."

Miss Carter beamed as she responded. "Then you must come with us. You have always had a clever eye for haberdashery, Miss Baxter. Come to think on it, the bonnet you wore to services last Sunday had me quite curious how you came by the design."

Susan smiled her response rather than revealing she had pulled apart two cast-off bonnets from charitable neighbors to create something of her own. Despite her financial circumstances, she had a great weakness for lovely bonnets and straw hats. Making her own hats had been something she took great delight in when her father was alive. He used to tease that she would make a better hatter's daughter than a vicar's.

The familiar squeeze of her heart, which occurred every time she thought of her father, was less painful than it had been in years past, but it still came.

Susan realized Miss Carter's smile had dimmed as she waited for Susan to volunteer more information about her hat. "I saw two designs I liked in a magazine, and I combined the upturned brim from one with the braided blue ribbons of the other."

The younger woman's smile returned, bright as the sun. "How exceptionally smart of you."

Though Susan did not miss the tone of Miss Carter's voice—she spoke as she would to a favored pet or child—she chose to ignore it. She held her basket a little higher. "I must beg to be excused, as I need to make my way home and see to our meal preparations."

Miss Fletcher gave Susan an apologetic smile, well aware of the slip in her former charge's tone. "Of course. Good day to you, Miss Baxter."

Susan walked away from the market stalls and headed east to the river where the trout had come from before it met its destiny as her dinner, and returned to her mother and their leased rooms above the bookshop.

First, she ought to see if Mr. Tipperman had taken in any books he might allow them to borrow and read. They had finished *Leonora*, new to them though it had been in print for over a decade, and needed something new to read together after dinner.

As she entered the shop below her home, the bell above the door chimed merrily to announce her presence. The smell of ink, paper, and leather new and old alike, hung in the air around her, welcoming her to this place that she loved as much as she did the home she shared with her mother.

She spied a customer, a girl with long, loose hair beneath her utilitarian straw hat and a rather determined, youthful voice, already standing at the counter.

"Thank you for seeing to my father's order, Mr.

Tipperman. While I am here, do you have any books on hand that we might have this very evening?" The girl bounced lightly on her toes, though she clutched a reticule in lace-gloved hands. She charmingly combined youth and propriety in her person.

Mr. Tipperman looked over the child's head to meet Susan's eyes. "I cannot say I am entirely certain what a young lady like yourself might enjoy, but perhaps Miss Baxter might be of help. Miss Baxter, have you any thoughts on especially entertaining reading material?"

The girl turned around, her bright blue eyes sparkling with interest. "The book is for my father too. We take turns reading before dinner."

Having never laid eyes on the child before and not knowing who the girl's father might be, Susan had to give the matter a little more thought. "Do you like adventures far from England, or things that could happen in this very county?" She walked to the counter to rest her basket on it. "Is your father someone who prefers a good moral to his tale, or does he wish only for entertainment?"

"It appears we have asked the right woman." Mr. Tipperman puffed out his chest and walked to a shelf behind the counter where he kept the used books he purchased from estate sales and schools. "Miss Baxter knows well what is stocked in my shop too."

Susan folded her hands in front of her and regarded the girl with raised eyebrows.

"Papa says that until I am old enough to have clearly developed tastes, I ought to read a little of everything. We read *The Life of Nelson* most recently." The girl's nose wrinkled briefly before she schooled her features into a serious frown, likely learned from her literary papa.

"How did you find the biography?" Susan tried not to

smile, drawing her eyebrows together and pursing her lips with some severity. She supposed Admiral Nelson deserved all manner of pomp and soberness.

The girl hitched one shoulder upward, albeit briefly. "Informative?"

"But perhaps long in facts and little by way of entertainment." Susan raised a finger to tap at her chin. "How do you think you would like a story about a family of girls? Two older than yourself and one about your age, the story relating all they must learn when their fortune turns from good to bad."

Rocking forward and backward on her heels, the child gave the matter some thought. "I am not certain my papa will like a book about girls."

"Oh, there are men too. Good men and bad. Clergymen, soldiers, and kindhearted neighbors. The girls also have their mama to look after them." Susan watched as the child went from being skeptical to being intrigued. Her blue eyes snapped as she gave her reticule strings a twist.

"Then he might like it." She looked toward the corner where Mr. Tipperman dusted the shelves housing old titles. "I think I will take the book Miss Baxter described, sir. If you have any copies in stock."

"A three-volume novel, yes. Let me see." Mr. Tipperman met Susan's eyes and shared a knowing smile with her. Susan had read *Sense and Sensibility* a number of times since it had arrived in his shop. He found all three books, bound in dark green with the title embossed on cream paper and their pages cut long, and put them before the girl. "I will put this on your father's account. If he is not pleased with your choice, you may always bring them back, but be sure to tell him they came recommended by a vicar's daughter."

The owner of the bookshop turned away to go back to his dusting. Susan's heart clenched at the mention of her father and her former honored position in the community, but she smiled when the girl gave her a skeptical look.

"You are a vicar's daughter? But I thought they only read sermons and wore spectacles?"

That image startled a laugh from Susan. "I am afraid I do neither of those things. Does that make me a failure amongst my kind?"

The girl blushed and a genuine smile appeared on her face, revealing a dimple in her left cheek. "I suppose not. I've only met a few vicars' daughters, and I've read the way they are described in books."

"I completely understand," Susan reassured her. "My kind comes in many shapes and sizes, I am sure. I am rather plain and freckled." She pointed to her nose where she knew she had a smattering of spots, which scattered from there, across her cheeks, and on her forehead.

"Papa says freckles can be avoided if one wears a hat and carries an umbrella." She shook her head, her long blonde hair shimmering in the light from the window. Susan had no doubt the girl would grow to be a beauty, based upon her hair and eyes alone. But that dimple would likely break hearts. "I would rather freckle than carry an umbrella with me everywhere."

"Alas, that was also my undoing." Susan carefully regarded again the girl before her. Something about her was quite familiar. "I have never seen you on our streets before, miss. Are you and your father newly arrived to Totnes?"

The child nodded eagerly. "Only last afternoon. We have taken rooms at the inn." She pointed behind her at the door, then her mouth dropped open.

Susan turned to look at the distraction causing the girl to pause.

Standing outside the door, with arms crossed and looking in with raised eyebrows, was a tall, blond gentleman without hat or gloves.

Mr. Stonecroft.

"Is that your papa?" Susan nearly choked on the question. Given the matching hue of the child's and the man's hair, she ought to have realized it before. Mr. Stonecroft glanced away from the child, his eyes meeting Susan's through the window.

The eyes were as cold and blue as the day before, but this time, something other than a shiver affected her upon seeing him. There was a most *distinct* flutter. It entirely discomposed her.

The girl came to her senses first. "I was supposed to hurry. Papa only let me come alone because I promised I could be back in ten minutes' time. Thank you for the books, Mr. Tipperman. Good to meet you, Miss Baxter." She curtsied before snatching the slim volumes from the countertop and rushing from the shop, the bell above the door bouncing merrily as she hastened to join the man outside.

Rather than reprimand the girl, Mr. Stonecroft grinned widely at her and bent to offer her his arm, escorting her across the street to the inn. And that grin transformed him completely.

He looked back once at the bookshop. At Susan? No, of course not.

"Dear me." Mr. Tipperman came back, a book in hand. "To have such energy again! Can you even imagine moving at such a speed?" He shook his head sadly and held the book out to her. "I thought your mother might enjoy this one. *The Mysteries of Ferney Castle*. It came in yesterday."

Susan looked at the slim book and nodded. "It sounds promising. I will let you know how we like it." She tucked it into her basket, then went up the back staircase to the rooms belonging to herself and her mother.

Having multiple entrances to the home proved an advantage many times, allowing her the ability to come and go without too much notice. She could enter from the bookshop's alley door, the bookshop itself, or the door at the street.

Yes, their little home had its advantages.

Once entering their home, she climbed the stairs and went to the kitchen, thinking on the little girl and her perplexing father, hoping the novel written by A Lady would prove interesting to them both.

Three

COLLIN DID NOT IMMEDIATELY knock on the door the innkeeper said would take him to Mrs. and Miss Baxter. He stared at it for a time instead.

The green-hued paint, which covered most of the door, had obviously been there a long time, but the swirling pattern of purple ivy in the center of the door hadn't been there the day before. It swooped and twirled outward, nearly reaching the edges of the door with its heart-shaped leaves.

Someone had taken time to add elegance and beauty to this very plain door—a door he might not have noticed at all had it not been pointed out to him. He had a feeling he knew exactly who had added the elegant detail to an otherwise inelegant door.

"Miss Baxter is plain," Beth had said the evening before. When he had fixed her with a severe look, she'd hastened to add, "Papa, she said it herself in the bookshop. Plain and freckled."

He had only glimpsed the woman in the bookshop, but he knew she was Miss Baxter from the day before. She hadn't seemed plain to him on their initial meeting. He'd thought her rather lovely. He had thought of her more than once and of his horrible manners to her.

Miss Baxter had his sympathy. Not only did she care for an aged mother in reduced circumstances, but she was severe upon herself. It seemed horribly unfair for a woman to describe herself in such a way.

That thought brought him back to his purpose. He had decided to ask Miss Baxter to act as a caretaker for Beth for a short time. He would pay her handsomely, of course, and not require her to leave her mother alone. But someone had to keep an eye on Beth while he went about his business in Totnes, meeting with all his new tenants and going over the accounts.

He'd rehearsed what he would say in front of his mirror that very morning. She was well respected; the Hatchers had assured him of that. The additional income he could provide would also be a great boon to both the Baxter ladies. And it certainly had nothing to do with the strange flair of curiosity he'd felt when he spied her speaking with animation to his daughter.

Collin knocked.

The window above opened, and he stepped back to look up, sweeping his hat off his head at the same moment. A woman with grey curls and spectacles perched on the end of her nose looked down at him. "Good afternoon, sir."

"Good afternoon. Do I have the pleasure of addressing Mrs. Baxter?" He ought to have asked the innkeeper to introduce them, even the innkeeper's wife. But the two were hard at work with a large party newly arrived from London, and Collin needed to see to Beth's needs sooner rather than later.

"Indeed, sir. Who might you be?"

Had Miss Baxter not mentioned him yet? That was oddly disappointing.

He looked up and down the street, noting a few curious glances as people went about their business. Although the network of neighborly gossip had likely spread news of his arrival, he hadn't intended to announce it himself in this way. He kept his voice as low as possible, pitching it to reach her above him and hopefully not much farther. "I am Mr. Stonecroft, lately come to Totnes."

The woman did not appear shocked. Indeed, she smiled as warm of a welcome as if she had expected him. "Do come in, Mr. Stonecroft. Up the stairs, if you please." Then she disappeared from the window, closing it behind her.

Collin followed her instructions, making his way up a narrow staircase with well-worn steps. Someone had thoughtfully added a handrail, the wood new and finely polished. When he arrived at the landing, which was a small square measuring no more than three feet in length, a door opened in the semidarkness, flooding the stairwell with sunlight.

A woman stood before him—not the grey-haired, white-capped female who had greeted him at the window. Instead, he laid eyes upon Miss Baxter. She was younger than Collin, he would wager, with a fresh-faced look and freckles, which made her appear almost impish. Warm brown eyes gazed into his own, her height a near match to his.

She wasn't at all plain.

She wore a drab brown dress with a clean apron, and she transformed her appearance from simply pleasant to pretty when she smiled.

"Let him in, Susan, so we can all be properly introduced." Mrs. Baxter stood beside a chair, her chin high and her eyes bright.

Susan—who appeared far too young to be a daughter to Mrs. Baxter—stepped aside and lifted a slender hand to welcome him into the room.

Collin tore his eyes from her and came inside. Sunlight streamed in from windows on both sides—the room running the length of the building, with doors along the walls not facing the street or alleyway. There were sections of the room, which were easily defined by a table and chairs at one corner, two comfortable chairs near a fireplace, and a small writing desk and chair at a window overlooking the street. One settee sat in such a way that it could belong to the grouping near the fire.

"Thank you for agreeing to see me, Mrs. Baxter."

With a bow to Mrs. Baxter, Collin noted more details of the state of the room and of her clothing. The rugs were worn but the colors were bright, and his nose detected not a speck of dust. The woman's gown was dark, not in current fashion but clean and edged in embroidery that would make many a London woman's head turn.

"You are most welcome, Mr. Stonecroft. The neighborhood has been quite curious about your arrival, especially after all the confusion of whether that solicitor and land agent would ever find our new landlord."

The slim woman came to stand beside the widow, her eyes lowered demurely. Collin kept his focus on his hostess, though he would much rather study the woman at her side.

"Allow me to introduce my daughter and only child, Miss Susan Baxter."

So she hadn't told her mother of their first meeting. All suspicions confirmed, Collin bowed to the woman. "A pleasure, Miss Baxter."

Her curtsy was perfectly correct, her posture impeccable. Though the fashionable world in London might call her plain, as she had so designated herself to his daughter, Collin couldn't apply that term to her at all.

Why wasn't she older? Mrs. Baxter was easily in her

sixties, and was elegant and mature with all the softness of face and shape a woman of that age had rightfully earned. Miss Baxter ought to have been somewhere above forty years, wearing dark colors, spectacles, and a pinched frown.

Miss Baxter met his stare and tipped her head to one side, the angle betraying her curiosity. "Is something the matter, Mr. Stonecroft?"

He pulled his gaze away from her, grateful he had grown past the age of blushing when caught in a lapse of manners. "Forgive me, Mrs. Baxter. I have come to thank your daughter for assisting mine in the bookshop yesterday."

Miss Baxter's soft exhale brought his gaze back to her, and she wore that transformative smile again. "You are most welcome, sir. She bears a strong resemblance to you. I can see that now, with your same-colored hair and eyes."

That comparison wasn't unusual, and the familiar response gave him a moment to collect himself. "Yes, I am afraid she takes those from me. Thankfully, she is as pretty as her mother was and just as clever."

The woman's eyes danced, and he realized they were coffee-hued in the warm sunlight. "She struck me as a thoughtful child, and she quoted you with some diligence."

Mrs. Baxter gestured to the chair nearest him. "Please, sit down, sir. Would you like some tea? Coffee?"

"Do not trouble yourself on my account, madam. I won't stay long." He took the offered chair, turning his hat in his hands, his fingers running along the brim. "Though I thank you for the kindness."

Both mother and daughter sat down too, with Mrs. Baxter in a chair and Miss Baxter on the settee. The elder of the two spoke first. "We know so little about you, Mr. Stonecroft. As we are some of your tenants, I hope that if you wish to know anything about us, you will ask. I imagine it takes a great deal of trust to allow someone to live at your properties without knowing who they are."

"With all sincerity, I am not sure what it will take to be a property owner. I have no experience being a landlord." He rubbed his hand on the arm of the chair for a moment. "Before the solicitor found me, I was an accountant at White's. I managed their bills and balances. The numbers and mathematics are the only thing familiar to me at this juncture." And he had not found pleasure in the work. Totaling up bills for men with more money to spend in a day than a family needed to survive in a year had soured him against those old families and their old money. Their continual insistence on family history and pedigree being the defining reasons they were admitted into the club itself had eaten at him.

Simply foolish men spending money in foolish ways when they could have been improving so much of the world around them instead.

"I did not even think of such a thing—a gentleman's club employing accountants. But I suppose they must, with the amount of money it must cost to run such an establishment." Mrs. Baxter's cheery tone was accompanied by an approving nod. "You must be quite clever with figures, Mr. Stonecroft."

"Perhaps." He shifted in his seat, sparing a glance to Miss Baxter. She sat primly, her hands folded in her lap, completely at ease.

If she was calm, why did he feel so unsettled sitting near her?

"As the rest of the business is new to me, I am afraid I must spend a great deal of time studying it. The contracts, the expenses of repairs, and matters that concern the Totnes council. I am uncertain how long it will take—weeks, perhaps. I intend to keep rooms at the Seventh Star Inn with my daughter, but she is still young enough that being inside all day is akin to torture for her."

At that, Miss Baxter released a light laugh, a most pleasant sound. "I think anyone not occupied with something they enjoy would feel the same. Is that why she ran the errand for you yesterday?"

"Yes." He couldn't help but sound rueful. "And why she has petitioned for permission to run errands for the innkeeper's wife too. I left her busy drawing in order to come here, and I know that will not hold her interest for long. As she is only ten years old, she is not of an age where I can let her run loose in a strange town."

"Totnes has grown swiftly this last decade," Mrs. Baxter added, shaking her head. "I do not know people the way I used to, and it seems more new families arrive every day to work at the river docks."

"The town is still quite safe." Miss Baxter spoke with a tone and an expression meant to set him at ease. "We have a kind magistrate and constables with families, so they are invested in keeping order. Though I agree with you that ten is much too young for her to go about on her own. There are several families who live outside the boundaries of High Street with daughters near her age."

Collin leaned forward in his chair, grateful her conversation had set up his offer. "I am relieved to hear it, Miss Baxter, and I will confess to hoping you would know of such families and children. I have not mixed in their company yet, and my business will keep me from visiting right away to make proper introductions. I wonder if you might be of some help to my Beth in the meantime."

Miss Baxter's eyebrows drew together, and she looked to her mother. "Me? How can I be of help?"

This was the part that was tricky. Despite their circumstances, the Baxters were gentlewomen. He could not offer to hire them as he might hire a maid or a coachman. Offering insults to women in their circumstances would be unforgivable by Society—and by his own conscience.

"I would consider it a very great favor if you would take Beth under your wing, Miss Baxter. Mr. and Mrs. Hatcher assure me that your reputation is above reproach, and they say that all who know you respect you. I have also heard it said that you are excellent with children, and Beth's interaction with you yesterday proves that point. She liked you a great deal, even after just a few moments of conversation." He clasped his hands and sat back a little, realizing he couldn't appear too eager, despite his desperation for help. "If you could help me by minding Beth a few hours each day and perhaps introducing her to other children as your schedule allows, I would be most grateful. I should even be happy to pay you for your valuable time."

Miss Baxter exchanged a puzzled glance with her mother before responding. "You wish me to act as a temporary companion to your daughter? Would it not be better to hire a governess for her?"

"That is my plan in the future. When we return to London, I will seek a governess from an agency there."

"You do not intend to stay in Totnes?" Mrs. Baxter murmured.

Did he imagine the disappointment in her tone?

Collin forced a smile. "I am considering the purchase of a cottage, if only to have a more comfortable place for Beth and me to stay when we come to Totnes for business. But I intend for us to spend most of our time in London."

When Miss Baxter responded, her tone held what sounded like forced cheer. "That seemed to make the most sense for your predecessor too. Except for the cottage part." She brushed at her apron, though it seemed as spotless as when he first entered the rented rooms. "I will be happy to watch after Miss Stonecroft for you, sir, as long as necessary.

And you needn't pay me. Consider it only one neighbor helping another."

A weight lifted from his mind, and Collin could not help but relax into the chair a little more. Yet he could not take advantage of their generous spirits. How could he make it right?

"Thank you. I cannot explain how much this means to me; it is a very great favor, and I intend to show my gratitude somehow, even if it is not through payment." He stood, eager to tell his daughter the good news, then hesitated. "Perhaps we might begin with a formal introduction at dinner this evening? You are both invited to take a meal at the inn with my daughter and me in our private parlor. Will that suit?"

Both women had come to their feet with him. Miss Baxter answered at a nod from her mother. Her dark eyes, flecked with lighter dashes of amber, brightened once more. "Of course, Mr. Stonecroft. We look forward to this evening."

He found he looked forward to it too.

Sitting before the small dressing table in her room, Susan met her mother's eyes in the mirror. "I suppose it was too much to hope that our new landlord would want to be a part of our community." Mother tucked Susan's dark hair into place, securing the modest style with ribbons and pins. They had acted as lady's maids to each other since Father had passed away.

Mother gave her handiwork a final study. "As he has no special ties to Totnes, I am unsurprised. London would call a man such as him back—he is familiar with the streets and people there. Totnes isn't nearly as interesting a place."

"I only wish we had a landlord who knows and understands our ways. Think of all the businesses and families dependent upon him and the decisions he makes." Susan rose from her chair and went in search of her favorite shawl, which also happened to be her second best.

"I agree with you, my dear. But the man will do what he feels is best for himself and his daughter." She went to the door, and once Susan secured her deep blue shawl, she followed. They descended the front stairs together and exited out into the street. Seconds later, Mr. Hatcher showed them up the Seventh Star's beautiful staircase.

"I'm glad to see you ladies here this evening," the inn's proprietor told them. "If Mr. Stonecroft comes to know the best of us, he'll be a better landlord. Make no mistake." He knocked on a door leading to one of the upper parlors.

Susan and her mother had both assisted the Hatchers from time to time. If an unexpectedly large party arrived without warning, Susan had made beds and laid fires alongside Mrs. Hatcher. If a guest needed mending done, Mother had lent her steady hands and clear eyes to the task. Yes, they knew the inn well.

The door opened, and Mr. Stonecroft greeted them. "Mrs. Baxter, Miss Baxter. Thank you for joining us this evening. Beth and I are delighted for an opportunity to come to know you both better."

As he swept aside, gesturing for them to enter, Susan had to temper her surprise as she had when he visited them in their home. Apparently, the frowning man she had met on the street was not who he really was, given the abundance of good manners she had witnessed since.

Then she nearly laughed at the sullen expression Beth wore. The girl appeared far from delighted, though she curtsied prettily in welcome.

Susan addressed Beth with genuine enthusiasm. "It is wonderful to see you again, Miss Stonecroft. Mother, this is

Miss Elizabeth Stonecroft, the young lady I told you about from the bookshop. Miss Stonecroft, this is my mother, Mrs. Baxter."

"How do you do," Beth said, her face stoic and somber. The child seemed to think they had come as executioners rather than friends.

"It is a very great pleasure to meet you, Miss Stonecroft. Have you started your book yet? *Sense and Sensibility* has become one of my favorites."

A flicker of interest came and went in the girl's expression. "We began reading last evening." She looked over Susan's shoulder, likely meeting her father's eyes, before she added, "I think it horrid that the awful brother did not give his half-sisters anything when their father died, just because they are girls. How is that right or fair?"

A cough from behind interrupted anything Susan or her mother may have said on that score, which could have been a lengthy sermon on what women could and could not inherit. Not that either woman would release such a diatribe on anyone, as they had rarely spoken of the injustices even between themselves.

"Ladies, dinner should be here in a moment. I asked that Mr. Hatcher serve it as soon as you arrived. Won't you please sit at our table? It is not much, but I hope you will find the meal and company welcome." He went to the table near the window, covered with as fine a tablecloth as the inn could boast, along with four place settings. The table was circular, but Beth went to a seat with an air of having long since claimed it as her own.

Mr. Stonecroft pulled out a chair first for Mother, then for Susan. Then he went around the table to help Beth into her seat before taking his own across from her. That put Mother on his right and Susan on his left. The door to the hall opened again, and Mr. Hatcher came in with two of the men employed at the inn, and laid out covered dishes on the table. In a synchronized motion, the men removed the lids from the dishes.

"I do hope you enjoy your evening. Please ring for us when you finish." Mr. Hatcher bowed as his employees went out the door behind him, covers in hand.

Steam rose from the still-hot food, and Mr. Stonecroft invited the ladies to serve themselves rather than wait on him. He began a conversation with Susan's mother, asking her questions about Totnes and her time in the town. Susan watched Beth, noting how the child feigned disinterest in the conversation as well as her food.

With voice lowered to not interrupt the conversation already taking place, Susan leaned closer to Beth. "I am exceptionally happy your father came to see us. I have a great curiosity about you."

The child appeared unimpressed by this statement. "Father said you would mind me while he works. Like a nursery maid."

"Is that what he said? The nursery maid part?" Susan allowed her amused smile to show. "I had not at all thought of the arrangement that way. You and I are both only daughters to gentlemen. I thought I might show you Totnes and introduce you to a few girls your own age, acting more as a companion if you'd like."

The frown fell away, and the girl's inquisitive expression from the day before returned. "Really? You mean I needn't sit quietly in your parlor all day?"

Susan laughed. "Dear me, of course not. That would be exceptionally dull."

The other two had noticed their conversation. Mother chuckled too. "Even I do not sit quietly all day when I can help it. I think you will enjoy yourself with my Susan, Miss Stonecroft. She keeps quite busy."

Mr. Stonecroft appeared more relaxed when Susan turned to face him, that strange tumbling feeling in her stomach making it difficult for her to sound natural. "I suppose an accountant must sit quietly all day while doing sums in his head. Do you enjoy silence as a rule, sir?"

"The working of sums is more favorable that way. However, when I close my book for the day, I am happy to surround myself with all manner of chaos."

The man's true, unhindered smile appeared for the first time, and Susan's heart stuttered. His daughter had inherited her dimple from him—Susan had guessed correctly when she saw it on the child. On her father's face, it was absolutely charming. Most definitely capable of breaking hearts. She hadn't been so affected by a man's smile in ages. And certainly not by a near stranger's pleasant expression.

With determination, Susan ignored the unexpected reaction, and looked instead to Beth. "The Totnes races are a fortnight away. I cannot think of anything louder than that—they always hold the registration to enter the races at the inn, so you will see much of the comings and goings involved with it. Will you still be here in a fortnight, Mr. Stonecroft?" She glanced his way with what she hoped was casual indifference.

"I think so . . . perhaps. I cannot imagine settling the matter of the cottage and the rents before then." He lowered his fork and considered his daughter. "What say you to the races, Beth? Should we attend?"

"Yes, please!" She bounced forward in her chair. "Do they hold the races every year?"

"Indeed, they do," Mother answered. "People come from all over to the course. There is always a to-do of weighing jockeys, frightening off dogs, and moving carriages away from the race grounds. This year they are in July, some years, August. But there are always three races. The Totnes Race, the Totnes Devonshire Cup, and the Ladies' Cup."

"Then there are the balls," Susan added, memories of years gone by drifting like dancers through her mind. "Two of them in all: one on the first night of the races and the other on the last. Though I suppose you are not yet interested in attending such events, Miss Stonecroft."

The girl actually giggled. "Not yet. Papa says I will have dancing lessons in London."

"What a wonderful thing to look forward to," Mother said. "I learned how to dance in London too. Here, we have a dancing master who teaches all the young people. Mr. Doughtery taught my Susan."

"Years and years ago," Susan added, dismissing the passage of time with a wave of her hand. "If you'd like, tomorrow I can show you where they will hold the balls. As you are so newly arrived, you must have a tour of our town. We will walk all the way up Fore Street, pass beneath the East Gate, and enjoy the delights of High Street. Then you must see our castle ruins. Every proper English town has a castle somewhere, you know."

Beth's earlier moroseness had vanished entirely by the time they finished dinner. The child had dozens of questions to ask about Totnes and what they might see the next day. When the clock struck seven, her father instructed her to say goodnight and go to her room to prepare herself for bed. She curtsied and promised to arrive on Susan's doorstep directly after breakfast.

When her bedroom door shut behind her, Mr. Stonecroft released a heavy sigh. "Thank you, ladies, for giving up your time for my daughter. As you can see, she is talkative and has a nature that requires her to stay busy. I think today was torturous for her, trying to sit quietly hour after hour."

"I think we will all get on quite well." Susan did not quite meet his eyes, hesitant she might again feel that strange stirring. Instead, she looked at her mother. "Won't we, Mother?"

"Decidedly so."

With Beth retired and dinner over, there was no reason for them to remain a moment longer. Mr. Stonecroft escorted them down the stairs and out the door, all the way across the street to be sure they entered their home safely. He bowed, ready to take his leave, when a shout came from across the street.

"Good night, Miss Baxter and Mrs. Baxter!"

They all looked up to see Beth at her window above them. She grinned gleefully before closing the window and disappearing from sight.

"That was my room," her father murmured, shaking his head at his daughter's antics. "She likely looked forward to doing that all evening."

Susan and her mother exchanged amused smiles before the elder of the two said, "I had best get upstairs by the fire. Even summer nights can be too cool for me as of late. I look forward to seeing you again soon, Mr. Stonecroft."

He said goodnight to her, then fixed Susan with a frown. "You will tell me if she is too much for you—or your mother—won't you? As much as I am glad to have things arranged, I would not put either of you in an uncomfortable position."

"Mother gets cold easily, but her energy is usually a match for my own," Susan reassured him, unable to look away now that it was only the two of them. "She has been speculating all day on what games Beth might enjoy should it rain and trap her inside with us. Besides, I think Beth and I are going to get along splendidly."

Mr. Stonecroft met her gaze, capturing her with those

lovely blue eyes. "Thank you, Miss Baxter. Especially for speaking to Beth this evening. I think I offered her grave insult without meaning to when I told her of spending time with you."

Susan's heart softened toward him. She could well imagine what it would be like, a father raising a daughter all alone, both of them being thrust into a new situation by his inheritance, the little girl removed from all that was familiar to her.

It was no wonder he had seemed cross at their first meeting. Everything had changed for both of them.

"She is the woman of the house. I am certain she feels old and wise and quite without any need for a nursery maid. Never fear. I will make certain she has a lovely time."

Mr. Stonecroft nodded his thanks, then stepped away. "But if you need anything at all . . ."

"I will speak with you, of course." She put her hand on the latch. "Good evening, Mr. Stonecroft."

"Good evening, Miss Baxter."

When she closed the door behind her, Susan leaned against it for a long moment, telling her heart to settle and hoping her stomach would stop its strange dips and dives. She had grown past such foolishness long ago. No matter how attractive she found Mr. Stonecroft or how sweet he was in his care for his daughter, she would conduct herself properly and avoid acting like an infatuated girl of sixteen.

It was for the best, perhaps, that he would not be long in Totnes to distract her.

Four

THE FIRST DAY WITHOUT Beth underfoot, Collin met with four of his tenants. The brewer down the street, a doctor with medical offices, the bookshop owner, and the owner of the bakery. They each presented him with their leases, discussed past arrangements with the former landlord, and reassured him on the subject of continuing payment. None of them assumed the rents would change. None of them thought anything would change, even though they lived and worked in buildings older than the current royal family's claim to the throne.

Collin's account book filled with numbers and figures, with the names of the businesses on Fore Street, and people who lived in buildings under his responsibility. He meant to examine each property after he had other facts and figures recorded because some of them needed to go. They ought to be replaced with modern architecture. Keeping something around merely because it was *old* wasn't a good enough reason for him. The older a building, the smaller and cramped it felt. He knew that from his own experience, boarding in a house built in the 1500s for a grand family, then repurposed to house members of the working class at exorbitant rates with little room for moving about.

When Beth arrived home before dinner, she trailed the scent of flowers and fresh bread into the parlor with her, making him think of a warm hearth and summer gardens.

"Papa, I have had the most marvelous day. Miss Baxter took me to the castle ruins and the East Gate, and we met so many people. Mrs. Giles, the baker's wife, let me help make buns covered in seeds. Oh, here." She held out the brown paper package in her hands. "I brought the one I made for you."

He took the small package from her. "Did you take tea with anyone in particular?"

"We met a Mrs. Innes and her four children at the teashop, and Mrs. Innes has a little girl named Daphne who is my age. I am to visit them the day after tomorrow." She rocked forward and backward on her heels, swinging her hands as she spoke. "They live at the Priory, which is an *ancient* house north of Fore Street."

"Wonderful. I am glad you had a productive day." Collin ordered their dinner while Beth kept talking, describing everything she had seen from window displays to a three-legged cat up on a roof. He hardly spoke a word and, instead, contentedly took in his daughter's happiness.

The next day, he met with three more business owners and two tenant farmers who lived south of Totnes near the river. The farmers shared concern about their crops, but they made assurances that they would pay him the proper rents. One of them lived on land with a ruined mill and seemed quite proud of the fact. "One of the oldest properties in Totnes, and that stone mill likely ground the flour for a king's bread at some point," he'd said.

Beth returned full of cheer like the previous day, this time to tell him all about the Butter Walk and the Brutus Stone. "It's in the street with a little plaque. It says that Brutus escaped Troy and came here to Totnes and built the first house. And that he was the first Britain."

"Is that so?" Collin tipped back a little in his chair, crossing his arms over his chest. "I am not certain I agree with that history."

"Miss Baxter doesn't either." Beth swung her small basket, this time filled with flowers from a garden they had visited with permission. "She says it is a local myth. Then she said it's fun to make believe that strange stories are true."

"Did she?" Collin smiled a bit to himself, picturing the way Miss Baxter's eyes had twinkled up at him two evenings before when she assured him his daughter would enjoy her time in Totnes. "Perhaps I ought to pay Miss Baxter another visit," he murmured.

"Tomorrow we are going to explore Totnes more before I visit the Innes family," Beth reminded him, dropping into a chair.

"Oh." Collin lowered the chair back down to all four legs. "Perhaps I should come. Just for the morning exploration."

"I thought you were too busy to make visits." Beth's forehead wrinkled. "That is why Miss Baxter is introducing me to everyone."

"Yes. Quite right." He sighed and looked to the stack of books and paper on the table. He needed to clear it off before dinner. "Too busy for visits, but not too busy for a little adventure."

"You would have liked the Butter Walk," Beth said, her tone sounding thoughtful. "Tomorrow is only a visit with other girls. Mrs. Innes said we should visit at one o'clock. I suppose you could come with me until then." Beth jumped up from the chair, snatching up her basket again. "I'm changing clothes for dinner."

"You can't adventure all day in one dress and take dinner in the same," he agreed. "I will clear our table for dinner's arrival." He scooped up the books and papers alike and took them into his room where he had a desk to work on. The parlor had been more inviting, however, given its larger size and the table's position near the windows.

Collin went to the window in his room to draw the drapes closed when he spotted the window across the street open, Miss Baxter sitting inside. He opened his own window on a whim. "Miss Baxter?" He did not raise his voice to the same strength as his daughter had before.

Miss Baxter turned and a smile appeared on her gentle face, the same smile that had reassured him Beth was in excellent hands. "Mr. Stonecroft. I see you wish to make use of your window yourself now."

He chuckled and leaned against the windowpane. "Terribly ill-mannered of me I know. I wanted to thank you for spending time with Beth today. She is as happy as I've ever seen her."

"I am pleased to hear it." She peered down at the street, then back up at him. "She is a lovely girl. Her manners and good nature do you credit, sir."

A measure of fatherly pride made his grin widen. "I think her goodness must come from elsewhere. I was an impatient youth at her age." He still was, given his chosen method of communication. "I would like to accompany Beth tomorrow morning, if that is all right."

"Oh?" She drew herself up, and though he could not be certain from their distance, she seemed rather flustered. "Of course. You are always welcome. I look forward to seeing you tomorrow. Both of you."

"Thank you. Until then, Miss Baxter." He closed his window as she retreated from hers. Had he said something wrong?

The next morning, he arrived with Beth at the green door with its deep purple ivy. Beth pulled the cord that rang a bell above them, the sound a cheerful announcement of their arrival. Collin half expected the window above to open with one of the Baxter women popping out to invite them up. Instead, after a quiet moment of waiting, the front door opened to reveal Miss Baxter dressed to go out.

Her brown hair was curled beneath her straw bonnet, and she had a basket tucked beneath one arm. "Good morning, Mr. Stonecroft. Miss Stonecroft."

Beth left his arm the moment Miss Baxter closed the door behind her, slipping her hand into the woman's as though she'd always done so. Miss Baxter glanced at him, eyebrows raised as though to ask if he minded the child's choice. Collin allowed one corner of his mouth to creep upward and shrugged. His daughter had a mind of her own. And Beth was an excellent judge of character.

"Where does our quest take us today, Miss Baxter?" He had joined them with a mind to sit in the parlor for a time and listen to the ladies talk or work on small domestic projects, as his wife had done when she had filled her mornings with embroidery or playing their small pianoforte. But it seemed Miss Baxter matched his daughter for energy and movement, not sitting idle when she could be out of doors.

"I promised Miss Stonecroft a walk to the Leechwell." Never had anyone said the word leech in such a pleasant tone; Collin felt certain. In fact, he did not quite believe what he had heard.

"A *leech* well?" He winced.

Beth giggled. "That is what I said yesterday."

Miss Baxter started off, and he walked a pace behind the ladies on the narrow walk. "Yes, Leechwell. But not the horrid, squirmy sort of leech you two are thinking of. It is a holy well. Or people thought it was, ages and ages past and perhaps some still do to this day. Legend has it that in the time before the Norman invasion, early Christians found the natural well, which comes from three different springs. The water cured them of many ills. It has been a part of our town since the Middle Ages, and it has survived, even though the castle has not, with town wardens assigned to keep the well clean and preserved."

Beth appeared completely besotted with Miss Baxter's historical explanation, looking up at the woman with eyes glowing and a smile on her face. "It doesn't really heal people, does it?"

"I cannot say. In my life, I have heard claims that the water heals maladies. It is certainly sweet to the taste, despite springing up at the edge of our town." Miss Baxter glanced over her shoulder at Collin, turning enough to present her profile. "I should always consult an apothecary or physician before consulting waters for my ills though. What do you think, Mr. Stonecroft?"

"I think people are absurdly besotted by *old* things." When she frowned at him, he continued in a tone more matched to hers. "Though I know people believe that taking the waters at Bath can restore many ills. Why not the waters at Totnes?" He liked the way she raised her eyebrows at that, her smile a reward for taking the conversation the right direction. "Does anyone own the well?"

"It is on private land that belongs to a lovely family. They are quite pleased when people visit the well, though Mrs. James asks the children *not* to leave offerings for fairy folk." That last piece of information was obviously for his benefit and amusement, as Beth's expression turned lofty.

"There isn't any such things as fairies."

"If you say so, dear." Miss Baxter pointed up. "Here we are, beneath the East Gate again."

Collin looked up, noting the archway stretching from one side of the street to the other, the houses built up on either side of it. "Was this part of the town wall in the past?"

"Yes, back when the Normans built the castle," Beth answered smartly. "People live in the archway rooms now, above the street." His daughter began to explain the importance of walls to the Normans and Saxons and everyone who came after. She chattered on with interest and pride in her newfound knowledge obviously gained from Miss Baxter.

The group turned down a narrow side street, walking southward, then down another track covered in dirt rather than stone. They left the houses and businesses behind, and the land on either side of the road was obviously farmed.

They left the road for a lane, and Collin finally drew even with Beth. He looked over her head to a cheerful Miss Baxter, who didn't seem at all put out by his daughter's conversation. She had left talking of walls and castles to instead share what she knew of orchards, which now surrounded them on either side of the lane.

Miss Baxter kept a steady pace. "Ah, the orchards are quite pretty, aren't they? Leechwell Cottage has very fine orchards."

"Is that why you have a basket?" Collin asked.

"Not at all. A woman should always carry a basket, I find. She never knows when she might need it to carry something home." She swung the empty basket. "The orchards here will not have anything other than leaves and tiny green apples at present."

They rounded an ivy-covered wall and there Miss Baxter stopped. "Here we are. The mysterious healing springs." She pointed down rough-hewn steps, and Collin realized with some surprise they had come to an ancient structure. Stone surrounded the well on three sides, the fourth allowed passersby to step down into the cool shelter of the grotto-like structure.

Against the rear wall, three holes appeared in the stone, all of them emitting water from the hidden springs. Ivy grew from one of the walls, creeping upward. Three stone cisterns, carved from stone and smoothed by both time and water, held the tiny pools. The gentle sound of water falling made the small place peaceful.

Beth released Miss Baxter's hand and hurried forward to kneel against one of the basins, and Collin nearly reminded her not to muss her dress. But Miss Baxter stepped closer to him, diverting his thoughts.

The cool air drifted toward them from the shadows of the well, the smell of moss and damp stone wrapping around them, which was not at all unpleasant. It was the smell of life and growing things. He imagined that ancient druid caves and the first stone sanctuaries of monks and saints would evoke a similar feeling.

Miss Baxter's voice lowered, as though they spoke in church rather than in the open air. "You can see why Totnes would not develop the same reputation as Bath. Our pools are small and humble, nothing for the Romans to make grand and glorious."

Collin studied her freckles, the slight turn of her nose, and the dark lashes framing her pretty brown eyes. When he spoke, he matched her tone. "Now that I am here, it does seem rather fairylike."

She looked up at him, skepticism in her gaze. "I think that is the nature of old and beautiful things. They stir our imagination and wake something in our souls. Early Christians saw the springs as miracles. The superstitious see them as the homes of fairies."

"What do you see?" he asked, leaning a touch closer, finding those flecks of amber in her eyes again.

The woman's smile returned, charming and unassuming. Did she not see the temptation she presented, standing there speaking of fairies?

"I see a little girl having an adventure." She nodded to Beth, who had taken a blossom from the ivy, watching it float in one of the little pools. "This was a favorite place of mine when I was her age. I used to come here with my friends to play."

"A charming childhood." He leaned away from her, supporting himself against the stone wall and crossing his arms over his chest. "I grew up in London. My father was an accountant for Lloyds Bank." He had spent his time playing at a little park far from his home where his betters looked down their noses at him. Then he'd been put into school, which was far from home, and given an adequate education until his father thought him old enough to learn how to put arithmetic to use.

There hadn't been gardens, rock walls, or teasing about fairies, only industrious work. The rare walk along a country lane had given him something to hope for. Daily rushing down bustling streets, which teemed with people, noise, and scents not at all as pleasant as moss and spring water, had nearly crushed that hope for better days ahead.

Now he was away from the crowds of London, away from the people who looked down on him and treated those like him as worthless merely because they did not have old names from old families. Totnes felt different, though he could not say why.

Maybe he ought not to be in such a hurry to return to London.

Mr. Stonecroft had grown quiet as he watched his daughter amuse herself with petals and pools, his expression changing from wistful to mournful. His thoughts had pulled him far from Susan, but she did not take it to heart. Sometimes a person needed a moment of quiet to think. She would wager he spent every scrap of time without Beth working through his books, leaving little time for his mind to rest.

At last he spoke, a rueful expression appearing on his handsome face. "I am sorry, Miss Baxter. I lost myself just now. My Beth has spent much of her childhood in a place . . . not as charming as this."

"Your daughter is a happy child, Mr. Stonecroft." She spoke that truth easily and was rewarded by his full attention once more. "I think you have smoothed the difficult path for her thus far."

Mr. Stonecroft leaned closer—as he had a moment before—her stomach again turning into a confused jumble of sensations. Then Beth darted up, dusting her hands off and recalling the attention from them both.

"I like it here," the child declared. "It's lovely. Papa, can we try to purchase Leechwell Cottage? Then I could come and visit whenever I like."

Her father pretended to consider, adjusting his hat atop his head as he did so. "I cannot think it a wise purchase to have a home named after leeches."

"Oh, Papa." Beth came toward them, pressing her hands together in a pleading gesture. "Will you at least ask? Please?"

"You know people around here better than I ever will, Miss Baxter. What do you think? Will the owners of Leechwell Cottage ever be tempted to part with their holy fairy spring?" he asked, bringing her back into the conversation, his eyes dancing with amusement.

"I sincerely doubt it," she answered gently, meeting Beth's eyes. "They love this place very much and have owned it longer than I've been alive."

"How long is that?" Beth asked, tipping her head back.

"Beth—" her father began in a voice of warning.

"Eight and twenty years." Susan had no trouble admitting her age. One look at her and most would know her place in Society: a spinster, too old to be looked at by most men, unless they needed a second or third wife to raise a gaggle of children.

Her cheeks warmed at the thought, realizing she had nearly included Mr. Stonecroft in such matrimonial prospects. *He* would not be the sort to look at a woman of her age and humble position. He was still young enough, and as handsome as Adonis, to have his choice of fresh-faced women with dowries and families of high standing, especially since he had inherited property and a small fortune.

Susan turned away from the well, leading the group back the way they had come. "If you are tired of the well, Miss Stonecroft, I have something else to show you."

Why had her mind even traveled down that old, nearly forgotten path of marriage? She knew her role too well to allow flights of such heights. Mr. Stonecroft, single and handsome, saw her the same as he would a governess or companion, someone to keep his daughter out of mischief, nothing more.

Beth and her father followed Susan around the other side of the well's walls to a small field left uncultivated, waiting for the Leechwell's owners to improve it with more orchards. At present though, it held a great deal of appeal to Susan. And likely to Beth too.

"Oh," the child breathed. "Wildflowers."

The green meadow grass was thick with daisies, buttercups, and ragged robin, as well as white campion and hay rattle. Lazy bumblebees tumbled out of one flower to seek out another, undisturbed by the two-legged visitors.

Susan offered her basket to Beth. "This is why a lady should always carry something like a pail, reticule, or basket."

The child's grin was full and quite contagious as she accepted the basket. "Thank you, Miss Baxter. May I bring some to Mrs. Baxter? And Mrs. Hatcher?"

"Of course. And if you'd like, we can make daisy crowns too." Susan took off her gloves, tucking them into her reticule. Flower picking would leave marks on them that even she would find difficult to remove.

"I've never made flower crowns before." Beth's eyes widened most comically. "Will you show me how?"

"As soon as you've gathered enough." Susan clasped her hands before her and bent closer to Beth. "So you had better get started."

Beth's eyes flashed with joy, an obvious acceptance to Susan's challenge, and she skipped away to a clump of oxeye daisies, her smile as bright as sunshine.

Mr. Stonecroft stepped near, his shoulder nearly brushing hers. "I think *you* might be the fairy, Miss Baxter."

She ignored the way his nearness made her heart pound and her cheeks grow warm. "I think you ought to apologize for suggesting such a thing." From the corner of her eye, she saw his dimple appear, and she had to divert her gaze quickly. "I am a vicar's daughter. You'd cause a scandal if you went about claiming I was from the fairy world."

His answer was a flirtatious grin, which, she told herself, was not at all meant to be as endearing as she found it. The man obviously did not know the havoc his very appearance could create in a woman's heart and mind, even if he had been married before. That, or he knew precisely what he did and simply did not care.

She needed to change the subject to something dull,

something mature and capable of proving she had no interest in flirtations—ah, she had it! "How do you find the leases on your properties, sir? Are they quite in order?"

The grin lessened to a smile and made that disastrous dimple vanish. "The records everyone has kept, including my predecessor's and his man of business, are quite thorough. I will tour the properties tomorrow to look into their upkeep and possible replacement."

Though the word replacement rang as an alarm in her ears, Susan kept her expression pleasant. "You will make an inspection?"

"Something like that." He looked up into the sunlight, then let his gaze wander to his daughter plucking flowers for her crown. "It is my duty to see to property upkeep, but I need to be sure the land and buildings maintain their value too. I had numerous meetings with the land agent and property agent my predecessor employed. Both of them are older gentlemen, ready to hand their clients and accounts down to their sons. It will take time for me to sort everything out on my own."

Susan stared at him in surprise. It was rare enough men spoke to her of weightier matters, but rarer still for her to hear a member of the opposite sex admit to any uncertainty.

He took in her surprise, and the troublesome dimple reappeared. "Do you think me a terribly unfit landlord?"

The question startled a laugh from her. "No, not at all."

"Thank you. I fear others may not feel the same before long."

"I cannot imagine why. You have gone to great lengths to meet everyone, and it shows thoughtfulness to come in person rather than send an agent to act on your behalf." Though his continual references to the buildings' ages and rents worried her, it wasn't her place to comment on such things.

He lifted one shoulder in a shrug. "I need to understand

everything, especially if I am to turn a greater profit. The rents have not been raised on any of the properties in almost a decade." As he spoke, he removed his gloves and put them in his pockets.

An unfamiliar feeling took hold of her then. It felt as though a stone had lodged itself deep within her stomach. "Mr. Fairchild never visited Totnes that I can remember. I think he depended on others to determine proper rent. I know our leases here are not as expensive as in London, where there are fewer empty places and many more people."

Mr. Stonecroft bent down to the ground, plucking a long oxeye daisy that grew near his boot tips. He gave the stem a twirl between his fingers. "You are correct. Totnes and London are far apart in terms of expense and the availability of housing." He presented the flower to her, his pleasant expression returning. "Forgive me, Miss Baxter, for discussing business on such a beautiful day."

She accepted the daisy, hardly aware she did so until their bare fingers touched. As a girl, when she'd accidentally brushed hands or shoulders with a young man she'd admired, she had blushed and stammered; her skin grew hot and interaction became awkward.

This touch was different.

Everything went quiet within and without, and as her gaze rose from the daisy and met his, everything else fell out of focus. She saw only him and everything about him, from the slight wrinkles at the corners of his eyes from time spent smiling, to the way his lips parted with a sudden inhale. The world shifted, but not with quakes and tremors. With subtlety.

Susan tried to speak, to say something, to say anything. What had they been discussing? She could hardly remember.

"Miss Baxter," he said, breaking the silence first.

She blinked, breaking the strange spell that had fallen upon her. Surely, she seemed a strange creature to him. She stepped back, flower in hand, and tilted her chin upward.

"Thank you, Mr. Stonecroft. I'll add this to your daughter's basket." By some miracle, she forced her legs to move and walk away from him. She crouched down near Beth, ignoring the man behind her. Instead, Susan concentrated on gathering flowers for a daisy crown, pretending nothing had happened.

Five

NOTHING HAD HAPPENED AT the meadow. At least, Collin tried to convince himself of that while he and Miss Baxter let Beth make half a dozen crowns and nearly as many daisy chains. She stacked them upon her head, looped them over his hat, and placed the best of them on Miss Baxter's bonnet.

When he handed Miss Baxter that daisy, it had been a weak offering meant in jest, yet in the moment their fingers touched, it had felt like the most significant event in the history of . . . not the world, surely, but in the history of Totnes, perhaps. Brutus the Trojan notwithstanding.

As his thoughts blundered about, he watched Miss Baxter and Beth sit together in the meadow, the shadows of their bonnets protecting them from the sun. They worked together with flowers spread about their skirts, their fingers twisting long stems, and their conversation passing pleasantly. When they put their gloves and hats back on and rose to return to town—Collin to his work and the ladies to prepare for their visit—he remained quiet.

Beth slipped up next to him and left Miss Baxter to walk

a step behind. "Papa, are you going to walk into town with the flowers still on your hat?" She sounded delighted at the prospect.

His father would not have countenanced such a thing, which made Collin all the happier to give his response. "Of course. Soon it will be the height of fashion for a man to wear flowers on the brim of his hat."

His daughter giggled, her sweet voice pulling him from his thoughts. Though she had lost her mother too long ago to even remember, Beth had his late wife's good humor in abundance. Mary, his late wife, hadn't always been content in their simple life, but she had loved to laugh. She had found the good in any situation up until the illness that took her away seven years ago.

Seven years was a long time to be alone.

Collin glanced over his shoulder at Miss Baxter. He knew well enough why he hadn't remarried. He had stayed too busy providing a living for himself and Beth and making his daughter the center of his world. Why had Miss Baxter never wed?

And why did he feel a pull toward her, which was too strong to ignore?

As they passed beneath the clock of the East Gate, Beth released her father's hand to skip forward down the walk. He watched her go ahead, the daisy crown atop her bonnet a cheery banner to all who saw her.

Miss Baxter came alongside him with matching daisies on her hat. "We must make quite the spectacle with our attempt to start a new fashion." She peered at him from the corner of her eye, her lips pursed playfully. "I did not expect you to keep your flowers, sir."

A gentleman walking the opposite direction met Collin's eye at that moment and smirked, not saying a word, though his condescending expression spoke volumes. A subtle attempt at mockery had little effect on Collin, not after the cutting glances from the gentlemen and lords at White's when he had dared leave his offices with them nearby.

In fact, Collin laughed right there walking down Fore Street. He offered an amused Miss Baxter his arm too. When she took it, his good cheer grew.

"My daughter gifted these flowers to me, Miss Baxter. There is nothing as important to me as her happiness. Wearing daisies on my hat for a quarter of an hour will do no harm." He had no one to please anymore but himself. That happy thought had come the moment he knew his inheritance existed and not just on a piece of paper. It struck him anew that very day.

Miss Baxter's expression softened, and she looked forward again at Beth, who had arrived at the green door with its painted purple ivy. Beth did not wait for them before going in—the lapse in manners likely due to her excitement to present Mrs. Baxter with flowers—so when they arrived at the doorstep, Collin had a decision to make.

Miss Baxter released his arm, her hands clasped together before her. Her eyes still danced with her good humor. "Thank you for escorting us on our adventure today, Mr. Stonecroft. We will have tea, which will be something to tide Beth over until her visit at the Innes's, and I will see she is home in time for dinner."

"Will you come for dinner too?" he asked, the invitation spilling from him unexpectedly. He did not need to examine the thought for longer than a moment though—he wanted her to come. The draw he felt toward her would not go away on its own. He needed to understand it, and that meant coming to know Miss Susan Baxter better.

A pretty blush appeared beneath her freckles. "That is very kind of you, but—"

"Your mother must come too. Beth would like to play hostess to you both, now that she knows you better." Perhaps it wasn't fair to use the appeal of his daughter, but Collin didn't want to play fair at the moment. "Won't you come?"

She diverted her gaze toward the riverfront where the tall sails of a fishing boat drifted away like a cloud. Then she appeared to gather herself for her answer and delighted him by delivering a firm nod. "Very well. We will come to dinner tonight."

Collin had no intention of waiting for her to change her mind. Bowing deeply, he took his leave. "Until this evening, then."

She slipped through the door to her home before he made it across the street, and when he swept off his hat to hand it to a member of the hotel staff, he had to grin at the daisy crown wrapped around the brim. The lad who accepted the head piece stared until Collin carefully removed the flowers. "Thank you. I'll keep these."

He went up the stairs to his account books with a lighter heart than he'd had before. The hour and a half he had spent with his daughter and Miss Baxter would be the best part of his day. Until dinner, of course.

―⁓⁓―

Susan and Beth were not the only visitors at the Innes's household. Miss Carter was present too, with her companion, Miss Fletcher. They were visiting the eldest Innes daughter.

Mrs. Innes, a kindly mother and hostess, immediately offered to take Beth to the garden where her younger daughters played. This left Susan in the parlor with the other women. Thankfully, she knew them all well enough to settle herself comfortably and enter their conversation on the upcoming races and balls.

The Innes family was of excellent reputation, and the Priory was one of the finest houses in the neighborhood.

The moment Mrs. Innes returned, she sat with an exclamation. "Miss Stonecroft is an extraordinary child, I think. I have never heard a little girl speak with such maturity, and as I have raised four of my own, I think that should speak to something."

"That is what comes of being an only child," Miss Fletcher said with a significant glance at her pretty young companion. "Miss Carter was much the same when I met her, and she was near the same age. I think it must be their greater exposure to adults in the household, since they've no other children to play with."

"A likely explanation." Mrs. Innes raised her eyebrows at Susan. "Do you think you were that way, Miss Baxter? You are an only child too."

"And a vicar's daughter at that," Miss Carter put in with an airy laugh. "Yours a solemn and mature upbringing, I would wager."

Susan smiled and shook her head. "I am not certain about solemn, but my parents did spend a great deal of time conversing with me. My father and mother were my teachers. I believe Miss Stonecroft's father is the master of her education to this point in her life."

"That says something rather good about him," Miss Innes said, tossing her coppery curls as she turned to look at her mother. "We are to have him to dinner soon, are we not, Mama?"

Susan folded her hands quietly in her lap, anticipating that this part of the conversation would need little of her help. A new neighbor, and a gentleman at that, was bound to cause a stir.

Mrs. Innes fiddled with the broach that gathered her fichu before her. "Indeed. Mr. Innes met him yesterday, and I am determined that we find out all about him. It is no small thing to come into the property that he has. A single, handsome gentleman of his maturity will be quite responsible with it. Especially with a daughter to look after." She met Miss Fletcher's gaze and exchanged a knowing smile. "And it cannot hurt to introduce him to my daughter."

"Mama," Miss Innes cried, blushing in such a way as to take on the appearance of a cherub. The girl had always been quite a beauty. She looked even prettier at that moment of maidenly modesty. "I do not know why you hint at such a thing. Every mother in Devon County will set their cap at him on behalf of their daughters."

Miss Carter sniffed. As an only child and heiress, she had little interest in marriage, and said so as often as anyone would listen. This time, however, she surprised Susan by pointedly turning to where she sat. "What do you know of the Stonecroft family? I heard you were out walking with Mr. Stonecroft this very morning."

All the women stared at her then, the quiet, as they waited for her answer, becoming most awkward. Susan spread her hands in her lap helplessly. "Not much. I was not out walking solely with Mr. Stonecroft. Beth wanted to see the Leechwell, and Mr. Stonecroft asked to accompany her. I imagine he is quite tired of being cooped up in his room at the inn."

That seemed to satisfy Mrs. Innes and her daughter, but Miss Fletcher continued to press. "He must have spoken to you. Tell us, is he a well-educated gentleman? Polite and thoughtful? I heard from Mr. Gregston that Mr. Stonecroft wore flowers on his hat. I did not believe him, but he said you had a matching ring around your bonnet too."

Mr. Gregston, a lawyer who had his sights on marrying the uninterested heiress, *had* passed them on their return from the meadow.

Susan saw Mrs. Innes's deep frown and a less certain version of the same on her daughter's face. Did they think her competition? How unusual! No one ever saw her that way. Not anymore.

She clasped her hands more tightly together. "There were flowers, yes. Miss Stonecroft made daisy crowns at the meadow by the Leechwell. Mr. Stonecroft indulged his daughter by wearing one, as did I." She tried to make it sound unimportant, though she had found it quite endearing at the time.

"Oh dear. A man should never indulge his daughter so much," Mrs. Innes said with a quick shake of her head. "Nothing good can come of it." She frowned at her daughter. "Mark my words, a spoiled child can make a home most unpleasant."

"I do not think he spoils her," Susan said quickly, then pressed her lips together. She had corrected someone higher than her on Society's ladder. Given Mrs. Innes's sudden firmness of jaw, the matron did not care for her words either. Susan quickly continued. "They are strangers in a new place. I think he only meant to give her some cheer." She turned to Miss Carter who had a knowing gleam in her eye. Perhaps Miss Carter would be an ally. What else had she asked about Mr. Stonecroft?

"He is very well spoken, and I believe he must have had an excellent education. Prior to his inheritance, he worked in a respectable position as an accountant for White's in London. He is most thoughtful too. His interactions with my mother prove his kindness." She twisted the finger of one glove. "I find it a shame he will not be a permanent fixture in our neighborhood."

"What?" Miss Innes squeaked. "What do you mean? He told Papa he means to buy a cottage or house near Totnes." She looked at her mother. "That is what he said, isn't it?"

"I have heard Mr. Stonecroft say the same," Susan hastened to explain. "He also said he intends to return to London as soon as possible and take up a lease there too. Totnes will not be his primary home."

Mrs. Innes narrowed her eyes at Susan. "You know a great deal about his personal business for someone who claimed to know nothing at all."

Susan felt her face grow cold, then hot, though why, she did not know. What might be Mrs. Innes's reaction if she learned that Susan and her mother would take dinner with the Stonecrofts for the second time that evening?

Miss Fletcher came to her rescue, inserting herself into the conversation by bringing up a brother who owned three houses all across the country and visited each of them four months of the year. She kept her cheerful chatter going until Miss Carter and Miss Innes joined her, their voices rising and falling like songbirds chirping in the trees.

Mrs. Innes eventually turned her attention away from Susan. Mrs. Innes and her daughter had clearly already formed notions and hopes about Mr. Stonecroft. The thought did not distress her though. Instead, she soon found herself smiling as she thought of the moment he had taken her arm in the street, laughing with his daisy-covered hat. Then he had invited her and her mother to dine with them.

He was a gentleman and a charming one at that. Because he would leave soon, Susan did not worry overmuch about forming an attachment, even if it would be easy. He would be gone before genuine affection—one-sided as she guessed it would be—could take root in her heart.

His daughter was a joy to look after. He was kind. That was all that mattered at the present.

Six

AS THE DINNER HOUR approached, Collin kept fidgeting with his pen. He had already sharpened it, had swept his work away, and dressed for the evening too. Beth sat at the parlor window, watching for their guests to open their door across the street. She wore one of the slightly wilted daisy crowns in her hair and her favorite yellow dress to match. She had been full of conversation about her time with the Innes children, assuring him she had enjoyed her time with children her own age tremendously.

Finally, Collin put his pen down and rose to join his daughter at the window. "Watching will not make them come any sooner."

"I know. But it is something to do, and there are other interesting things that happen in the street." She pointed to a barrel tipped on its side outside the bookshop. "There is a cat in that barrel. Every time someone passes, it reaches out a paw to swipe at them. People always look, but never see the cat."

Collin focused on the barrel in question just in time to see two women hurrying past. The cat paw appeared, caught one of the women's skirts, but released it and disappeared as the woman turned to see if her dress had caught on something.

Beth giggled, and he had to grin too. "A clever and mean-spirited little animal."

"I doubt he is mean. He is probably only bored. Or lonely." She pointed to the Baxters' window. "Oh, look. The light has gone out."

Anticipation tickled his stomach as though he had swallowed a loose feather. "You really ought not to spy on our neighbors." Never mind that he wanted them to come as much as she. Something about seeing Miss Baxter again put his mind in an excitable state. Though they barely knew one another, he had the feeling that he truly *wanted* to know her.

"It isn't spying," she protested, pressing her nose to the window to watch the green door. "Not if we are waiting on them."

His daughter was as eager as he was to begin the evening. "You left their company less than an hour ago."

With the sweet simplicity of youth, she smiled up at him without a hint of chagrin. "I know. I like them so much that it seems much longer than that."

He understood the sentiment perfectly. When the purple-ivied door opened, Collin leaned forward with as much giddiness as his daughter. Mrs. Baxter came out first, dressed for dinner, then Miss Baxter closed the door behind them. She wore a deep blue gown and a daisy tucked behind one ear.

They both looked up, and Beth waved merrily while Collin tried not to grin like a fool. Miss Baxter waved back at Beth, though her eyes met Collin's and stayed there for a moment. What did she think about catching him watching her?

"Why don't you save Mr. Hatcher trouble and escort them up?" Collin asked Beth, though the temptation for him to go down and be the first to greet Miss Baxter came to mind first.

Beth slid off the window seat and left the room in a hurry. Collin took the moment of solitude he had bought to compose himself. He stood and tugged at his coat, pulling it down at the sleeves and waist. Then he ran a hand through his hair and released a slow breath.

There was nothing to be nervous about inviting two women to dinner. Even if one of them had captured his attention in a way he could not begin to understand, let alone explain. But for the first time since he'd lost his wife, he felt an interest in coming to know someone else—coming to know Miss Baxter. And he had time, too. He wasn't working at White's to balance the books from sunup to sundown. He didn't have to sacrifice his own social needs to see to Beth's. His inheritance had gifted him with all the time he would ever need to spend with his daughter *and* find his own path again.

When Beth entered with the ladies behind her, Collin stepped forward and bowed to them. "Mrs. Baxter, a pleasure to see you again. I am delighted you could come this evening."

"As am I. Thank you for having us again." The woman tucked her shawl a little closer, then put her hand on Beth's shoulder. "Miss Stonecroft wanted to show me the daisies in her room. Would that be all right with you, sir?"

"Of course. Please." He gestured to Beth's door, and Beth wasted no time in taking Mrs. Baxter by the hand to lead her into the room.

"You must have one of the crowns," Beth said brightly. "Even if you don't wear it to dinner."

Miss Baxter wore a soft smile, which communicated her happiness of the scene as her mother and Beth disappeared. "Your daughter is as kind as she is clever."

He stepped nearer to her, deliberately moving slowly. "Thank you. I am grateful you do not mind her company."

"Mind it?" Miss Baxter scoffed cheerfully. "Your sweet Beth is a breath of fresh air in our home. My mother adores her too."

"I'm glad. The feeling is mutual. Beth adores you both." He stood less than a pace away from her, enjoying the way the later afternoon sunlight bathed the room and her frame in shades of gold. The sun wouldn't set for several hours yet, but he wondered what she would look like in the softer light of the lamps.

Miss Baxter kept her eyes on his, her height making it an easy thing for them to squarely meet each other's gaze.

"It's interesting how one can come to feel they know someone so well after such a short time," she murmured, her dark eyes studying him.

Did she guess he felt that way about her?

⁓⁓⁓

Susan didn't know when the world had grown so quiet, only that it had. She didn't know how long she stood there either, looking into Mr. Stonecroft's glimmering blue eyes. He didn't seem to mind her staring, given how still he stood, letting her look her fill. Could he guess at the strange turn in her thoughts when it came to him?

She turned away first and went to the window, looking down at the street. She saw Mr. Tipperman's cat up to its usual tricks in the barrel, and the amusement it stirred set her more at ease.

There was no reason to be nervous. Totnes was her home, the innkeeper and his wife were her friends, and Mr. Stonecroft was the father of a sweet little girl. Yet when she turned again, ready to ask him how he had passed his afternoon, she found him watching. All the strange feelings of anticipation she'd had bubbled up inside her again.

Perhaps he felt something too. He looked away, a sheepish smile tugging at his lips. "I apologize. I was admiring your hair ornament. I cannot think of where you could come by such a unique piece."

She reflexively put her hand to the daisy tucked behind her ear and laughed, the sound breathier than she liked, but at least it broke some of the tension. "I promised Miss Stonecroft I'd wear one of our daisies when she told me she would keep her crown on for dinner."

He folded his arms across his chest, one corner of his mouth higher than the other to hint at that dimple she liked far too much. "It suits you both. Miss Baxter, you may call her Beth if you wish. She is still quite young."

Susan lowered her eyes to the richly patterned carpet, its floral pattern and whirls as confusing as her thoughts. "Perhaps, if she wishes it."

A knock at the door announced their dinner, served by Mr. Hatcher and his male servants as before. Mother and Beth came out of the child's room at the same moment, with the elder woman wearing a daisy chain over her fichu. They were talking cheerily about Beth's day, and after the bustle of everyone taking their seats and filling their plates, Mr. Stonecroft joined the conversation.

"It sounds as though I will enjoy taking dinner with the Innes family tomorrow evening, based on your report, Beth."

"They seemed quite eager to meet you," Susan added, thinking of the dark frowns Mrs. Innes had sent her way as if Susan was competition for the younger, prettier daughters of that family.

Beth, with no preamble, blurted out, "Daphne Innes said her oldest sister wants to marry you, Papa."

The three adults at the table froze, and Susan's lips parted, though she could not think of what to say about the announcement. Her mother's eyes widened, and she looked to Susan as though for confirmation of the statement.

Mr. Stonecroft startled them all when he released a deep, rich laugh. "Does she now? Brave of the girl, considering we've never met. I believe she's all of eighteen years old, too." He looked to Susan for confirmation, and she nodded once, still startled by his reaction. "And how does the child's mother feel about that decision?"

Before Susan answered, Beth did. "Daphne says it's all they've talked about since they found out you weren't an old man. She said one of her sisters could be my stepmother. Papa, you aren't going to marry one of them, are you? Daphne says that Miss Innes is horrid to her, always calling her a baby. I'm the same age as Daphne, and I'm not a baby."

Susan watched him with fascination. Most gentlemen of her acquaintance would have interrupted their children before so many words spilled out and certainly would not have treated the situation with humor.

"Beth." He covered his mouth with his napkin a moment, looking first to Mother, then to Susan, his eyes still dancing with good humor. "I have no intention of wedding someone as young as Miss Innes. I hope that puts your mind at ease. Now, we need to apologize to Mrs. Baxter and her daughter for having such a personal conversation with guests present."

Susan relaxed. "It hasn't unsettled us in the least, Mr. Stonecroft." In fact, she grew more comfortable in the room. More comfortable near him.

"Not at all," Mother agreed. "Beth obviously needed to address her concerns."

Beth blushed and dipped her head lower, but Mother soon had the child engaged happily again by relating stories of Totnes when she first came to the town as a bride.

When the dinner hour ended, Beth pleaded to spend more time with their guests. Her father agreed to another half hour sitting by the fire. He rang for servants to clear the table while Susan, her mother, and Beth settled more comfortably near the hearth. Beth and Mother took the settee so Beth could show Mother a sampler she had begun to work on before leaving London.

Susan and Mr. Stonecroft settled into identical chairs a few feet away on the other side of the fire. He leaned over the arm of his chair toward her. "Thank you for coming this evening. I hope you didn't mind the dinner conversation."

"Beth has learned to speak her mind." Susan kept her eyes on the child across the room from them, trying to ignore how close the father sat. If she looked him in the eye, she might stare as she had before. Though he hadn't seemed to mind, she couldn't allow that to happen again. It was rude, uncalled for. It made her stomach do strange things.

"Do you think that a fault or a virtue?" he asked, voice lower still. She could practically feel his gaze on her, watching her with those handsome eyes of his. Men had never looked at her with the openness Mr. Stonecroft did. Their gazes were always uninterested in her, except when it pertained to her purchasing their wares or offering a polite greeting. She was normally quite invisible to members of the opposite sex.

"I think it a talent, but one that might need practicing. She will have an easier time of things if she does not always speak her mind in company with those who do not know her character."

The art of conversation was something her parents had taught her well. As a vicar and vicar's wife, they often had to put others at ease by saying the correct thing at the correct moment. And her father had counseled many a person on private matters, she knew, with gentleness and understanding.

"Beth is bold. That is a good thing for anyone. She will never shrink away from an unpleasant topic, I think. But she should learn there is an art to keeping silent too. Or discussing things in more private settings. I hope you were not embarrassed."

She finally looked at him, feeling her cheeks warm as she realized she was telling a man too much about his own daughter. It wasn't her place at all. Not ever.

And yet, he was staring at her with that open expression again, studying her as though she were an interesting painting from which he hoped to glean some deeper understanding of the scene presented.

His chin came down a notch, so he looked up at her from beneath golden eyelashes. "Perhaps Beth isn't the only one in our family who behaves too boldly." He cleared his throat before continuing. "I have a question for you that might seem presumptuous, Miss Baxter. I hope you will answer me with honesty, without worry of giving any offense."

As Mother and Beth were undoing a bit of embroidery, heads bent low over the project, and discussing what had apparently gone wrong, Susan knew at once this would be a private question. Warmth curled in her stomach and she finally nodded. "You may ask, sir. I will do my best to always give you an honest answer."

He leaned a little closer, his eyebrows drawn together tightly. "May I call on you, Miss Baxter? Just you. Perhaps for a carriage ride or a walk. Or we might take tea at the shop on High Street if you wish."

He couldn't be asking her this. No man had. Not for years. And the last man who attempted to court her had rained insults down on her the moment he became aware she would not leave her mother alone to wed someone.

His handsome smile faded, hiding his dimple, the light in his eyes dimming. "Never mind, I can see the idea alarms you." His lips twisted more ruefully. "You must forget I asked." He turned away.

Susan reached for his hand, bare as it was, where it rested upon the arm of the chair. It brought his attention back to her, though all hope had left his features. "Please—that is not it at all. I am only surprised."

He stilled beneath her touch, staring at her, and Susan sensed rather than saw that the other two in the room were finally paying attention to what was happening only a few feet from them.

"Are you in earnest?" she asked, hardly daring to breathe while she waited for his answer.

He turned his hand over so he could wrap his fingers around hers. "Very much so. Won't you allow me the privilege of coming to know you better?"

"Say yes," Beth whispered loudly from across the room.

Susan looked at the little girl, Beth's eyes wide and eager as she bounced forward to the edge of her seat. Then Susan looked up at her mother, who appeared surprised but pleased. She looked back to Mr. Stonecroft, who waited most patiently while holding her hand. "Then yes. I would like that. More than anything." She hadn't imagined the way he looked at her after all. Every time her stomach twisted, her cheeks warmed, and she felt as though she might burst from an emotion she could not name, it had meant something.

"Tomorrow afternoon," he said, then looked to his daughter and Mrs. Baxter. "If you do not mind watching after Beth for a little while, Mrs. Baxter."

Mother clicked her tongue against the roof of her mouth before answering. "Not at all. I am certain we can get up to plenty of mischief on our own."

Beth grinned her answer, and Susan lowered her gaze to her hand tucked into his. She bit her lip only to keep from grinning.

Seven

THE QUESTION OF WHETHER or not to return to London became more complicated with each passing day. Collin had taken Susan Baxter on two carriage rides across the Dart River and through the countryside, and spent another morning rambling through town with her and Beth. They had even eaten dinner together twice more in the week since he braved asking to call upon her.

Susan had a gentleness about her, even when she spoke without reserve, which drew him to spend more and more time in her company. Beth did not seem to mind in the slightest either. She never offered a word of protest but had given him a sly glance a time or two.

Something about Susan had enchanted them both.

It rained the last week in July, and the skies had taken on a dreary cast even when it wasn't raining. Many of the farmers were confused by the unseasonable weather, and a few of Collin's tenants had been concerned enough to seek him out at the inn.

He sat downstairs in the Seventh Star's open dining hall

at a table near the wall. The tea before him grew cold as he again looked at the sheets and sheets of numbers he had gathered in his time at the inn. He put his pencil down and scrubbed a hand across his cheek, then through his hair.

He likely looked a fright. Maybe it was time to hire a valet.

Spread before him, held in place by his account books, was a sketched map of Fore Street. The buildings he owned, including the inn and bookshop, were inked in red stripes. The buildings he meant to tear down were filled completely in crimson. Pulling down old shops to make way for the new, and making breaks in-between the buildings for alleyways struck him as the best idea for Totnes's future.

The town had long been established, but with the growth in industry, there was also growth in Totnes. There had even been talk of a gasworks going in near the river. If the town modernized and brought in more workers, the shops ought to attract more people. What better way to do so than to update the architecture? It would also mean raising rents, as he thought he must.

His predecessor hadn't left a large emergency fund for times when his tenants found themselves unable to pay rent or to improve buildings beyond small repairs.

Collin had to come up with the capital himself . . . through rents.

The familiar scent of summer rain and wildflower-filled meadows drifted in the air before him, and Collin looked up to see Susan standing above him with an umbrella under one arm and her customary basket in the other.

"We made sweet scones." She held the basket toward him. "Beth suggested I deliver a few to you." Her slight smile appeared hesitant as usual when she first saw him each day—as if she needed reassurance that he welcomed her, which he was perfectly happy to give.

Collin stood and gestured to the chair across from his own seat. "I accept the offer of scones and request something more. Would you keep me company for a few moments?"

After she sat, he watched her shoulders go from stiff and taut to round and soft. Susan smoothed an imaginary wrinkle in the tablecloth, a smile playing on her lips. "I hope I am not interrupting. You seem . . . absorbed by your work."

"That is one way of saying that it has consumed me, mind and body." He took a beautiful golden scone from the basket and enjoyed a large bite. "The odd weather is putting people out of sorts, including me."

"I've always enjoyed the rain, but the cold in July—that I could do without." She leaned over the table to look at his sketches. "Oh, Fore Street. Are all your properties marked?"

"Indeed." He pointed to the bookshop, striped rather than solid. "Your home included. I am preparing to meet with an architect."

She glanced up from her perusal, a small wrinkle on her brow. "Architect? Whatever for?"

He tapped the bakery and haberdashery, both in dark red. "I have plans to take out some of these old buildings, and we will replace them with something new and more modern."

She stared at him, then looked down at the sketches. "The dark red properties? But half of them are filled in."

"Yes, I think Fore Street could use some improvement. Nothing has changed here in nearly two hundred years." Collin shook his head and pointed out the East Gate. "There are relics from the time the castle wasn't in ruins. The obsession people have with old things—it is one I do not understand."

⁓⌣⌣⌢

Susan's heart constricted. "I do not think the people of

Totnes are *obsessed*." She looked at the red squares on his paper, each one so much more than an old building: the bakery, the haberdashery, the dry goods store with a family of six living in the rooms above, the stationery shop. She looked back up at him. "Though we do honor the history of our town."

"Like the Brutus Stone," he muttered, shaking his head and making another mark on his paper. "And the Leechwell."

He sounded dismissive, distracted. Susan folded one hand on top of the other on the table, trying to form an explanation he would understand. "Precisely. Those things matter to us—to me."

Collin looked up, raising his eyebrows at her. "But they are ridiculous stories."

Susan shook her head, watching his blue eyes turn from dark to light as he studied her. "The Brutus Stone makes us feel like a part of something so much older than our families, than Totnes itself. It reminds us that this land has existed, that this village has stood, for centuries and centuries. That people before us lived and died here."

"As they will continue to do." He tapped the bakery's square. "And so the town must change to suit those who will next arrive."

With a wince, Susan looked out the window at their side. "There is change here and there, but there is also comfort in some things remaining the same. Is there something wrong with those buildings, aside from their age?"

He put his second scone, only half eaten, down on the table. "Is that not reason enough?"

"I can only imagine the vast expense of tearing something down only to build anew in its place and surely cannot be justified if the buildings themselves are sound." The words spilled out, sounding entirely reasonable, but when he leaned back in his chair and stared at her, Susan felt heat rise up her neck and creep into her cheeks. "I overstepped myself."

He waved away the concern. "In London, I lived in a very old, very unpleasant house. Its history and age did not enhance the charm of the leaking roof or rotten timber."

"Is that a problem here?" she asked.

He hesitated, then shook his head. "Not at present. From what I have seen, the interiors of the buildings might need some small repairs, but they have been cared for. It is not that way in London."

"We have a clear advantage over the people who live in London." Susan looked at her hands folded so primly, but her eyes strayed again to the splotches of red on the paper, marking buildings she had known all her life to face their end. "We look after our town the way we look after each other."

"What do you mean?" he asked, leaning forward again. When Susan dared to raise her eyes to his, the intensity of his gaze gave her hope. Perhaps she could make him understand why tearing down pieces of history was such a terrible idea.

"When my father died, my mother and I were certain our income would see us to a pauper's house. But our neighbors and friends found little ways to help, which let us stretch our income. They gave us the time we needed to plan and make safe what funds we had left. Our shops and houses, these little buildings, which you might see as no more than windows filled with ribbons and paint-chipped doors, are part of us too. We care for them. They make Fore Street our home."

Collin's expression sank into a frown. He tapped an open book beside his sketches, pointing to where the figures all lined up in columns and rows. "Do you remember me saying the rents hadn't been raised in a decade?"

The air between them grew somber as Susan nodded. "You mentioned the need to change that."

He nodded once, his shoulders sagging downward. "They must go up for everyone, not just the farmers. The income on the properties is too low to continue sustaining everything as it must. I have gone over all the numbers multiple times."

"I think people must expect some small adjustments." Susan lowered her eyes to the book where his hands rested, her eyebrows pinching together. "I know nothing of business matters, of course. But . . . leaving the buildings as they are and making small improvements to modernize things must be better than changing entire structures."

He put his hand out, covering both of hers as though to reassure her. "If you are concerned about the rent for your home, please don't worry. I would not touch your lease."

Susan stared at him with slowly widening eyes. "I am not fretting for myself, Collin." She'd never said his Christian name before. Somehow, she thought when she did so, it would be under sweeter circumstances.

He tried to explain. "My predecessor didn't set much of his income aside for troubled times or for renovations to these old houses. And why continue to fix something old when something new and without damage might be put in its place?"

"Must your predecessor's lack of care now punish the people who live and work here?" she asked, voice plaintive. "I understand things must change. If a building had rotten timbers, if the foundation was weak, if the roof leaked, everyone would understand replacements such as that." She pulled in a deep breath. "But raising rents in order to put people out of their homes so you may tear down structures, which have stood for centuries and are known to all, is so unnecessary."

Collin sat back in his chair, staring at her as though she could not possibly comprehend the situation.

"It is a complex issue, Susan." Her name on his lips ought to have filled her with joy. Instead, she felt tears gathering behind her eyes. He bent forward, lowering his voice, though the room was quite empty. "If we replace the old buildings with new ones, it will be better for everyone. A small raise in rent wouldn't be enough. A larger raise . . . well, everyone would eventually see the benefit to that."

"You do not know us if you think that is true," she argued, slipping her hands from beneath his. "These people are my friends. We all look out for one another. That has always been the way of things in Totnes and something that Mr. Fairchild likely never understood, given we never saw him. Everyone spoke of him as one would someone guilty of neglect. I hoped it would be better with you, considering how determined you were to come to know each of your tenants—to know Totnes."

"Perhaps it is something a man brought up in London cannot understand." He took back his empty hand and put it beneath the table, his tone pained. "And it could be the very reason Mr. Fairchild and other landlords kept their distance from their tenants."

"That doesn't seem right." Susan leaned back, studying him. Surely, she had not misjudged him so, that he would raise the rent for his own benefit without thinking of those who would struggle.

His expression closed. "I will do what I think is best for my properties. They are an investment for Beth's future. And mine."

Susan gave a slow, firm nod. "I see." She rose from the table, her throat closing painfully. She managed to choke out her excuse. "I had better return home."

Collin stood quickly and put his hand on her elbow, asking her to wait with the touch. "Susan, it isn't a simple matter. I am not trying to hurt you or anyone else, or line my own pockets. Do you understand that at least?"

"I understand you are under no obligation to explain yourself to me, sir. If you will excuse me, Beth is waiting." She stepped back, and Collin let his hand fall to his side. She gestured to the basket. "Enjoy your scones."

She left as quickly as she could, determined not to turn and face him again when tears spilled down her cheeks. She left the inn, hurried across the street, and rushed through the green door to her home. But she did not go up the stairs right away. Instead, she stood there, breathing deeply, trying to push back the tears.

Though it made little sense to her, the knowledge that Collin Stonecroft wanted to pull apart the street she loved—her neighborhood, her home—without regard for what it would do to the people who lived there hurt her. She had grown up in Totnes. She had accompanied her mother down the Butter Walk from a young age, played amid the castle ruins, made flower crowns in the meadow by the Leechwell.

The buildings he had inked in red, marking them for destruction, were friends to her. They had watched over her as she walked to and from the fish market, up to High Street, and down again toward home. They were old, yes, but they were beautiful. And the people who lived and worked beneath their roofs were proud of their history.

If only Collin could understand that there was more to Fore Street than pavement and timbers.

Eight

BETH SAT CURLED ON the settee beside Collin, book in hand, frowning darkly at the pages she held. "Everyone is horrid to Elinor Dashwood, Papa." She closed the book with a snap and glared at him. "And why isn't Margaret in the story more? Do children count so little in books?"

He took the slim volume from her and put it aside, draping his arm over her shoulders and drawing her close. "Margaret doesn't have any big adventures, it's true, but that is only because this story is about her sisters. Why not imagine what you think Margaret's story would be? Perhaps you could write it down for yourself."

The girl pulled away enough to look up at him. "Would you read it?"

"I would," he promised at once, and she grinned before settling in against him again.

"Good. And I would not make it such a sad story. I think Margaret must enjoy things more than her sisters, since she has fewer things to worry about. She probably spends her time playing in the meadows and streams near their cottage. Will we have a stream near our cottage? Will you look for one with a stream?"

He thought again of the house he had found for them, not far down the main road that would take them to Leechwell Cottage. There were meadows, a pear orchard, and a brook that wound through the land until it reached a larger stream, which eventually joined the Dart River. A beautiful place to make a home with his daughter, and—someday, perhaps—a wife.

Susan Baxter's likeness filled his thoughts; her charming eyes, framed in dark lashes and freckled cheeks, were a part of more than one daydream as of late. She would know of the cottage that he meant to make his own. She had likely visited the pear orchard at some time in the past, exchanging pleasantries with neighbors at its gate. She would be a fine mistress of such a place.

He ran his hands over his daughter's head where it rested on his shoulder. He knew by the way her weight had shifted that she had nearly fallen asleep, exhausted as she was from a day spent wandering the world with Susan. Despite the rain, they had explored the river looking for all manner of fowl and animals along its shores. Beth had returned with wet boots and muddy stockings but a smile larger than any he had seen her wear before.

Susan had barely spoken to him when he fetched Beth the day before or when she returned Beth that rainy afternoon. Her smiles had been weak, though her eyes had sought his with something urgent in their depths. As though she tried to see if he had changed his mind.

And he had. A dozen times. She was right. The buildings marked as replaceable did not need to be destroyed. It would save some of his expense if he left them where they stood. He could keep the rents lower that way too.

Yet sacrificing modern designs and preferences to preserve something merely because it was *old* made little sense to him. Especially with Totnes growing larger every year. A larger bakery with places to sit and eat, like the coffee houses he had seen in London, would attract more customers. The baker would make more money, thus paying the larger rent with ease, and that ought to make everyone happier.

Putting an alleyway where the haberdashery had stood would create a firebreak. And it would create a place for people to slip more easily from one street to another too, instead of having to walk nearly all the way to the East Gate before there was a road wide enough to take southward. His plans for all the structures he had looked over were sound.

He even thought it worth looking into replacing the front of the Seventh Star's building with a facade reminiscent of the houses of Grosvenor Square, pulling people into the inn with a promise of luxury. Not that there was anything wrong with the inn as it was, he conceded in his thoughts. He and Beth had been most comfortable.

But as more people crossed the bridge over the river, wouldn't they rather see bright new buildings in a style similar to what he saw happening in the finest neighborhoods in London?

His thoughts came to a grinding halt.

Beth sighed in her sleep, shifting so her head bobbed lower on his shoulder. Collin carefully maneuvered the sleeping child into his lap, then stood and carried her to her room adjacent to their little parlor. How many nights had he seen to Beth this way? From the time she'd been born, he'd tucked her close to his chest and rocked her to sleep, then carried her to her cradle, then cot, and now bed.

After he removed her shoes and made her comfortable enough to sleep, he tucked the blankets over her and stood a moment. The late summer sun cast a weak orange glow through the heavy clouds, giving him enough light to see his little girl. At ten years old, she didn't remember the mother who gave her life, except through the stories he told. She had grown into a lovely girl, despite their circumstances. Despite London's cramped streets, its large houses looming over them, and parks too far from their home to visit with regularity.

In Totnes, Beth finally had room to grow into the woman she was meant to be.

He had thoroughly rejected the idea of returning to London, where his modest inheritance would not mean grand houses but merely respectable neighborhoods. But despite the rejection of the city that would never welcome them, he had wished to change parts of Totnes to suit London tastes.

Disturbed by the direction of his thoughts, Collin left the inn. He barely remembered to put on his hat, and he did not stop to look for gloves or an umbrella. He went out into the fading light and paused when he saw lamplighters before the inn, plying their trade and bringing dim light to the darkening streets.

The gasworks would come. He had no doubt of that. And then the town would be forced into changes. But would that mean turning Totnes into a smaller version of London? London, with its dirty streets and its crowds of poor, did not fit well with what he'd learned of Totnes.

As he walked up Fore Street, his eyes went to the windows above the businesses where families lived. He had met all his tenants, spoken to their children. Beth had spent more than a week walking up and down this street with her hand in Susan's, learning the history of the East Gate, the Brutus Stone, and the castle ruins.

He paused beneath the East Gate when he gained it, looking eastward to the river. With the slight curve of the road, he could barely see the inn at the opposite side of the street.

Thunder sounded in the distance, reverberating against the buildings, and a moment later, a fine mist fell. Collin didn't hurry his steps as he walked back the way he had come, taking in once more the cobblestone streets, the ivy crawling up the sides of a few buildings, the flower boxes in upper-story windows.

The people of Fore Street took pride in their houses. They swept the streets in front of their workplaces. They proudly told newcomers of the Brutus Stone, the river, the castle, and everything that made their village beautiful and unique in their eyes.

"Mr. Stonecroft," a voice called, interrupting his thoughts. He turned to see the owner of the women's hat shop open her door. "Sir, would you like to borrow an umbrella?" She held one out to him.

She was one of his tenants. Her husband owned the haberdashery adjacent the bakery, selling men's hats and articles of dress. She did the same for the ladies of Totnes. She waited for his response, the umbrella held out toward him.

Any of the tenants he had met would have offered him the same, if they would have caught him wandering around in the rain like a fool.

And that was what made London and Totnes so different. The people, as Susan had tried to explain, looked out for one another and now for him too.

He smiled and shook his head. "Thank you, but no, Mrs. Harpin. I do not mind the damp." He touched the brim of his hat to her, then walked twice as fast down the road.

He needed to speak to Susan.

"I cannot help but notice," Susan's mother said hesitantly, "that you have been quiet these two days past. Something is troubling you."

Susan sat in the window, watching the raindrops gather and join before racing down the outside glass. "I am perfectly well." She rested her forehead against the cool surface and tried to banish her thoughts.

"You might be able to hide your feelings from Beth, but you cannot hide them from me. I have known you all your life." Mother came closer, standing at Susan's side. She put her hand on her daughter's shoulder. "What is it, Susan?"

Dare she tell her mother about Collin's plans to level parts of their beloved street? And for no other reason except to make unnecessary improvements to the old buildings? She did not think it greed, not after coming to know him and his daughter as she had. A man like him didn't wish to prosper while others suffered.

But he wanted to change things to match what he thought a proper town should look like. Never mind that Totnes had been a proper town for far longer than either of them had been alive.

When Susan answered her mother at last, it was with some reluctance. "I am not certain Mr. Stonecroft understands our ways here."

Mother surprised Susan with a laugh. "Understandable. It took me years to feel at home here, despite being the vicar's wife. The poor man has been with us less than a fortnight. He hasn't even seen the races yet."

Susan leaned against the window frame. "It took you years? Why? Did you miss London?"

"Sometimes." Mother sat on the window ledge next to her. "I missed knowing where I fit in the world. Totnes has its classes, but they are less clearly defined than in London. The roads are different, the buildings too. It's as though Totnes didn't change centuries when London did. To be sure, you can find many old streets and buildings in London, but they are rarely in the finer neighborhoods. Not like here, where there is more history in a cobblestone than one would imagine."

Though that thought made her smile, Susan wrapped her arms about herself to stave off the cold. "Mr. Stonecroft spoke to me of making changes—sizable changes—like knocking down a building to replace it with something new."

Behind her spectacles, her mother's eyes widened. But then she tucked her hands in her lap. "I suppose he must do what he thinks is best. The buildings and land beneath them belong to him now."

"Mother, think of how much would change—" Susan tried to protest.

"Things are always changing, dear one." Mother put her hand over Susan's folded arms. "Sometimes we can see the change coming, sometimes it takes us by surprise. Such as your feelings for our landlord." She raised her greying eyebrows, and Susan lowered her gaze to the carpet. "Give him time and grace, Susan. He is learning his way about the world the same as you are. If change comes at his hand, have faith he is doing the best he can."

Susan's shoulders sagged. "I love our neighbors, and Fore Street, precisely as they are."

"As do I. That does not mean if changes come, we will not grow to love the new ways too."

"But our neighbors—" She pulled in a breath, meeting her mother's steady gaze. "Their lives would be upended. Like ours were when Papa died."

Mother nodded slowly. "Perhaps. And then we would be there for them to help them find new lodgings, to support them in their new endeavors. Just as they were there for us. I must also say that I doubt your fine gentleman would throw anyone out into the street. He would do things the best way. I can tell."

Why did her mother have to make everything seem logical, even reasonable? Susan turned to look across at the hotel again, noting the light still behind the curtains of Collin's room. She dropped her gaze as a blush rose into her cheeks and saw Collin standing on the pavement below her window. She gasped, and her mother looked down too.

"Oh my. What is that man doing out in the rain?" Mother murmured, stepping back. "Perhaps you ought to go speak to him."

Susan was already across the room, picking up the umbrella from its hook as she went, and hurrying down the steps. She opened the door, then the umbrella, and stepped out to hold the cover over Collin's head.

"Collin, it's raining," she said, somewhat helplessly.

"I can see that." He stepped closer so she could bring the umbrella over both their heads. He looked down at her, his blue eyes comfortably cool and water dripping from his golden hair. He swept off his hat and shook it, the droplets flying everywhere.

"Well." Susan stared at him, her heart racing and her mind turning the same thoughts over and over again. "I missed you," she blurted suddenly, then blushed.

His smile appeared, growing slowly. "Did you? I missed you too."

She took in a steadying breath. The dimple hadn't appeared yet. There was hope for her to say what she needed to say to him. "I was upset. And I am sorry for it. I am afraid the idea of change is not entirely welcome. Not yet."

Collin's expression softened and he put his hand out, covering hers, supporting the umbrella above them. His fingers were warm, despite being gloveless, and they held hers with gentleness. "You needn't apologize. My ideas were startling, I'm certain, and lacked any kind of sense to you. I understand that now. I also think you must be right."

"I am?" Susan blinked in confusion, stepping closer to him, certain she had not heard correctly. "About which part?"

He chuckled, a flash of dimple appeared, and he bent closer as he spoke. "Making the decision to demolish buildings after only a fortnight in Totnes—it is foolish. I need to study things out, speak to those who live here, and perhaps the town council too. Totnes has been the home to many others, some families even for centuries, and for me to make such a change without understanding how it would impact the others would be irresponsible. I do not know Totnes as you do. Owning a few pieces of it might give me the right to do as I wish, but as I wish to make it my home, I have no desire to offend my neighbors."

"Your home?" she repeated, her heart rising with hope at every word he said. "You mean to stay?"

"I am going to buy Pearsfield Cottage," he admitted with a sheepish shrug. "I decided this evening. A few moments ago in fact." His nose was but a hand's breadth away from hers now. "You know Pearsfield?"

"Of course I do," she whispered; the fine stone house was only a little older than she was. It sat upon a hill outside of town, overlooking a bend in the river. "It's beautiful."

"I'm glad you think so," he whispered, his lids half closing and that mesmerizing dimple appearing. "Susan?" He caught her free hand with his. "Susan, I cannot promise what will come next. I don't know that yet, though I can promise you that I wish to understand. I want Totnes to be a home to Beth, and to me, as it is for you. Will you be patient with me? Will you teach me the history of all the streets and houses?"

A relieved laugh bubbled up from her chest. "Only if you promise to make me a daisy crown." She didn't know what would come next either. But when he smiled at her that way and bent so close she could feel the warmth of his breath on her cheeks, she was willing to give him more than a chance.

"Susan?"

"Hmm?"

"Might I kiss you?"

She answered by lifting her chin and leaning in, pressing her lips to his, making it their very first kiss.

Eventually, and after thoroughly kissing Susan, Collin asked to see her inside. She blushed far too much, but Mother thankfully did not comment. Perhaps she remembered what it was like to be young and in love.

Mother warmed them both with tea and sugared scones, without saying a word.

Epilogue

COLLIN CAME THE NEXT day with Beth and stayed all morning long, despite the rain and the work that waited for him at the inn. Then he came the next day, and the next, and did not let a day go by without making certain Susan felt cherished and loved.

A fortnight after their first kiss, Collin took all of them—Susan, her mother, and Beth—to Pearsfield Cottage to walk the empty rooms and then the modest gardens. Beth danced along the lane, occasionally bending to pick a wildflower to add to her newly acquired basket. Mother sat on a chair in the garden, sketching with paper and pencil what ought to be done to the flowerbeds.

"The cottage is beautiful." Susan leaned into him, her back against his chest. They stood together at the end of the lane, taking in the house with its old-fashioned thatched roof, her mother and Beth in the foreground, and the rare blue sky above.

"But terribly empty," Collin murmured in her ear.

Susan looked over her shoulder at him, her lips tipped

upward in one of her prettiest smiles. "There are plenty of shops in Totnes to help you see to your furnishings."

"True. But I wasn't thinking of chairs and tables, Miss Baxter. I was thinking of a grandmother to sit near the fire and tell Beth stories, and a mother to make daisy crowns with her . . ." He felt her catch her breath, and smiled as he added the most important thing of all. "I am also very much in need of a wife to advise me, to take me on long walks, and to teach me how wonderful life can be when I'm not buried in numbers and ledgers. Do you know anyone who might be willing to take up such a demanding position?"

Susan turned slowly, and he settled his hands upon her waist while she rested her palms against his chest. "I might know someone. But she is a spinster, and you know how they are. Noses stuck in books, spectacles on their noses, and rather plain to look upon."

"That isn't at all what I have heard." He bent a little closer, trying not to smile, though his heart was lighter than it had ever been. "In fact, I know a spinster who is more beautiful than anyone I have ever known, because she is kind and gentle, intelligent and truthful. Do you think, if I asked, she would marry me?"

Susan put one hand on his cheek, and he felt her finger gently caress a particular spot. "She would be silly to say no. Especially if you smile, because spinsters are quite helpless against a well-placed dimple."

He laughed and kissed her nose. "Susan Baxter. Will you marry me? If you do, I promise to smile just for you, every day, for the rest of my life."

She leaned up, and just before her lips brushed his, gave the answer his heart longed to hear. "Yes."

Not long after, Susan and her mother became permanent members of the family. Beth thrived beneath her new grandmother's instruction and her stepmother's kindness. And Collin went to bed each night with Susan in his arms and counted himself blessed. He hadn't expected, when he arrived at the Seventh Star Inn, how his life would change so much for the better.

Calculations were made, and the tenants of Fore Street and their landlord came to an understanding. Fore Street stayed much the same as it had been before Collin came, except for a small rise in rent, some fresh coats of paint, and a few much-needed repairs. The people of Totnes looked after their own, and that now included Collin and Beth.

Hardly a day went by that Susan, Collin, and Beth didn't walk hand in hand from High Street to Fore Street, sometimes past the Seventh Star Inn and all the way to the river. Together learning the history of the river town and making memories for the future.

Sally Britton is sixth generation Texan, received her BA in English from Brigham Young University, and reads voraciously. She started her writing journey at the tender age of fourteen on an electric typewriter, and she's never looked back.

Sally lives in Arizona with her husband, four children, and their dog. She loves researching, hiking, and eating too much chocolate.

Visit Sally online:
Website: www.authorsallybritton.com
Instagram: authorsallybritton

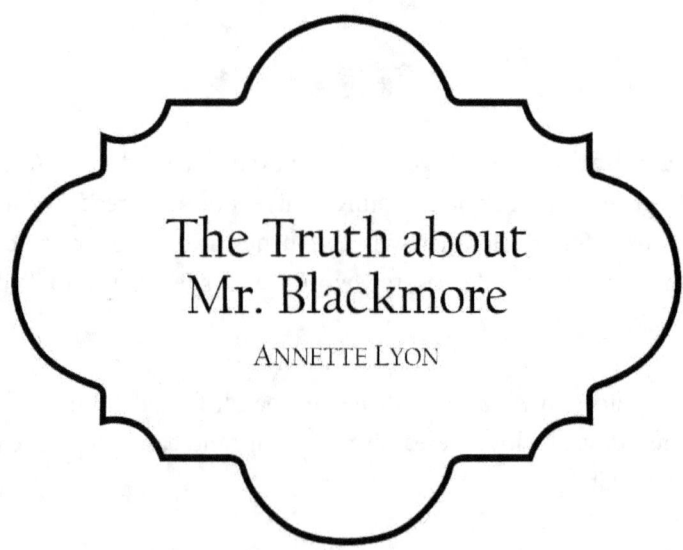

The Truth about Mr. Blackmore

ANNETTE LYON

One

A CHILLY BREEZE KICKED up about Leigh Cutler's skirts as she sat atop the hill that she and her father had once named the Ogre's Hump. She leaned against a rocky tor that overlooked the green valleys and drew her wrap a bit more tightly to ward off the cold around her. The sun had dropped close to the horizon, telling her she'd best be leaving. She had to be back to the inn in time to help with supper preparations. And if the sudden lowering clouds were any indication, a storm might break before reaching shelter.

Reluctantly she slipped a pencil between the pages of her notebook to mark her current sketch—a ragged tor in the distance that, to her eye, looked like a sprite turned to stone—then she tied a ribbon tightly about the cover to hold it all together.

She stood, brushed off her skirts, and headed down the hill along the dim path, which was created mostly by her own footfalls as she'd walked between her favorite tor and the Old Grey Inn over the years. She sighed, wishing she could linger. Perhaps one day Aunt Edyth would let her stay away in her magical happy places past sunset, and Leigh would get to see how the pink and gold light played on the landscape's rocky shapes. As a child, she'd often imagined them to be friendly giants who came to life after dark. She'd invented names for many of them, and she'd told her father about the games the giants played at night when humans weren't around to witness them.

"You're a masterful storyteller, little Leigh," he'd said more than once. He'd also told her she had an astute intellect, allowing her to quickly solve problems.

She hadn't heard praise like that—or praise of any kind—since his death over a decade before when she was not yet ten years old. As an orphan, she'd been left in the care of relatives who viewed her as a burden, no matter how hard she worked for her keep.

Another gust of wind kicked up, and again she held her wrap close, nearly tripping on a protruding rock as she did so. *Better keep my eyes on the path.* She couldn't risk hurting herself and thereby delaying her arrival for chores.

When she reached the village, the skies opened and poured heavy rain upon the earth. Small puddles were forming, and thunder boomed nearby. She hugged her notebook close and ran for the inn. She entered the village square and noted a man searching for something. He looked up at a few signs here and there but clearly didn't find whatever he sought. He drew a hand down his face in frustration, then returned to a trunk resting on a street corner.

He's already quite wet, she thought. *If he stays outside much longer, he'll catch his death of cold.*

Save for Leigh and the stranger ahead, the cobbled road was empty. Approaching him, she asked, "Sir, may I offer you assistance?" She wiped raindrops from her cheeks and awaited his reply.

He dipped his head in a small bow. "Yes, please. I am definitely in need of some help." If not for his hat, rain would be dripping down his face too. As it was, his clothing was already damp—tailored like the ensemble a gentleman wore, though he didn't hold himself as an aristocrat, and something in his speech didn't sound as polished as his clothing, either. Questions about him increased in her head.

Working at an inn with all manner of travelers over the years had taught her how to size up people with few available details. She could often guess within miles from which county someone hailed. Not this man, however. He was a complex mixture of several qualities: refined, educated, and common, all at once. "How can I help?"

"I rode a mail coach into town, and my driver had me alight here. He left because he had a schedule to keep."

"Ah." Mail coach drivers always had the risk of losing their position in the back of their minds, so they often raced along without rest to deliver the mail on schedule.

"He said the town has an old inn with good food and accommodations. It's grey, I believe. I don't dare leave my trunk to search, and I haven't had any success seeking it out from here. Do you know of the inn he means?"

"I believe I do." Leigh hid a smile. "He likely meant the inn's name, not its color." She pointed behind him, where the inn stood visible a block down the road: a long, white building with a thatched roof. "The Old Grey Inn, named after the man who founded it centuries ago."

He turned about to look. "There's even a sign." He cleared his throat with a mixture of laughter and embarrassment. Even with the cold, his cheeks pinked slightly.

"Not easily readable from here," Leigh assured him. "I'm headed there now. We'll send someone to retrieve your trunk. I'm sure it'll be safe for a few moments."

"You're right. It's rather heavy, so one would-be thief couldn't whisk it away from here so quickly. Thank you, miss." He dipped his head again.

Leigh wasn't used to being bowed to by anyone of name. She hid her fluster by continuing to walk. "Come with me." She finished her journey with the stranger at her side and wondered idly whether she'd best worry about gossips—not that she *would*, but whether she *should*.

The town of Kellettshire was small. Everyone knew the girl at the inn, that she was an orphan working for her keep. She certainly had no grand reputation, though she supposed a scandal could sully her name, but a short walk with a man staying at the inn was certainly not anything the townsfolk would whisper about.

She had no future to protect—not really. She'd almost surely die a spinster. Living in Kellettshire wasn't ideal, though she loved the countryside in this part of England. With her physical needs met by her aunt and uncle, and her soul somewhat fed by sketching landscapes, she had a decent life. Many women would view her circumstances as a luxury. After all, she never worried over having food to eat, clothing to wear, or a roof to sleep under.

She acknowledged those things with gratitude in prayer each night, yet she still yearned for more.

At the door of the inn, they shook off the worst of the rain and went inside. Leigh went behind the main desk, where she left her wrap on a hook, then reached for the ledger to assign the stranger a room. "Guests pay for at least one night upon arrival, though you may pay for your entire stay now, if you wish. How many nights do you anticipate staying at the Old Grey Inn?"

He stomped his feet and wiped his boots on the mat by the door then joined her opposite the desk. "A fortnight."

"So long?" That was quite unusual. Kellettshire was usually an interim destination. To be fair, the Old Grey Inn wasn't nearly as busy and chaotic as the George Inn, where guests were likely to be awakened at all hours by stages coming and going. This inn was a quiet place to stay on the way to somewhere else. Tourists sometimes spent a night here to admire castle ruins or ride through what had to be the most beautiful landscapes in creation. She'd never known a guest to stay more than a few nights.

"At *least* a fortnight," he said. "Possibly longer, but I'll pay for fourteen nights today, including meals."

Surprised and pleased for the inn's sake, Leigh filled out the ledger, then turned it toward him. "Sign here," she said, offering a quill.

He took it, dipped it into the inkwell on the counter, and signed. Leigh turned the ledger back around and read his name. "Well, Mr. McGrady—" *Mattias McGrady*, she thought, remembering his signature—"I hope your stay will be pleasant. Let us know if there's any way we can make it so." She added up the costs of the room and all the meals for fourteen days, and he paid the large sum without so much as a blink. What would life be like to have such money?

As he was a lone guest, she'd planned to put him in one of the smaller rooms, but his wealth changed her mind. She found a key to a larger one, wrote the number on the ledger, and held out the key. "Up the stairs, to the left, and down the corridor. Number seventeen."

"Thank you." He took the key, looking into her eyes the whole time. "I look forward to getting better acquainted, Miss . . . ?"

"Cutler. Leigh Cutler." Goodness, she must look ill-bred to have offered her Christian name. Perhaps she *was* ill bred; after all, she wouldn't soon forget that *his* Christian name was Mattias.

He gave a crooked smile, which lifted slightly higher on his right cheek. "Lovely to meet you. Thank you again."

"My pleasure," Leigh said, then remembered his trunk. "I'll be sure two of our boys retrieve your trunk and bring it to your room."

"Thank you," Mr. McGrady said again. She already thought of him as Mattias, which could be a problem in the days ahead. She couldn't embarrass her aunt and uncle by referring to their guests by given names.

As he headed up the staircase, she wondered about the mystery that was Mattias McGrady. His name could belong to the humblest of origins. She had no recollection of any with that surname of the upper class or nobility. McGrady hinted at a Scottish or Irish history, which might explain the whisper of a lilt in his speech.

What was he doing in Kellettshire for a fortnight—possibly longer? Paying for all meals meant he didn't plan to leave for any significant portion of his days. The mysteries compounded: why was he here, alone? What would he do here? Could a constable be in pursuit of him? If so, an obscure country inn such as this one could provide refuge. She blew on the ledger ink to ensure it had dried before closing it and placing it back in the drawer.

She looked forward to solving these mysteries. If Father were here, he'd say she had an intellect worthy of the challenge.

Sighing, she got to her tasks at hand. She instructed Jack and Will, two of the older pages, to fetch Mattias's trunk, then checked the clock on the wall. She needed to hurry. At least Aunt would be pleased with the reason for Leigh's tardiness—more money for the inn.

Leigh quickly fetched her sketchbook, wiped it dry with her sleeve, then hurried up the first flight of steps to the landing. Instead of taking the stairs to the next floor, she went to the wall and pressed a certain spot on a wood panel that led to a secret priest hole dating back centuries. Only she knew about the spot. The catch released, and the panel opened. The dark space before her was her escape from life at the inn when she couldn't visit the Ogre's Hump.

She still marveled that centuries ago, a Catholic priest had hidden here. She marveled further that her aunt and uncle knew nothing of the hidden room. Her father, however, had been particularly clever, noting how the inn's exterior dimensions, doors, and windows didn't quite match the dimensions of the inn's interior. The outside appeared slightly larger than the inside. He'd been correct, of course. After he found the priest hole, it had become a sanctuary for them both, and even more so for her since his passing. The priest hole truly felt different from any other place she knew—safe, quiet, away from trouble. She didn't know exactly how to describe the feeling, but *holy* fit. Perhaps something of the divine had been left in the stones by a priest, his prayers soaking into the stones and bricks themselves that now protected her as they had once protected a man of God.

Once inside, she closed the panel, then went down the short flight of steps and crossed to the makeshift shelf her father had made and where she now kept her notebooks and a few treasured books. A few small gaps in one wall let in a little light, likely intentional—the gaps appeared to be disguised from the outside. The storm dimmed what little light there was. Leigh, however, didn't need much light to find her way—a good thing, too, because she hadn't time to spare. Aunt Edyth would be impatiently eying the clock. Leigh placed her notebook and pencil onto the crowded shelf and headed back up the steps.

Usually when tardy, she prepared a speech to avoid the

ire of her aunt, but this time as Leigh slipped out of the priest hole, closed the secret panel, and rushed to the kitchen, her thoughts were otherwise engaged.

I'll learn your secrets, Mr. Mattias McGrady.

Two

MATTIAS FOUND HIS ROOM without any trouble—number seventeen. Was that good luck? According to biblical scholars, seven was lucky, holy, or some such. But what about seventeen? He unlocked the door and pushed it open, the hinges squeaking slightly. He stepped inside the room—clean and modest, with plenty of space for one man.

The room held a bed, a chest of drawers with a basin and pitcher atop, and a mirror on the wall above that. He walked about the room, noting its details—an extra blanket folded at the foot of the bed, the smell of a newly sanded floor, a mug and brush hidden behind the pitcher. His eyes landed on a coat rack beside the door. He removed his coat and hat and settled them there. They'd done their job well, but the cold had gotten into his boots. Hopefully the servants would be up soon with his trunk, and one would light a fire.

His quarters had a window and small table and chair—a must for his work. He'd forgotten to ensure his room had a writing table. He'd been flustered after being left in an unfamiliar village during a rainstorm. Then Miss Cutler's appearance had taken any room his mind would have had for such matters, and she continued to be in his thoughts.

What fortune it was she'd passed by and was the kind of woman willing to help a stranger. That itself was no small thing. Without a chaperone, many women would avoid speaking to a man they didn't know. She'd been eager to help another despite social rules.

During their brief encounter, she hadn't seemed to mind the rain, though she'd clutched a book of sorts she'd protected from getting wet. He understood *that* quite well. He sensed she'd been returning from an outing, perhaps from reading whatever book she'd carried. If she enjoyed the outdoors and clean air as much as he did—a welcome respite from the polluted miasma of London—perhaps they'd enjoy some of those things together during his stay.

Mattias stared out the window. How long would the rain last? The driver had bemoaned the storm, worried he'd break a wheel or get stuck in the mud. Mattias did not envy those whose livelihoods depended upon elements outside their control.

He shot a bit of gratitude toward the heavens for his ability to pay for personal expenses and have a decent-sized amount saved as well. Born of Irish parents who'd been poor beyond comprehension, Mattias had learned early that the slightest unexpected expense could be devastating. Like the cost of the physician who examined Ma, bled her, and gave her medicine. Whatever concoction had been in the bottle only made her sicker. The cost was so great that his father had been sent to debtor's prison when they couldn't pay rent that month. 'Twas not Da's first time there. Despite his comfortably deep pockets today, he'd never forget that life was uncertain.

Mattias turned from the window and his thoughts. While

waiting for his trunk to be brought up, he might as well get his work things arranged. He considered starting a fire in the small fireplace but decided that might raise questions. Men of his supposed breeding did not know how to start a fire.

He propped the door open so the pages could bring in the trunk, then sat at the writing desk. From his satchel, he removed one of three corked inkwells as well as a tied leather wrap, which held his papers together. A tin holding several quills came last. Later, he'd sharpen each quill so he could work longer without having to stop. He could tell he'd want to have uninterrupted time, for though he'd been in town scarcely an hour, already he felt inspiration waking in his mind and the whisperings of a story itching to be told.

Perhaps he'd spin a tale about a young woman in the rain, holding her wrap close as she hurried through the square. With a fresh sheet of paper and a sharp quill in hand, he began scribbling ideas, which came faster than he could write them.

Sometime later—seconds, minutes or longer, he couldn't have said—a knock sounded, followed by the door slamming open as two men carried the trunk between them. "Room seventeen?"

The interruption yanked Mattias out of the current the story had pulled him into. After returning to reality, he set to quickly gathering his papers, caring nothing about smudging ink if it meant the servants didn't see his writing. They mightn't be literate, but he couldn't risk anyone discovering that he was the novelist publicly known as Simon Blackmore.

"Where do you want her?" one of the servants asked.

Mattias quickly tied the leather straps and stood, pointing toward the corner opposite the bed. "There," he said, though it was the only spot in the room his trunk would fit. The young men set it down, and the second swiped his palms on his trousers.

"Thank you," Mattias said.

The servants glanced at each other so briefly Mattias almost missed it. *Blast.* Men in his position didn't say thank you to servants. "That is . . ." He dug into his vest pocket for a few coins for each. "Here you are."

They tipped their heads as if wearing hats, murmured thanks, then turned to leave, but the shorter of the two turned around. "Nearly forgot. Miss Cutler said to tell you that supper is served six to eight o'clock on the main floor."

Mattias nearly thanked them again, but he clenched his jaw to prevent the words until he trusted himself to continue. "I'll be down. Please thank Miss Cutler for me."

As the men closed the door behind them, he wished he could call them back and chat like chums at a pub. Instead he walked to the door and locked it. He felt far more at ease with common men like them. He'd worked many a job like theirs, though they'd never guess it.

He looked at his papers, all gathered haphazardly and tied in a mess. The spell of writing had been broken, and he'd need time to reenter that world. 'Twasn't time yet for supper, and with the rain still coming down, a walk was out of the question.

He remembered something else in his satchel: a small stack of letters and pieces of mail. In his urgency, the driver had entrusted the items to Mattias, offering him a crown to deliver the letters to the local coaching inn, the George Inn. He'd need to ask Miss Cutler about the other inn. She could show him how to get there.

He withdrew the letters and let his imagination go free, inventing stories about the messages each contained. He never knew where his next book idea would come from, but they always appeared in his mind after these kinds of mental play.

The top letter was thick, clearly made of several sheets of

paper. They were all soft ivory on the outer layer, so the sender was surely of the *ton*. The delicate handwriting was angled, like a woman resting against a tree, and it had gentle loops, as if a bird had drawn them. Perhaps the author was a woman, and the recipient the object of her love.

The next letter was thin, with writing that looked like spikes. Was the author angry? Was the letter a threat? So many possibilities.

Likely, none of his imaginings were close to reality, but he enjoyed the exercise all the same. Such dreams provided his living. When he was a boy, adults other than his parents viewed such fancies as odd or worse: the devil's handiwork. Surely Mattias must be slothful, they said, if he'd time to conjure such lies.

He idly flipped through the rest of the stack, then stilled at the final letter, which was addressed to Mattias McGrady in Kellettshire. Only one person knew of his intended destination, and only one person wrote with that distinct script. Only one person could have penned the letter: Harold Shriver, his editor. Harold knew how Mattias worked, writing a dozen or more installments of a novel at a time and taking several weeks to do so. Harold knew that he intended to go to Kellettshire, but not even Mattias had known about the Old Grey Inn until an hour ago. Fortunately, he'd been the unwitting carrier of his own letter.

With his stomach souring from worried anticipation, he slipped the letter out of the stack, which was bound by twine, and set it on the table beside his things. The letter nearly burned his fingers. Mattias needed to read it right away. There had to be an important reason for Harold to send an urgent letter.

He sat down, took a deep breath, and cracked the gold wax seal. After unfolding the single page, he read.

Dear M,

I hope this letter finds you well and in the midst of a flurry of creation we will both benefit from.

I am writing to inform you of an invitation I have accepted on your behalf: attendance at Mr. Edward Campton's annual banquet. It is there he decides which individuals he will become patron to for the forthcoming twelve months. You must know what an honor and opportunity this would be for you.

However, as you'll recall, Simon Blackmore is engaged to be married. Therefore, he'll be expected to attend with his fiancée. Do not think for one moment that appearing without a woman in that role would be acceptable. I have every confidence that you'll find a way to make such an appearance possible.

The banquet will be at Campton's country manor, Woodland Park, but a short drive from Kellettshire, on the evening of the twenty-eighth of July.

Barring a complication as dire as death itself, I trust that you and a fiancée of your arrangement will both attend.

Yours, H

Mattias sighed. *Barring death, indeed.*

Harold was correct that an invitation to Campton's annual banquet was an enormous honor. Every modern man of letters had heard about the annual banquet at Woodland Park, and every one of them with even the slightest hint of ambition yearned to be invited to one. Without exception, the fortunate man chosen to receive a patronage from Campton had his life changed forever. Harold's life could change too.

If Mattias was chosen, he'd have even more money. He could buy a house of his own, not a room he let. Perhaps a townhouse in a respectable part of London, or a cottage on the outskirts of the city. He could employ servants, giving work to those who, for a myriad of reasons, lacked the opportunity to find it otherwise. And he'd pay them well.

He could travel to the continent and visit Notre Dame, the Colosseum, perhaps even travel north to see from where the Vikings had hailed. Riding in coaches across the English countryside often provided inspiration for his stories, so how much greater might his inspiration be after weeks or months spent in the shadows of far-flung places he'd only read about?

Mattias stared at the letter, rereading the words as if the text might change, that he'd discover he hadn't been invited to the banquet after all.

An invitation is not a patronage, Mattias reminded himself. *Best not to put the cart before the horse.*

Campton invited three or more artists each year. An invitation alone helped anyone's standing. But being chosen? He could hardly fathom what being chosen for the patronage would mean across the kingdom's territories around the world. No wonder Harold had accepted the invitation without speaking to Mattias first.

Though he was loath to leave his work for any reason, the Campton banquet would be cause enough for an exception. A few problems lingered, however, and they were difficult enough that his stomach twisted at the odds he'd be able to solve them.

Harold had invented Mattias's pen name, knowing that *McGrady* would be assumed to be lowborn and therefore wouldn't sell books as easily as a more noble-sounding moniker would. Along with having Blackmore's name came a history for the faux man, which Harold created as well. Harold never lied to the papers, but he certainly did not correct assumptions, and he was happy to make his client sound mysterious, rich, and handsome.

Mattias snorted at the thought. He was most certainly none of those things.

While Simon Blackmore had supposedly been born of landed gentry in northern England, Mattias McGrady was born to poor Irish parents in Dublin. Unable to find work in Ireland, the family had come to London when he was but ten years old. His parents worked their fingers to the bone to earn the money needed to survive, but more than that, Mattias's parents wanted him to have a better life than they'd had.

"I don't want people to know how little money your family had simply because you opened your mouth," Da had said.

And so Da and Ma instilled the desire—nay, the requirement—that he lose any hint of an Irish accent *and* that he learn the Queen's English as much as possible. That was, Ma declared, the only way he'd have a better life. To that end, they spent evenings reading from books, Ma often correcting his pronunciation. She spoke with a strong Irish accent herself, but she worked for a powerful family in the *ton* and knew what proper speech should sound like.

Ten was young enough for Mattias to learn some of the educated ways of speaking, but also just old enough that his Irish lilt, and sometimes Irish words and poor grammar, slipped through.

His life today bore little resemblance to the one he'd known as a child. He ate better now than at any time in his life. His clothing was sewn specifically for him from high-quality materials and could be replaced whenever something tore or even whenever fashions changed. He doubted he'd ever get used to that—not after growing up wearing clothing until it was hardly more than rags, with patches atop patches. His life now was, by every measure, better than he could have dreamed.

Yet it remained a lonely life—no family, Harold as his only friend and the only person who knew his hidden identity. Harold was a business associate who made a decent living from Mattias's success. Could such a person truly be called a friend?

With a sigh, Mattias slipped the letter into his satchel. Eating supper at a country inn would be familiar and comfortable to him. At Campton's banquet, he'd be expected to wear a coat with tails and a white tie. Every moment, he'd worry about saying or doing something to ruin Simon Blackmore's reputation and career.

Could he successfully portray Simon Blackmore for an entire evening? Could he speak and act—even *eat*—with the manners and fashions of the highborn English, and do it so well he'd fool an entire room?

And if he managed such a feat, how in the world could he find someone to portray his fake fiancée?

Three

AS LEIGH PREDICTED, HER arrival in the kitchen was met with a snide lecture from Aunt Edyth, which ended with a decided *harrumph*. Since the outburst was entirely expected, the disapproval didn't touch Leigh's mood as she went to the counter to prepare squabs for supper. She ignored the derisive remarks about her rock friends.

"I found a man in the square who needed lodging, and now he's taken a room for at least a fortnight," Leigh said. Though facing the counter, she could well imagine her aunt's reaction.

"Tell me the man has paid for at least one night," she said. "You didn't give a room to a vagabond, did you?"

"I believe you'll be happy to have him staying here."

"Is it His Highness the Prince himself?" Aunt Edyth *hmphed* again, adding in mock worry, "Whatever shall we do?"

"No one quite so grand," Leigh replied. "But he paid in advance for fourteen nights and all meals. He may stay even longer."

Something dropped to the floor, and Leigh turned to see that Aunt had dropped the wooden spoon she'd been stirring the sauce with. Aunt was so shocked, she paid no mind to the spoon or the sauce. Pleasantly shocked, no doubt.

The inn had seen a significant decrease in guests in recent months thanks to a new road, which made a stop in Kellettshire less likely for those going long distances. Upkeep and other costs had increased in recent months, yet they brought in less money than ever. The business wasn't in dire circumstances, but it was heading that direction if something didn't change. A guest staying a fortnight and eating all meals at the inn would certainly help.

"Mercy," Aunt Edyth said, practically staring through Leigh. She clasped her hands almost as if in grateful prayer. Only then did she pick up the spoon and clean the mess. When she returned, clean spoon in hand, to the sauce on the stove, she said, "W-who is this guest?" Now she was stirring the pot too quickly; it might spill over if she didn't slow down.

If I did that, I'd get a lecture.

"His name is Mr. McGrady," Leigh said. "Not of a notable family, as far as I'm aware." Leigh finished cleaning out one of the squab's insides, collecting the organs in a bowl for later, and took another bird from the pile.

The reality remained that she couldn't get Mattias's blue eyes and quirky smile out of her mind. Nor could she forget how his wet hair curled and fell across one eyebrow. She'd keep those thoughts to herself, as she did so many others.

Steps sounded on the stone floor, and the women turned to see Jack, one of the pages Leigh had sent to fetch the trunk, enter the kitchen. "Mr. McGrady's in the dining room."

"Already?" Leigh looked at the clock above the arched doorway—not quite five o'clock. "Did you tell him that supper isn't for another hour?" To emphasize their unreadiness, she held up her messy hands, which were covered with blood and other remnants from the squabs.

"I told him." Jack lifted a shoulder in a shrug. "He's in the dining room all the same. Took a table by a window. What should I do?"

Leigh turned to her aunt for direction, but she looked confused, likely wanting to chide a guest expecting dinner so long before it was scheduled. Knowing that treating him with brusqueness could cost them a valued guest, Aunt said nothing, so Leigh took matters into her own hands.

"Tell him we'll bring him supper momentarily, if he doesn't mind simple fare."

"You certain he won't balk at that?" Aunt said.

"It'll be fine." Leigh washed her hands in a basin and dried them on a small cloth beside it. "I'll warm up the colcannon in the buttery. There's enough left over from the Irish family who requested it yesterday, and we still have soda bread. If he's hankering for something sweet after, I believe we have some scones, clotted cream, and marmalade remaining from tea."

Aunt Edyth groaned. "Colcannon for a wealthy man's supper? Such food is beneath him."

"No one could think your food beneath them," Leigh assured her aunt. The statement was true enough; Aunt's skill in the kitchen had won the Old Grey Inn a reputation for its food. Leigh headed to the buttery to confirm how much of the colcannon they still had.

The movement broke Aunt Edyth's frozen state. "See that you don't burn it." She huffed and returned to the stove.

"Of course." Leigh's step stilled in the buttery. She sighed, weary of constantly deflecting such barbs.

She's just afraid of losing a guest—and his money, Leigh thought as she collected items from the shelves. She'd recited thousands of similar thoughts over the years, times she'd tried to not be hurt by Aunt's and Uncle's words. She'd long-since abandoned hope of receiving any compassion from either of them.

Some minutes later, with the food heated, Leigh arranged a tray for Mattias complete with a pint of ale, fresh butter for the soda bread, which she'd sliced and placed into a small basket, and the colcannon.

Just as she picked up the tray, Aunt Edyth interjected, "What if he wants tea?"

"I'll ask him straightaway and let you know if he does." Carrying the tray, Leigh went through the arched doorway to the dining room.

"Don't spill or break anything, or you'll pay for the damages."

As if I'm ever given payment for my work with which to pay her.

According to Uncle Cloyd, Leigh had years of work ahead to pay back how much they'd spent on her and her father before he died. Leigh gripped the tray more tightly and willed her patience to grow. "I'll go slowly."

"No dallying!" Truly, one could never please the woman.

"Yes, Aunt."

In the dining room, just as Jack had said, Mattias sat at a table beside a window, gazing outside thoughtfully. He didn't look impatient—a good sign. Truly, during their brief time together, he hadn't seemed like a man to get his feathers in a fuss over something as small as having to wait for supper.

"Here you are, Mr. McGrady," she said, approaching his table.

Her voice jolted him out of a reverie. He looked away from the window and blinked a few times, as if getting used to the light of the dining room. "Thank you."

The sight of his handsome blue eyes—filled with intelligence and friendliness—looking straight into her own eyes startled her, making her nearly tumble to the floor when the toe of her slipper caught a chair leg. Somehow he caught her about the waist before she hit the stone tiles, and he steadied the tray with his other hand. He placed the latter atop the table, then turned back to look at her.

Silence settled over the otherwise empty room. They stood awfully close to each other, gazes locked. Goodness, his eyes were like the sky after a storm. His hair was as dark as a black sheep's wool. And his scent . . .

Stop, you ninny. She cleared her throat and stepped back. Her neck felt hot and was surely flushed. He released her just as quickly, muttering an apology.

"Thank you for saving me." She gestured toward the table and laughed. "You saved your supper, as well."

"I didn't expect a full meal, truly," he said, still standing beside his table. "It's not supper time, but—"

"You're hungry after a long day of travel," Leigh supplied.

"Exactly." His mouth curved into a smile that hinted of relief and more, something like camaraderie. He looked at the tray. "Colcannon with soda bread? I couldn't have requested a better meal. It smells just like the kind I had as a boy."

"Truly?" Calling his statement surprising didn't capture the half of it. Was he Irish, then? Considering the common English hatred of the Irish, that wasn't something one asked of a stranger. He couldn't know whether she held the prejudices others did toward those from the Emerald Isle.

He took his seat, then gestured across the table. "Care to join me? I'd welcome the diversion. Conversation with someone like yourself would be a pleasant way to end my day."

"I'd love to"—he had no idea how much she wanted to—"but my aunt needs my help in the kitchen." Goodness, she sounded forward. She felt her face flush.

She didn't think they'd have a particularly large group of dinner patrons tonight, but that wouldn't matter to Aunt Edyth. If *she* had to work, Leigh would too. Mattias lifted a hand, looking at someone. She turned to see Jack walking toward the kitchen but stopping when Mattias beckoned him.

Jack approached the table. "Yes, sir?"

"Could you inform Mrs.—" He turned to Leigh, brows raised.

"Forster," Leigh said, answering his unspoken question.

"Could you inform Mrs. Forster that Miss Cutler will be keeping me company as I dine? Tell her I'd be most appreciative if she'd allow the inconvenience." Mattias reached into a pocket of his burgundy waistcoat, pulled out a couple of coins, and held them out in his palm.

Jack's eyes widened. "I'll be happy to relay the message. Thank you, sir." Jack gave a quick bow, took the coins, and hurried to the kitchen.

"You didn't need to do that." Why had he? Did he pity her? Did he really wish to have a companion for dinner?

"I didn't need to," he agreed. Mattias smoothed a serviette on his lap, his smile changing into something mischievous. "But I *wanted* to." Then his forehead wrinkled in concern as something occurred to him. "Unless you'd rather not stay. I don't want to impose on your time. I thought a conversation would be a pleasant diversion for both of us, but if you'd rather be in the kitchen, please—"

"I'd be delighted to stay," Leigh said. She called for Jack and asked him to bring her the remaining colcannon and soda bread for her own meal. She slipped into the chair across from Mattias, feeling rather mischievous herself, as if she were a young girl breaking a rule. Which, in some respects, wasn't inaccurate. "It's been so long since I've had enjoyable, intelligent conversation with someone *not* old enough to be my father."

He reached for a fork, but he paused and cocked his head. "I'll take that as a compliment," Mattias said with amusement.

"Do," she said. "It was meant as one." She added butter to a bit of soda bread and took a bite, mighty glad that Mattias had come to the Old Grey Inn. She had a suspicion that the next fortnight would be far more enjoyable than usual.

Four

MRS. FORSTER CALLED FOR her niece from the kitchen doorway, and Miss Cutler hopped up to obey. "I'll be back in two shakes of a stick," she promised, her eyes brighter, if Mattias dared say so, than they'd been before she'd joined him.

"Do remind your aunt that she promised me your companionship."

"I definitely will," she said with a grin.

Mattias watched her go and marveled at the outlandish thing he'd done tonight. He was very much used to traveling and dining alone. He'd done so countless times in inns across England and Scotland. Yet tonight, he'd wanted company in the form of Miss Leigh Cutler.

I must be mad, he thought, adding some butter to a slice of soda bread. He had no intention of withdrawing the request unless Miss Cutler herself declined, which, so far, she did not.

What an odd life his had become—certainly not the existence he'd ever dreamed for himself as a boy working at a bootblack factory. Though his life was rather solitary, he certainly didn't pity himself. On the contrary, he remained very much aware that his was an enviable position to be in, isolation notwithstanding. Ever since the success of his first serialized novel, *The Milliner's Daughter*, he hadn't worried over money. Provided he didn't squander his newfound wealth on gambling, liquor, or other evils, he'd never again be forced to wear boots with holes, never again find himself sleeping on the streets because he couldn't pay rent. He'd always have warm food and a full belly. After his parents' passing, he'd spent years during which no meal or roof was ever certain, so he'd always marvel at such comforts.

He'd learned long ago that money could provide not only the necessities of life but also the simplest of things: choice. If his parents were still alive and fell ill today, he'd have been able to choose *which* doctor to call, *which* medicine to give them. Yet contrary to what many people assumed, money did not necessarily bring happiness with those expanded options. Enjoyment and pleasure, whether in the form of elegant clothing, rich food, or invitations from those in power, were *not* happiness.

Tonight he realized how much he missed companionship. Even in a ballroom or gentleman's club, surrounded by dozens or even hundreds of people, he felt alone. None of them truly knew him, though they assumed they did because they'd read his stories. Parts of himself were left on the page, but readers assumed much in error, attributing traits to the upper-class Englishman Mr. Blackmore, not poor, Irish Mattias.

He'd done much to eliminate any whiff of his true self when attending public events as Simon. On the advice of Harold, Mattias had worked with an elocution instructor to eliminate, as much as possible, any lingering Irish brogue. "You, my dear man, have an image to maintain," Harold had reminded him more than once.

But here, sitting at a table in the Old Grey Inn, Mattias could be himself. He could enjoy a plate of colcannon every bit as good as his mother's. It was precisely what he'd needed after a long day of travel.

Good thing I'm Mattias right now, he thought with a smile. Simon Blackmore wouldn't ask for colcannon. No one would think to serve him such a dish as lowly as Irish potatoes and cabbage. But Mattias didn't have to be Simon in an inn. Harold said that he should travel under that name, as news of Simon Blackmore's travels would spread, and word of his books would, too, likely increasing sales across the country. But Mattias was loath to lose his anonymity. Moments such as this one, where he could eat the kind of food he'd been reared on, proved his choice correct.

First, on every writing trip—he took several a year—he went to a place he'd never visited. No one knew his face or connected it to Simon Blackmore. He could experience small towns as a regular person and find inspiration in places where he couldn't as Simon. So long as he could leave the smog and crush of London, breathe country air, and see real people living their lives unfettered by city life, the muse found him and moved his pen.

What had compelled Mattias to invite Leigh to sup with him? He blamed his impulsivity on Harold's letter, which had him feeling restless and anxious—two things these writing trips were typically successful at avoiding.

As he took another delicious bite, Miss Cutler returned to the table, slipped into the chair and scooted it in.

Drat. A proper gentleman would have noticed, stood, and held out the chair for her. That's what Simon would do.

"Are you well, Mr. McGrady?"

How could she tell his mood was even slightly changed from a moment before? He shifted his gaze from his plate to her face and spoke, but not to answer her query. "This is the best colcannon I've tasted in years." He didn't quite dare say it was as good as his mother's, because that could open up a volume of questions he shouldn't answer.

Miss Cutler tilted her head ever so slightly, as if weighing his reply and noticing he hadn't answered her question. She let the question lie, smoothing her serviette onto her lap. She picked up her fork. "I'm glad you like it."

They ate in silence for a moment, during which time Mattias could not remember how to speak. For goodness' sake, he'd given hour-long speeches about his books in university lecture halls. But here he was, so taken by a young woman from the countryside that he could not think of a single topic of conversation.

"What brings you to Kellettshire?" she asked suddenly. Clearly *her* mind and tongue were functioning properly.

Even given a conversation topic, however, Mattias struggled to reply. He'd provided plenty of answers to similar questions in the past to various maids, servants, and innkeepers, all of whom had been satisfied with his vague replies. Miss Cutler was different. This moment felt different. Simply put, he couldn't abide the thought of misleading her.

Lovely. Perhaps my conscience has locked my tongue away next to my mind, wherever it is hiding.

He couldn't very well answer by beginning with, *Are you familiar with Simon Blackmore and his books? Well, I am he.* Among other things, such a statement would come dangerously close to the line separating honesty and arrogance.

In most company, no matter his conversational partner's position in Society, he gave not a single care what they thought of him. He'd likely as not never see them again. Miss Cutler was different in a way he could not precisely define or express, even to himself. Something in her eyes told him that she had a sincere interest in their conversation, limited as it had been thus far. He felt sure she wouldn't judge him if she knew the whole of his history.

That fact itself made the moment notable. How many times had he interacted with members of the *ton,* knowing with certainty which ones spoke to him for their own benefit? Whether it was to tell friends that they'd exchanged pleasantries with *the* Simon Blackmore or whether they wanted something from him—typically money, as they assumed he was indeed wealthy, or a favor—they had ulterior motives.

Miss Cutler, however, seemed interested in what he might say—what *Mattias McGrady* might say. Was such a thing possible?

"I'm here to escape the crush and dirtiness of London so I can complete some work in the beautiful countryside." He nodded toward the window beside them, the lush green landscape, rolling with gentle hills punctuated by craggy rocks that looked as if they'd burst through like crystals reaching toward the heavens in some story about the fae. The slightly wobbling texture of the panes in the glass made the rolling landscape and trees beyond look otherworldly, especially with the last rays of the sunset peeking above the horizon.

"You've come to the right place," Miss Cutler said, "and at the right time. Kellettshire is most beautiful in late summer. You'll see sunsets the likes of which you've only read about in ancient epics."

Mattias smiled crookedly—something Harold tried to train him out of, but at the moment, he didn't care to correct it. "I'm unaware of ancient epics lavishing praise on sunsets in particular."

Miss Cutler shrugged and smiled, lowering her gaze to her platter. "Well, perhaps not the ancient epics, but certainly poets throughout history have waxed long on the beauty of such sights."

She didn't look up right away, moving her colcannon about on her plate with her fork. If Mattias hadn't imagined it, twin rosebuds of pink bloomed on her cheeks. From pleasure? Embarrassment? Another emotion?

Most people—typical men and women who went about their daily lives—didn't analyze small, almost imperceptible changes in another's face. Or so he'd read in reviews. His attention to detail was often considered a strength in his work. Critics frequently mentioned his knack for noticing what others missed, and such things added enormously to his characters, making them feel real and vivid.

It was all well and good when writing about people who lived only in his mind and on the page, but what did an eye for detail accomplish for a man hoping to spark a friendship with a woman? Especially when he could not, in this case, determine which emotions had led to the pinking of her complexion?

Whatever it meant, she appeared to be enjoying herself, so he decided to find a way to ensure he'd see her again. "I heard that the area is known for wild berries."

"Oh, yes," she said with a nod. "Far more than one would guess."

"Any currently in season?" Oh, to be as subtle and charming as the heroes in his own books. What a travesty it was that even his heroes' words had to be slaved over, sometimes for weeks, to have the intended effect. He hadn't the luxury of days or weeks to find the perfect way to sway the woman sitting across from him. She grew prettier the longer he spent time with her.

Miss Cutler laid her fork on the plate and leaned forward as if she was about to impart a grand secret. "Wild raspberries are ripe for the picking, and I know where the best ones grow. They took hold several years ago, and as far as I can tell, no one else knows about that particular spot. I'll be gathering them first thing in the morning, before the dew is gone, so tomorrow, you can expect raspberry tarts on the menu."

"Divine." The word slipped out—Mattias was thinking it about Leigh, but he could have been referring to the raspberry tarts.

The two locked eyes for a moment, a brief span wherein Mattias could have sworn he recognized something inside her yearning for happiness and escape. Was she unhappy here? Or was the idea of escape merely leaving the inn for a walk through the dew-covered grasses while hunting for raspberries?

The patches of rosy pink on her cheeks deepened. She smiled hesitantly and, after a moment, lowered her eyes to the table once more. "I don't suppose you'd like to come? That is, I'm sure you have important work to do, and I wouldn't want to take you away from it. I understand completely if you'd rather not, but perhaps . . ." Her voice trailed off.

"Would I rather not what?" After a moment of tension in the air between them vibrating like a string on a violin, he encouraged her to complete the thought. "Perhaps . . ."

"You're our guest." Miss Cutler shook her head as if waving off whatever she'd been about to suggest. "I couldn't impose."

Please do impose, Mattias thought. Berry picking with her would be no imposition at all. If anything, time spent with her would likely prove to be inspiration for the book he was to write more of during his stay.

He followed her example, leaning forward slightly. To his pleasant surprise, she did not pull back. They sat there, faces but a few hand widths apart, and he finally spoke. "I find that a morning constitutional is helpful for me prior to my workday, but I have the misfortune of not knowing this area well.

If it wouldn't be too much of an imposition on *you*, I would greatly enjoy accompanying you while berry gathering in the morning. You could help me find a good path for my morning walks."

Miss Cutler's eyes brightened, giving him hope that the suggestion had been the very one she'd been contemplating moments before. "That would be lovely, Mr. McGrady. Jacob will likely come along. He can carry the filled buckets."

Of course, Mattias thought. *To maintain propriety.* A young woman walking about with a bachelor could start tongues wagging around town.

"Thank you, Miss Cutler," he said. "I will be anticipating the excursion."

"Don't sleep late," she said, standing and pushing her chair in. She began gathering their dishes. "I'll be waiting for you by the front desk at six o'clock. Don't want to wait until the day warms; we'll miss the best time for picking."

"I'll be here at six o'clock sharp."

Before turning toward the kitchen, she added, "I'll be going even if it's still raining. You won't need anything but your coat and hat. I'll provide work gloves and pails." After one more smile thrown his way—a sight that set his chest aflame—she left, disappearing through the arched kitchen doorway. He stared after her for a moment, half wondering if he'd imagined Miss Cutler.

Wishing it were already morning, he left the table and walked to the staircase. His work awaited him, but for the first time in ages, he had no desire to set his pen to paper. As he climbed the stairs, he thought of the story waiting for him, partially written. Usually his tales provided an escape from reality, a happy place where sadness and loneliness disappeared like the morning dew Miss Cutler spoke of.

He paused on the landing, hand resting on the newel

post, and looked over the rail, toward the main floor. Tonight Miss Cutler herself had been his escape, yet she was very much a part of the real world.

He reluctantly went to his door. Slipping the key into the lock, he wondered if perhaps fatigue from a long day in the coach was why writing didn't tempt him.

Or perhaps, he thought as he stepped inside and closed the door, *I have something—or someone—even more interesting capturing my attention tonight.*

Five

LEIGH NEARLY DIDN'T WAKE to the clappers of her alarm clock, and she had Mr. McGrady to blame for it. She groggily sat up and moved the little metal switch to stop the noise, then smiled at the thought of why she was so tired. For once she wasn't kept up late baking bread, sanding floors, or boiling and bluing bedclothes. Aunt and Uncle had been in a remarkably good disposition, allowing her to retire for the night at ten o'clock while they drank to their good fortune at hosting a guest of means.

Despite retiring early, she stayed awake for hours, remembering every moment she'd spent with Mr. McGrady. She relived every second, from the moment she'd first seen him in the square, to dining with him and saying goodnight, knowing she'd see him again to pick raspberries come morning. Sleep had been very long in coming, but a deep slumber had finally claimed her, as evidenced by the alarm clock yanking her back to consciousness.

She'd told Mr. McGrady to meet her at six o'clock sharp, which meant she had to be ready then herself. Her practiced hands quickly made her bed in the manner she'd been taught her whole life—precise enough to satisfy even Aunt Edyth. Leigh poured some water from her pitcher into the basin and splashed her face. If she hadn't been fully awake, the water, chilled from being near the window all night, would have performed the service adequately. Gooseflesh broke out on her arms, and she shivered as she patted her face dry with a soft cloth.

In the mirror, straight ahead of her, she analyzed her features. What did Mr. McGrady think of them? The cold would likely brighten her complexion and enhance her features, provided the redness wasn't solely on the tip of her nose and chin.

I'm foolish to think such things, she mused, setting her towel down. No man with the money Mr. McGrady had would ever see her as a possible match. She knew her future: merely an extension of her past and present. In ten years, she'd still live here. This would be her room. She'd still work for her keep. Hopefully, when Aunt and Uncle passed, the inn would be hers, seeing as they had no children of their own. That was her one hope for not becoming destitute.

A future as the owner of the Old Grey Inn was the best she could realistically hope for. No more thoughts of handsome men with crooked smiles and eyes that pierced her very heart and claimed ownership of it.

She combed her hair and arranged it into a simple bun, then dressed quickly, wondering what life would be like for a woman who wore dresses that required the aid of a maid to get into and out of. Oh, to wear gowns of fine fabric and lace, made of colors much deeper than the yellows, browns, and greens from plant dyes available to humbler folk.

With her slippers on, she left her room and headed downstairs, stopping at the landing. As she did each morning, she opened the door at the front of the grandfather clock and adjusted the weights to keep the clock running properly. She spared a glance at the panel that hid the priest hole, wondering if she should fetch her notebook. She rarely went outdoors without it, but she didn't yet know if her drawings and fanciful ideas would be safe with Mattias—rather, with Mr. McGrady.

Considering how close the priest hole was to commonly trafficked areas of the inn, it was nigh unto a miracle she'd never been caught entering or exiting the secret room. She fully intended to keep matters that way.

Her usual method of remaining undetected included pressing her ear to the panel from inside the priest hole, her eyes closed so she could give her energies entirely to detecting sounds from the other side.

If steps sounded, she'd count footfalls and note the floorboard's squeak on the landing. She'd wait longer than was likely necessary, counting to thirty slowly, to ensure that anyone who'd passed by had assuredly left. If no other sounds reached her, she'd slip the panel open, step onto the landing, and close the panel so quickly, she might as well have been performing a well-practiced dance. Which, in a manner of speaking, she was.

She decided against fetching her notebook this time and went downstairs instead. There, as promised, Mr. McGrady waited for her.

"Good morning," he said, standing from a chair in the dining room and walking toward her.

"Good morning," she replied, then begged any saints who might watch over the priest hole that her tongue would untie itself.

"Is this attire suitable?" he asked, holding out his arms for inspection. He wore what were probably common clothes for a man of his station, though they were much finer than anything she possessed. His hair looked damp, likely from his morning toilette, though he hadn't shaved the night's growth of whiskers. Perhaps he skipped that step to be on time, and he'd shave when they returned. She rather preferred this version of him. He looked more at ease, slightly mischievous, and, well, not rich. He was certainly more handsome this way.

"You look perfect," she said, then cursed the saints for *not* helping her avoid looking a fool. *I should have been more specific in my request,* she thought. *Saint, loosen my tongue* and *wake my mind.*

She gestured toward the back of the inn. "My boots and such are in one of the outbuildings, and so are the pails."

"Shall we, then?" Mr. McGrady asked.

"This way." She led the way through the front door, then into the courtyard through the gate the stages used. She could have gone through the kitchen, of course, but Aunt would be aghast if a guest entered her kitchen, and Leigh had no desire for the woman to know that Mr. McGrady had accompanied her this morning. The best way to stop wagging tongues was to prevent them.

They walked through the courtyard, cobbled with round stones. Along the way, they passed the relatively small mews for guest horses and carriages. The early morning light broke above the inn roof, lighting the way ahead. Leigh loved the beauty of this time of day, when the darkness of night made a gradual surrender to morning light.

In a small outbuilding, she found her own coat, gloves, galoshes so she wouldn't ruin her slippers, and a wrap for her head. She fetched two tin pails, one of which she handed to Mr. McGrady, along with a pair of leather work gloves.

"Wear these," she said. "I'd hate for your nice wool ones to be ruined by thorns and mud."

He took the pail and the gloves, and despite both of them

wearing woolen gloves, she could have sworn she felt a touch of warmth coming from his hand—a warmth that slid up her arm and settled in her chest deliciously. Their eyes met and he smiled at her, revealing dimples in both cheeks, something she hadn't noticed the night before. He took a deep breath of morning air and looked about them.

"Is that boy coming along—Jacob, I believe?" Mattias asked.

"He's otherwise engaged," Leigh said.

Mattias put on a comical expression of pretend shock. "Shall we go berry picking without a chaperone, then?"

"I dare if you do." Leigh spun on her heel and headed toward the lane.

He caught up, and they walked side by side. "I've always loved this time of day," he said. "It's almost as if this is the time fairy folk are still about, and if we could only look in just the precise place quickly enough, we'd spy their wings flitting away, or see fairy dust in the wind as they flee into their burrows until night falls and they emerge again." He took another deep breath and gazed at the landscape before them.

For her part, Leigh could not tear her gaze from Mattias, so stunned that he thought the very kinds of things she often did. She'd never met anyone near her age who dreamt of fairy folk. For that matter, she'd never heard another soul, excepting herself and her father, speak of things like fae people and magic hours, at least without derision unless quoting a poem or book. Aunt and Uncle were notorious about whipping such nonsense out of her, or at least they'd tried to.

She was quite used to keeping her flights of fancy to herself—stories of tors coming to life at twilight, along with her sketches of them and, yes, even fairies. She thanked the saints above for the fact that Mattias didn't notice her staring at him. She couldn't have stopped doing so if an actual fairy appeared before them and landed on her nose.

After several moments of gazing at his remarkably handsome profile, Leigh turned to look at the emerald landscape stretching before them. Mattias McGrady might indeed be the very kind of person she could entrust with her sketches and her imaginary flights of fancy.

This outing would be an opportunity to become more acquainted with him, and she dearly hoped her anticipation of finding a truly kindred spirit and friend wouldn't be for naught.

Six

MATTIAS FOLLOWED MISS CUTLER as she stepped off the dirt road and onto a footpath. They walked in comfortable silence for several minutes, a fact he felt grateful for, and he was lost in thought. He'd foolishly let thoughts of dawn and fairy folk slip out, and while she hadn't mocked, he chided himself. Such things were not for adult conversation; they were for books. He could talk about fairies all he liked in his stories—and someday hoped to write stories entirely about them—but no sane man discussed them aloud.

After a time, Miss Cutler stopped and turned to her left, looking out toward the trees and shrubs, surely searching for the place she wanted to pick berries. She stood in a perfect position for him to admire her profile. As the rising sun broke above the hilltops, it shone through her hair, revealing a hint of strawberry he hadn't seen before.

"There," she said, pointing to a spot only a few yards away, "that little hollow."

For the slightest moment, the word hollow made him think of the slight dip at the base of her neck, visible thanks to her scarf coming loose. Miss Cutler had a beautiful hollow. He couldn't help but notice such things. Observing people and the world around him were part and parcel of his work as a writer. Yes, Miss Cutler, with her touch-of-red hair and bewitching eyes, would find her way into a book. That was why he paid such close attention to her, or so he told himself.

She left the footpath, and he followed her to the bushes loaded with dew-covered fruit. Soon they were gathering raspberries, each in his or her own spot of the bramble.

"I'm glad you suggested these gloves," he said after a time. "Mine would have been scratched beyond repair." And he would have needed to find another set before going in public.

"The ones you're wearing are old, but they do the job well." She picked a few more berries, then added, "Though I cannot imagine a fairy or other magical sort having anything to do with old, torn gardener's gloves that date back to William the Conqueror."

Was she teasing him by bringing up fairies? He eyed her askance to gauge her expression, which appeared entirely pleasant and not at all derisive.

He ventured a reply, gambling it wouldn't be one he'd regret. "Fairy folk may well have something akin to work gloves. I imagine they have commonplace moments just as human folk." He moved to the next bush heavy with plump berries and waited expectantly for her reply to see if the gamble had been wise.

"How do you mean?" Miss Cutler asked, looking curiously over her shoulder. She genuinely wanted to know his thoughts about a flight of fancy.

She is no ordinary woman, this Miss Cutler.

She smiled before returning to picking, which gave him the gumption to elaborate.

"I imagine even fairy folk must clean, cook, and dispose of rubbish. They likely have magical ways that leave them with time and means of tending to humans who need them, whispering life into flowers, consoling a doe who has lost a fawn..." As his voice trailed off, and he recalled his words, he realized how daft he must sound. He'd spoken as if fairies were real *and* as if he'd given their lives a significant amount of thought. He didn't truly believe in fairies. Not usually. But he *had* given them plenty of thought.

Miss Cutler didn't reply for several seconds, seemingly in contemplation. He tucked his chin, bent over, and reached into a bush with canes that surely would have made holes in his own gloves. His face felt rather warm, and not from the sun. Goodness, he felt a fool. He'd learned time and time again to never speak of such things. He'd felt so at ease with Miss Cutler that he'd let his real views and ideas spill like an overturned glass of milk. Based on the changes to his bank account and living status, such things were acceptable in stories—but not in conversation. He could not bear to think of how Miss Cutler must think of him now.

When she spoke again, it was almost a whisper, which made him stop picking and look at her. She gazed upward at the sky and quoted, "*She wept for lost time, of moments forever slipped away like pearls falling from a necklace.*"

He knew those words. They were from *The Lady of Hawthorn Abbey*, his own book. Hearing words he'd penned coming from her mouth, he straightened and stared at Miss Cutler. She appeared to be viewing something beyond the mortal realm. As she continued, he mouthed the words along with her, which he knew as well as his own name.

"*Where was her guide, her angel, her fairy? Where was her comforter, protector?*" Miss Cutler stood in the same position for a moment before letting out a breath of wonder.

Did she know who he was?

She looked at him, a gentle smile curving her lips and her eyes brighter—even more beautiful than before—but without recognition. "Apologies. I couldn't help but think of that passage. It's from one of my favorite books. I've read it more times than I can count. Do you read much, Mr. McGrady?"

"I, er—" At such an early hour, he could not think clearly, not after hearing his own words spoken by a woman who could arguably be of the fairy realm herself.

"You must think me silly," she said, waving off her question. She bent to her raspberry bush again.

"I think nothing of the sort." Mattias abandoned his bush and pail and crossed the hollow to her. "You must think *me* silly. I do read often. I enjoy books very much, novels as much as anything else." If she'd read and enjoyed *The Lady of Hawthorne Abbey*, she must approve of novel reading rather than limiting herself to history, biography, and other "proper" books.

"I'm so glad to hear you say so," Miss Cutler said. "One of my favorite writers is Simon Blackmore. He authored the book I quoted a moment ago; your talk of fairy folk reminds me of him. Are you familiar with his work?"

"Yes," Mattias said. "I am familiar with him." That was arguably the grandest understatement of his life. Now to shift the topic of conversation enough to avoid dangerous areas. "Who else do you enjoy reading? I've personally rather enjoyed Jonathan Swift's work of late, though he's hardly contemporary." He wished he could take back his words and mention someone less controversial than Swift, a brilliant satirist. He was a man of the cloth, which made his work more palatable for Englishmen who did not look highly upon his nationality as an Irishman.

"You and I are of one mind," Miss Cutler said with a note

of surprise that mirrored his own feelings. "Many people think Swift is crude or unfeeling, when the precise opposite is the truth. Goodness, he intended his great essay as a way for mankind to soften their hearts toward their fellowmen. It was his plea as a clergyman for others to remember and care for his own flock. Sometimes riling an audience accomplishes the goal. He knew that."

"Precisely," Mattias said, impressed with Miss Cutler all the more.

Harold had often said Mattias needed to marry, to find a woman who was pretty to look upon but weak in mind. Such a woman could be on his arm at events but would not stir a bee's nest with such things as thoughts and opinions. Mattias could not bear to share his life with such a companion. He'd much rather join himself to an intelligent woman who challenged his ideas. The women Harold described had no more life in them than a fashion plate in a magazine.

Miss Cutler had the perfect combination: features that attracted him more than he wanted to admit, as well as a mind that could rival the best at Oxford. Harold would never approve, as she was of the lower classes. Undoubtedly, she hadn't had the privilege to attend a refining ladies' school—she'd likely had very little formal education, if any. In short, she was of the class he'd escaped. Rising in position, he was learning, was far easier as a man than as a woman.

"Tell me more about yourself," he said, returning to his pail. "Have you always lived at the inn? You said it's a family business, I recall."

"My grandparents bought the inn when my mother was quite young. They planned to leave it to her."

"Planned to?" he echoed. A story was buried in that statement; he was sure of it. "They didn't?"

"No. After she and my father met, they built grand dream

castles, which included life together in the City. Aunt Edyth inherited instead. When I was not quite two years, my mother passed."

"I am so sorry," Mattias said, imagining a young father of practically a babe left alone in the world.

"I wish I remembered her," Miss Cutler said. "After her death, Papa did everything he could for me. Eventually that meant returning to Kellettshire because he couldn't find enough work, and what he did find made him ill. So Aunt Edyth and Uncle Cloyd took us in."

"That was good of them," Mattias said, but with a note of uncertainty, as Miss Cutler spoke with a tone of discomfort as she related the events.

"It was," she admitted, but not with particular enthusiasm. "Father worked at the inn for our keep. He died when I was ten. I've lived there ever since." She never said so outright, but the uneasiness Mattias felt from her said that, in writerly terms, there was more to the story.

"Have you been happy here?" he asked.

"Not always." She paused in her picking but quickly resumed as if chasing away unwanted thoughts. "I'm grateful for their charity. Without them, I'd be without a home or even dead."

The story unspooled little by little. He wasn't willing to be done with it quite yet. "Naturally, you're grateful, but . . ."

Miss Cutler sat on a tree stump and thought. "I wouldn't call my life *happy*, necessarily. But I should be content with my lot."

Should be.

Her hesitance gradually melted, and he had no need to coax more, for she continued the thread on her own. "Some days are difficult. Aunt and Uncle say I cost them more than I help, that I owe them pounds and pounds from before Papa died. I doubt I'll pay off the debt. Truly, who am I to complain? Compared to many, my life is good."

Mattias's chest ached. She had the essentials for life but not the essence of living. Abandoning his pail, he sat upon a nearby stone to listen to her, hoping she could sense that he understood her feelings completely. Food, shelter, and clothing did not bring happiness. No matter what she did, she remained a guest in the only place she could call a home. No doubt she, too, understood the paradox of feeling lonely in a crowded room.

The precise circumstances were different—his took the forms of ballrooms and lecture halls, hers as an inn and dining room, in particular. Others wanted something from him. No doubt she experienced the same thing in the form of someone demanding one chore or another.

"We've gathered plenty," Miss Cutler said, standing. "We'd best head back so I can start cooking breakfast."

"Of course."

Soon they were walking back along the footpath, their pails laden with raspberries. When they reached the dirt road, he ventured, "I, too, have been on my own most of my life. My father died after a terrible year in debtor's prison, and my mother passed a few years later from consumption."

"Oh, I'm so sorry," Miss Cutler said, her step slowing. She looked at him, and something in her eyes said she knew what he was trying to say.

Revealing even that much about himself felt foreign, but surely the information would be safe in her hands. If his words helped her feel less alone, telling her was worth the risk. "Not having close family can be very lonely," he said.

"It certainly can."

Tell her who you are, a voice in his mind yelled at him. *Invite her to the Campton banquet.*

He pondered that last part, knowing he was daft to be considering such a thing. She'd have to learn that he was Simon Blackmore so she could play the part of the future Mrs. Blackmore. He could buy her a new gown, hire someone to arrange her hair, and teach her a few etiquette rules. She was plenty clever enough to act the part; he had no doubt of that. He could pay her aunt and uncle a few pounds to compensate for her absence for an entire day and into the night. He'd dreaded the banquet, but with Miss Cutler at his side, he might very well enjoy it.

They reached the gardening shed, where they returned the things they'd borrowed and fetched his nicer gloves. A few moments later, outside the inn door, they both paused before going inside, as if they had a mutual understanding that stepping across the threshold would put an end to their fairy-like morning together.

He ventured to propose his idea. "Miss Cutler . . ."

As forcefully as the idea of inviting her to act the part of his fiancée had occurred to him, worry latched onto his middle, echoing Harold's repeated warnings: *Careful who you trust, for secrets exposed can destroy you.*

He *thought* he could trust Miss Cutler with his identity and as his companion at the Campton banquet, but how could he truly know after such a short acquaintance? If he paid an actress to play the part, she would be under contract to never reveal the truth. Miss Cutler would be under no such obligation, and he couldn't imagine demanding she sign such a thing.

Might she inadvertently reveal his secrets? If circumstances put her reputation in question, would she reveal the truth about him to save herself? He could hardly fault anyone for doing such a thing.

When he didn't finish his thought, she questioned, "Yes,

Mr. McGrady?" and looked up at him with trust, friendship—and possibly more—in her eyes.

His heart quickened. Though they hadn't known each other long, he felt utterly at ease with her, drawn to her. He wished to be with her every day, not just at the inn but forever. To have her companionship—her humor, her intelligence, and yes, her beautiful face—with him always. He wanted to say so many things, to tell her everything about him.

But secrets were heavy, and giving her that burden wouldn't be fair to her. He should do what Harold expected: find a woman who could play the part convincingly.

Instead of inviting her to the dinner and revealing his identity, he instead asked, "Could we go berrying again tomorrow? Or perhaps go for an evening constitutional?"

"I'd like that very much." She stepped toward the door and turned the knob before looking over her shoulder. "And Mr. McGrady?"

"Yes?"

"You may call me Leigh."

Her words washed over him like a spring rain, fresh and livening and oh-so-welcome. He grinned. "Only if you call me Mattias."

She tilted her head, clearly pleased. "If you insist." She blushed and, with a smile, disappeared inside.

Seven

As Leigh reviewed the inn's income, guests, and ledger from the last week, she could scarcely believe that Mr. McGrady—Mattias to her, now—had come to the Old Grey Inn but five days ago. The reality stared at her in ink right there on the page of the inn's records, both in her hand and in his own.

For five nights, he'd stayed at the inn. Five mornings now they'd gone out together, though after the first two, they'd abandoned any pretext of requiring a reason like berry picking. For the last few nights, after a day of whatever work he did in his room, he insisted to Aunt and Uncle that she accompany him on his evening constitutional. "Without a guide such as Miss Cutler, I'll be terribly lost in the countryside." Or so he reported to her later with a glint of humor in his eye.

To Aunt and Uncle, and, indeed, anytime when others might be within hearing, he always referred to her as Miss Cutler. She was equally careful to never call him Mattias unless they were alone. And to her delight, they'd spent quite a number of hours alone together, something she'd never expected but had thoroughly enjoyed. She'd even shown him the priest hole, feeling certain he'd appreciate the secret space and view it as another piece of a magical world as she did. One might have expected her to worry over the impropriety, but she trusted Mattias, and she knew how to keep the priest hole a secret. No one would learn of it—or their time together inside—if she didn't want them to.

Others might view their time together as scandalous—especially their time in a secret room. But walks in public wouldn't be deemed improper. She'd often imagined life as a lady, and prior to that very week, she'd often wished for that life: with a four-poster bed of mahogany, lush draperies, and thick rugs from some exotic place in Asia. She'd imagined quarters with an enormous fireplace to keep her warm on the coldest of nights, by which she could read well into the wee hours—even after the flames had dimmed to coals—with no worry for how many candles she used.

Such flights of fancy kept her a half step removed from the mundane, burdensome realities of her real life. She had the books of Simon Blackmore to thank for giving her imagination a greater range, with vistas grander than any she'd have dreamed up herself. If she could not live such a life, then she could read about and escape into one through his books. Her drawings were another way to dreamland. Many had been inspired by Blackmore's stories. Her escapes, if only in her mind, had been to the kind of life she wanted, if she could have chosen one for herself.

But after the past few days, she'd come to realize how wrong she'd been. If she were from a family of means, she'd have more restrictions preventing her from things such as spending time with dear Mattias. Suddenly a life of having a maid to dress her in fine gowns, servants to cook rich foods, and never having a chore to perform, didn't sound so wonderful. Thanks to Mattias, the weight of her life and duties had lightened. After an hour's walk filled with enlightening conversation, debates, and much laugher, she could better face the humdrum realities of the day. She even found Aunt Edyth's lectures and Uncle Cloyd's anger more amusing than hurtful. Yes, even as she added numbers in columns of a ledger, Leigh was grateful that she was *not* a gentleman's daughter, for her position had allowed her to meet Mattias *and* spend time with him.

As she finished with the ledger, she absently flipped back a page and ran a finger along Mattias's signature. Would he stay the full fortnight he'd paid for? Would he stay longer as he'd hinted he might that first day? Oh, if she could leave the inn once and for all, have a life of her own choosing. Perhaps a life of *some* privilege if it meant a chance to meet a man she loved and have a family with him.

Someone, if she dared think it, like Mattias McGrady.

Before she could leave the inn, she'd need to know precisely how much of her father's debt remained and how much she owed Aunt and Uncle personally for caring for her all these years. *That* ledger was one she hadn't been given access to. That volume, Aunt and Uncle declared, was kept updated in their quarters.

We wouldn't be so foolish as to leave it within reach of the person who owes the debt, Uncle Cloyd had said, with variations of the same, on many occasions. As if she'd destroy the book or change the numbers. How could she ever free herself if she didn't know what she and her father owed? His debts, according to Aunt and Uncle, were large sums from Father's gambling, which she never could quite reconcile with the man she'd known.

Precisely what debts could *she* have incurred? She

worked most waking hours. Yes, she ate the inn's food and slept under its thatched roof. The inn's firewood kept her warm. Her clothing was purchased with money from the inn—when it wasn't merely cast-offs from villagers. Surely her work counted toward the debts. How could the scales always be tilted in the inn's favor?

A tear fell onto the dried ink above Mattias's signature. She quickly blotted it, wiped her cheeks, and tried to gather her emotions. A weepy woman at the front desk wouldn't be looked upon with kindness by Aunt and Uncle. The bell on the door jingled. She blew on the dampened page to dry it quickly, then closed the volume and looked up to greet the new arrival.

"Jimmy," she said in greeting to the boy from a nearby farm who had several gaps in his mouth from missing teeth. "I hope you're having a lovely day. Looks like you've grown since I last saw you. You'll be taller than me soon enough."

The shy boy straightened to his full height, clearly proud at her words. "Brought some mail that was left at our place," he said, holding out a small stack of envelopes. "The stage was in an awful hurry—driver said he was late—and said he'd give me a halfpenny if I promised to bring these to the inn right away. So here I am."

Leigh took the stack from him. "Lucky boy. Well done."

She held a finger to her lips, looked right and left secretively, then withdrew a couple of lemon-drops she kept in a drawer. "These are my thanks. Not as grand as a halfpenny."

He popped a sweet into his mouth and grinned, gap-toothed. "But more delicious. Thank ye, Miss Cutler." He tapped the rim of his cap and left. After the door closed, she flipped through the envelopes and found one addressed to Mattias. She hadn't seen him since early that morning, and she'd been careful to not interrupt him during his work hours except for tea, which he took in his quarters. He hadn't confided about what his work consisted of, and she hadn't asked, though her interest was certainly piqued. Each day after tea, he set the tray in the hall, and she took it away, not seeing him again until supper.

The envelope had one word written in large letters, underlined three times: URGENT. Should she interrupt his work or wait to give him the letter until he came down for supper in about an hour? *How* urgent was the missive? She glanced at the staircase, then back at the missive and its declaration of urgency. Could the contents be bad news? Would Mattias be able to finish his daily work after getting such news?

If he hadn't been so concerned about completing his work while at the inn—voicing doubts about his ability to do so at least once a day—she would've gone right up, knocked on his door, and handed it over. Most people would want an urgent letter as soon as it arrived.

Yet in so many ways, Mattias wasn't *most people*. He was uniquely wonderful and kind and handsome and hardworking . . . and *secretive*, which might have been part of the attraction she felt. He remained an exciting mystery to solve in the midst of a humdrum existence.

Perhaps she could compromise on the matter: slip the envelope under his door so he could see it and open it if he so chose, but do so without knocking so he could remain undisturbed. Yes, that might be the wisest course.

Decision made, she corked the inkwell, locked the ledger in a trunk for safe keeping, and then, letter in hand, went upstairs to Mattias's room.

Standing outside his door, she *wanted* to knock, to see him open the door and smile, to speak for just a moment.

Though she saw him multiple times a day, she always wanted more. The more she saw him, the more she wanted to. And rather than satisfying any desire within her, every encounter only increased her longing to be with him.

After arguing both sides in her mind, she forced herself to bend down and slip the letter under the door. When she straightened, she listened for any hint of whether he'd stopped working to read the letter.

During tonight's walk, would he tell her of its contents? For a moment she almost wished she had the ethics of her aunt, who knew how to open a letter by warming the wax and sealing it again after reading the contents. Leigh's conscience had never allowed her to attempt such a thing. She heard some steps, and a scratch that sounded like paper sliding on the floor. She wanted to lean her ear against the door to listen.

No, she thought, stepping back. *I won't invade his privacy, no matter how tempting.*

She walked quietly back down the corridor, careful not to tread on the squeaky floorboards, which would reveal her presence. As she descended the stairs, however, she heard his door open, and her heart jumped in her chest.

"Hello?" Mattias called. "Who left this under my door?"

Was he terribly cross, then, for being interrupted? She breathed deeply a few times to quiet her nerves, then walked back toward his room. "Mr. McGrady?" She turned. "Were you looking for me?"

His hair was mussed, looking as if his fingers had raked through it several times. "Could I speak with you for a moment on a rather urgent matter?"

Urgent? Something to do with the letter, then.

"Of course," Leigh said.

He grabbed his hat from the stand. "Let's talk outside." He needed privacy, and being outdoors would provide it.

She went down to the main floor, not bothering to tell Aunt where she was going. He strode quickly to the door, with heavy steps and a furrowed brow. Was the news in the letter so very terrible, then? Or was he put out at being interrupted?

She stepped outside and closed the inn door. Mattias had already begun pacing the cobbled road, back and forth. He raked his fingers through his hair, mussing it further, and his cheeks looked pale. Worry for him replaced any other concern. "Mattias, what ever is the matter?" she asked. "Did you receive terrible news?"

Facing away, he once more raked his hair, then sighed and turned about to face her. "Not terrible, exactly."

Leigh took a step forward. "Is it something I can help you with? You seem most distressed."

"I dearly hope you can help." Mattias licked his lips, stared at his boots for a moment, then raised his head. He steeled himself for whatever he was about to say.

"Tell me," she said. "You look like a man sentenced to the block. Whatever it is, let me help."

He drew a hand down his face, which only made him look even more weary and worried. He held up the letter, still clenched in one hand. "Explaining will take some time. I suppose the first thing you need to know is that—" He closed his eyes and took another deep breath, then looked up again, straight into her eyes. "I am Simon Blackmore."

Eight

MATTIAS HADN'T KNOWN WHAT to expect when he revealed his identity to Leigh, but laughter wasn't it.

She covered her mouth with one hand to diminish the volume, but when she lowered her hand, surely noting his serious expression—one he hoped didn't reveal the depth of desperation—the laughter subsided. Her eyes wide, she leaned forward. "You—you can't be in earnest."

For the space of a few heartbeats, they stood staring at each other, Mattias not knowing how to proceed, and Leigh looking entirely befuddled. Her eyes narrowed slightly. "Why would you jest about something like that?"

Mattias shook his head. "No, you misunder—"

"I trusted you," she interrupted. "Shared parts of my life no other living person is privy to. And now you use that knowledge to *mock* my love of books and the author I hold in the highest regard, the man who's helped me weather trying times, and—"

"Please," Mattias interjected. This knotted mess needed sorting quickly. "I'd never do such a thing, Leigh. Not ever.

You've come to mean a great deal to me—something I did not anticipate or believe possible in such a short time."

She pulled back slightly. The anger and confusion in her face softened a bit. "Go on." Doubt and suspicion laced the two words, justifiably. She had every right to question him. He *hadn't* been entirely forthcoming with her, though he felt certain that when she knew the whole of it, she'd understand why and even be willing to protect his secret.

"I truly am Simon Blackmore," he said slowly. "That's a *nom de plume*. My publisher believes my true name wouldn't sell as many books, and he's probably correct."

The inn door opened, and they both jumped at the sound. Leigh greeted the exiting guests and stepped to the side to allow them passage. She hurried to a copse of trees, and Mattias followed close behind. When they were certain of a measure of privacy, she stopped beside a tree, staring at its base. He couldn't read her expression, a mixture of a half dozen emotions, and none likely in his favor.

"Leigh—" He caught himself, realizing that if she believed him a liar, he shouldn't address her so intimately. "Miss Cutler—"

"Are you in earnest?" she asked. She looked up from the ground and gazed right into his eyes. "Are you truly Simon Blackmore, the novelist?"

Once more, he could not interpret her emotion, but she appeared more intent than angry. He decided to infer that as movement in the hoped-for direction.

"I am." He stood there for a moment, then beckoned her. "Come." He strode back into the inn, this time with Leigh following. They went to his room. She stayed in the hall as he retrieved the newest pages of his manuscript. "Here. This is what I've been working on."

She took the proffered papers with both hands and slowly

began reading them. As the minutes ticked by and he awaited a verdict, he wondered if he'd been entirely daft to show her the pages. Unpublished scribblings in his own hand wouldn't convince anyone.

He searched his mind for something that would be better proof. "I wrote my first book while working as a driver for a wealthy family. I often had hours of unfilled time, especially during the Season when I had to wait for them during a ball or another engagement. I spent most of my income on paper and ink, and I wrote most of the book sitting in various mews about the city. The pages surely smelled of manure. It's a wonder Harold ever read them."

"You wrote *The Milliner's Daughter* in stables?"

"Yes." Half of his mouth pulled up into a smile.

"Is that why Peter spends so much time with horses?" Her voice was lighter now. Was she beginning to believe him? The possibility made his heart leap.

"Yes. Most of the misfortunes that befall Peter are things I witnessed or experienced during that time."

Leigh smiled a bit wider. The lively glint he loved in her eyes had returned. "What about the man who tripped and fell into a pile of manure?"

"Alas, I did not *witness* that," Mattias said.

She covered her mouth and laughed from pure amusement. "I'm so sorry," she said, breathing between chuckles. "That's horrible."

"It was," he said. "But I figured it wasn't a lost experience if I could inflict it onto a poor soul in fiction."

She lowered her hand and tilted her head at him. "If memory serves, it's Mr. Carlyle who had that experience, and he is the last person in that book I would describe as a *poor soul*."

Indeed, Carlyle was the villain of *The Milliner's*

Daughter. Mattias chuckled and shrugged. "Poor soul, conniving miscreant . . . whichever."

Leigh's voice took a thoughtful turn. "You knew what I was quoting that first morning not because you'd read the passage but because you'd *written* it." Understanding of the full scope of what he'd told her was dawning.

He nodded and shrugged helplessly. "I didn't know what to say. I was flattered, certainly, but—"

"But you didn't tell me your true name."

"I did. Mattias McGrady *is* my true name. I merely kept my pen name private. It's the only way to travel without being easily found out. It allows me peace to write."

She nodded, but her brow furrowed again. "I understand. I think. And yet . . ."

What other concern might she have? Oh, that he could soothe it. "Yes?"

Once again, Leigh's gaze lowered now to the floorboards of the hall. "What else have you told me that isn't . . ." She swallowed as if struggling to voice the rest of her question. "*True?*"

With the difficult question spoken, she lifted her eyes to his, and they pierced his very soul. She was asking far more than whether he'd fibbed about small things. She wanted—nay, needed—to know whether the hours they'd spent together had meant something to him, as he'd said they did. Whether he'd lied about his past or his feelings. She might wonder if he was a rake, with a string of young women he'd fooled in inns across England.

"*Everything* else is true." What a relief to be able to say so! He stepped into the hall, leaving his room. Leigh surrendered the manuscript, and he set it on the floor of his room, caring more for her. "Everything else I've said about myself is true."

"Everything?" She stepped away from the wall toward him. Now their faces were closer. He could smell lavender and rosemary.

"Everything," he repeated. Though he wished he could kiss her—and could have without difficulty, so near they stood—forbearance would be the better path. He settled for taking her hands in his, something she readily allowed. His thumbs stroked the backs of hers, and she squeezed gently in return.

"I am an orphan like you," he told her. "When I was a boy, my parents brought me from Dublin to London. My father worked in a factory, and my mother as a maid in a fancy house in Belgravia. They both died of consumption, but they really died from poverty. If we'd had enough money to pay for their care, they might have recovered. And if they hadn't been so poor as to be nearly starving and frozen during winter nights, perhaps they wouldn't have gotten sick at all. My books are the reason I was able to escape a similar fate."

"So you didn't say those things in hopes of . . ." She glanced down the hall toward the staircase, where someone could happen upon them at any moment.

Another man might have tried to lure her into his room and have his way with her. He hoped she knew him well enough from their outings, which had been filled with opportunities another kind of man could have used to take advantage of a young woman. Mattias had so many flaws in his character. He'd never knowingly cause her harm.

"I wouldn't lie to you," he said. "You know more about me than Harold, my publisher. He's the only other person who knows both names. He's the one who invented Simon Blackmore."

Her brows furrowed as if an understanding had given her bad news. "You are engaged to be married." Disappointment threaded each syllable.

"No," Mattias said with urgency. "Indeed, I am not. That, too, is Harold's invention. He believes an unattached bachelor would sell fewer books than a family man. He told the papers about a fiancée, though she doesn't exist. Fortunately, he's never invented a name or history for my fictional betrothed. I convinced him not to when I pointed out that the less that could be exposed as false, the better."

"Oh," she said, weighing his words. Her tone sounded not exactly happy, but perhaps hopeful or relieved.

"Anything you may have read about Simon's life or childhood is Harold's creation, I assure you. Everything I have told you about my life is the truth. Every crumb." He took a steadying breath. "However, there's one more thing you must know."

"Yes?" Her caution had returned.

He held her hands and looked deeply into her eyes. "I've shared more with you about myself in the last few days than I have with any other living soul. I trust you. I know you'll keep my secrets. With you, I have genuinely, for the first time in years, felt . . . *safe*."

A single tear escaped her eye and trickled down her cheek. "And I with you," she said through a smile.

Their hands were still clasped, and though he knew that holding her hands without them both wearing gloves was already a breach of propriety, he wished he held her in his arms instead, that he could kiss her. Yet he did not want to presume anything, especially now, when she had so much to ponder and consider.

"Because I trust you entirely, I can tell you about the contents of the letter."

The turmoil of emotions over the last several minutes had made them both forget what had prompted this encounter.

"Is it dreadful news?" Leigh asked.

Harold's second letter brought a heavy cloak of storm clouds with it, but Mattias felt certain a bright beam of sunlight was shining through now. "It could have been, but there is a way to make it less so," Mattias said mysteriously.

Leigh's eyes narrowed in curiosity. "Should I fear that mischievous look you're wearing?" she asked with a laugh.

"I have been invited to a banquet hosted by a Mr. Campton."

Her eyes widened. "The Artists Banquet at Woodland Park?"

"You're familiar with it?" Mattias asked.

"Goodness, yes. Everyone in Kellettshire and beyond knows about it. It's the single most talked about event all year for leagues. That's splendid news. You needn't worry. The invitation alone will be enough to secure your position in Society for years to come, and I'm certain he'll select you for his patronage."

"There is a slight condition for my attendance," Mattias said. "You see, the invitation was extended for me and my affianced. When I first got the invitation, the banquet was two weeks hence, and I felt certain I could find some lady to play the role, but . . ." He released her hands and raked his fingers through his hair. "Campton has been called to the continent on a family matter, so the banquet has been moved to tomorrow night, and I have been working so hard—thanks in no small part to your company as inspiration—that I haven't given my supposed fiancée any thought at all. Would . . . would *you* come with me?"

"To Woodland Park? To the Artists Banquet? *Now* you jest." Leigh stepped back against the wall warily, eyes as round as teacups.

"I am most sincerely earnest." Mattias had to force

himself to stay where he stood, to not step closer after she'd withdrawn. "Apparently I either attend with my fiancée, or I do not attend at all."

"Why not?"

Mattias waved at the air, as if some nonsense hovered near him that he tried to swat away. "Something about having thirteen at a table being unlucky and how all of the other artists will be bringing their wives. Campton expects a couple, not a bachelor."

Leigh looked as if her mind was racing through a million considerations. She shook her head back and forth, but when she spoke, it wasn't a rejection of the invitation. "I haven't anything suitable to wear, and I don't know the first thing about doing my hair properly for such an event. And that's not even considering things like asking Aunt and Uncle to do without me for hours during the evening crush, or how I know only the broadest concepts of proper table manners and—"

She cut herself off by pressing her fingertips to her lips in thought. Lips he wanted to kiss—first gently, and then intently. Then kiss her cheek and work his way to her temple, trailing kisses the entire way. He forced his thoughts back to the matter at hand. Holding up the letter, he spoke again.

"Will you come?"

"How can I?"

"I'll manage if you're at my side," Mattias said. "You know more about me than anyone, and if your drawings and stories are any indication—and I'm certain they are—you can more than hold your own in conversation. I can help you with some of the rules for dinner. I'll buy a dress and shoes for you to wear, plus a necklace and any other things you might need. We can go to a larger village in the morning to find someone who can do your hair just so. I'll pay for it all."

With each point, her defenses appeared to lessen, so to

fully convince her, he added what he hoped would be the best part. "I'll pay your aunt and uncle for your time away. And I'll pay them any remaining debts they claim you owe them."

At that, her face lit up, and her eyes sparkled with unshed tears. "You would do that for me?"

"I would do anything for you." As he spoke the words, he recognized their truth—simple and pure and burning bright in his soul. "You deserve more than this life. I can help you start anew. Pay any debt—genuine or imagined by your relations—then help you travel to London, find a flat, and find work. You can start a brand-new life." Worrying that he might have overstepped his bounds, he let those words hang in the silence as he waited for her answer; it felt terribly long in coming.

At long last, she stepped away from the wall again. He waited for her to speak. Just when he feared she would leave without giving him an answer, she looked up into his eyes. Her cheeks had flushed pink, and she looked happier than he'd ever seen her.

"This entire endeavor sounds mad," she said, laughing nervously.

All he could do was laugh along and shrug in agreement. But then she nodded. "I'll do it."

Nine

THE NEXT DAY WAS nothing short of a flurry of preparations. Together, Leigh and Mattias took a two-hour drive to visit a dressmaker.

When Leigh stepped inside, her eyes lit up. She'd never seen so many elegant and beautiful fabrics, so many stylish and stunning gowns. Many were on forms, where a seamstress toiled away with needle and thread. Atop a table on one side of the room lay a gown of deep blue, slightly darker than Mattias's eyes.

"May she try that one?" Mattias asked the shop owner. He'd clearly noted how she'd been drawn to that gown.

The middle-aged woman looked at a loss as she scratched her head through a large bun using what looked like a knitting needle. "Sir, wouldn't you prefer to have a gown made to your wife's specifications?"

Leigh had to restrain herself to not react to being referred to as his wife, which was a valid assumption, considering they were a couple traveling together, although her old work dress didn't match the fine clothing Mattias wore.

"Ideally, we'd prefer a gown made for her, of course," he said, holding his hat in one hand and speaking with the air of a wealthy gentleman. His speech lost all trace of the Irish lilt she so loved.

Impressive, she thought. He was quite an actor.

"Alas, we had a trunk stolen during our travels. As you can see, she's had to wear an old frock an innkeeper had lying about."

"Oh, dear," the seamstress said, nodding in understanding.

"It was quite alarming," Mattias said. He looked to Leigh for confirmation, and she nodded dumbly. What could she possibly say that wouldn't spoil this ruse? "We can certainly replace the lost gowns when we return to London. Our regular seamstress has her measurements and can replace the lost items, in time, for my sweet wife." He looked to Leigh and smiled.

They were playfully putting on airs, yet his smile made her middle flip upside down anyway.

"We have an important social engagement that we cannot attend without proper attire. I'm sure you understand."

The woman poked the knitting needle straight into her bun and eyed Leigh's work dress, which was about as far from a gown as a rock was from a toad.

"I certainly do understand," the woman said, arms folded. "I have a few dresses almost complete, but they're made for specific women who—"

"Are not nearly as desperate as we are." Mattias drew banknotes from his coat pocket and silently flipped through them as if counting the pounds. "We are eager to compensate you for the extreme inconvenience."

Leigh, who was trying not to gape at so much money in

one man's hand, glanced at the shopkeeper. She still had the knitting needle jabbed in her bun as if a marksman had left a wayward arrow in it. The woman's eyes definitely flashed with greed at the sight of the money, but she quickly composed herself. "Desperate, you say?"

Mattias sighed and pocketed the notes. "Quite desperate, alas."

"Call me Mrs. Turley," she said suddenly, then took Leigh's arm and led her to the worktable, which held the blue dress as well as several others. "Try any of these you like. You're a mighty thin little thing, but I imagine that'll work in your favor; I can take in a dress much more easily than I can make one larger."

And that was how they returned to the Old Grey Inn that afternoon, with them a gown of vibrant blue precisely the color of the sky on a clear morning, altered to fit her perfectly. As promised, Mattias arranged for her hair to be done and both jewelry and slippers to be delivered to the inn.

That evening when she was ready to leave for the banquet, she bid goodnight to Uncle Cloyd, who sat at the front desk, nursing a pint. "Can't believe yer aunt agreed to this nonsense," he said, gesturing up and down her dress with his mug. "Stuff and nonsense. Don't think you can walk about with airs like yer better'n us after this."

Leigh was so filled with excitement, and Uncle's warning was so ridiculous, that she nearly laughed. She schooled her expression. "I promise I won't. I'll be back, cleaning and cooking and scrubbing in my usual way tomorrow." But hopefully not much longer if Mattias could truly pay her debts.

"Be sure yer up 'n' workin' at dawn." His voice bordered on a growl.

Just then, the clopping of hooves and the squeak of

wheels sounded out front. "I must go," she said. "Mr. McGrady is waiting for me."

"We're two workers down in one night," he grumbled.

With her hand on the door, Leigh turned to him. "Pardon?"

"Jack got hired out for the night. Edyth says he's filling in for a sick footman for a rich estate or some such. We'll be paid for his absence, but now *I* have to sit here at the desk, help in the dining hall, *and* suffer the old lady's wrath. She aims her complaints at me when there's no one else, you know."

Oh, Leigh knew. "I *am* sorry you're without both my help and Jack's tonight."

Right then the door opened, revealing Mattias in the finest clothing, from his hat to his boots, she'd ever seen. Was that waistcoat *velvet*? The cravat was most certainly pure silk. He turned to Uncle Cloyd as he held out an arm for Leigh, which she took.

"I apologize for the interruption, Mr. Forster," Mattias said. "Alas, I must spirit away your niece for the evening."

"Go on then," Uncle Cloyd said, huffing as he turned to a newspaper on the desk. On another night, his disapproval might have stung.

She and Mattias left the inn, climbed into one of the inn's coaches, which Mattias had let for the night, and were soon on their way. She'd seen it many times in the outbuildings, but never the inside. Under normal circumstances, she would have admired the woodwork, the colors, and the padded benches. But all of that paled in grandness with Mattias sitting beside her. She doubted she'd ever seen anyone as handsome.

More than half of the journey was on bumpy, hole-filled roads over which Leigh was nearly certain her teeth would rattle right out of her head. The last portion, on Woodland Park's own roads, were as smooth as the icing she drizzled over scones each Friday morning.

Had the jostling undone her hair? Oh, she hoped not. When the lady's maid Mattias had hired showed it to her earlier with a small mirror reflected into a larger one, Leigh had hardly recognized herself beneath the curls and twists. She reached up to feel them, and when her fingertips did not brush her hair, she was reminded she was wearing lady's gloves. So many things to get used to. Would she be unable to eat properly with gloves on? Would she forget which utensils to use for each course? Would she say something untoward? Her middle tightened uncomfortably.

"Are you well?" Mattias asked, looking concerned.

"I'm fine."

He tilted his head, clearly doubting her words. Trust Mattias to know when she wasn't telling him the whole of it.

"My middle is full of terrified butterflies, but I'll manage."

"They will adore you. You glow from the inside like a firefly."

"A what?"

"A firefly. I prefer the Yankee term. It's a much prettier image than our *glow worm*."

Leigh laughed in agreement; the release felt good. "*Firefly* sounds much more fairy-like than a *worm*." He'd compared her to a firefly. Was there a more magical creature? She felt herself blush. Was he complimenting her as a beau or merely easing her nerves so she could play her part well? He was arguably her employer for the evening.

Unsure how to reply, she held out her gloved hands, palms up. "I never thought I'd be grateful for needing to wear fine gloves. If anyone is to believe me a lady, they cannot see what my hands really look like." The calluses, scratches, and more would tell anyone, from the servants to Mr. Campton himself, that hers was a life spent in service.

"What do you think anyone at Woodland Park would say if they knew that Simon Blackmore went raspberry picking in the brambles?"

As one of Blackmore's greatest admirers before she'd met him, she understood the common side of him better than those at Woodland Park or, indeed, his readership could. She knew now how he captured the common life so well. He *knew* it. He'd lived it.

"Interesting that no one wonders how your ideas of nature and fairy spirits come to you if not from experience. I'm amazed that I never wondered before."

"I've heard rumors about Blackmore having spent his boyhood years exploring the Lake District, like Wordsworth and Coleridge. But they weren't born to poverty. They had educations and plenty of hours to while away in the wonders of nature."

"They likely had access to opium too," Leigh said with a laugh. "I understand it can help in such matters."

Mattias grew pensive. "I hope never to be a slave to such a thing. I've seen too many men in the arts lose their gifts by becoming chained to a substance like that."

"How different you are from other men, Mattias McGrady."

The coach rattled to a stop. Mattias drew the curtain aside, revealing Woodland Park. "Ready to play our parts, Miss Cutler?"

"Indeed, Mr. Mc—that is, Mr. Blackmore."

He smiled at her error as the coach door opened. After the steps were lowered, Leigh, then Mattias, alighted onto the drive. Before her stood a massive estate, which looked more like a castle than a residence. The odds were rather good that the outbuildings were large enough to hold the entirety of the Old Grey Inn. This must be one of the grand places she'd heard tell of with enough staff to inhabit an entire village. How many rooms were inside? How many fireplaces? Did it have a hall of old paintings of ancestors? She'd read about places such as this, including in Mattias's books. But seeing one was truly extraordinary.

Realizing that appearing awed at the sights around her would make her look low-born, she lowered her gaze. A true lady would *not* show wonder at things such as a mansion, liveried servants, or anything else beyond the doors. Chandeliers, surely. Rich foods the likes of which she could only imagine.

No matter what I see, I will behave as if I've seen the same things a thousand times.

With butterflies fluttering in her middle, they crossed the threshold, her hand in the crook of Mattias's elbow. He must have felt her trembling, because he rested his own hand atop hers in a simple, steadying gesture. They exchanged warm glances; his said he had every confidence in her, which warmed her to her toes.

I am not alone tonight. She stood taller, chin up, shoulders back. *Mattias is with me. Together, we will play our roles to perfection.*

They simply had to.

Ten

WITH LEIGH ON HIS arm, Mattias felt more and more at ease with every step. Together, they looked just like the upper-middle-class couple they sought to portray: a man and a woman from respectable families, with moderate educations but without large wealth or an inherited fortune.

The one thing Leigh had asked him to aid her with involved ensuring that all greetings were done in the proper order and manner. Mattias had a much better idea of who had titles and how to address fellow guests. He'd made a number of *faux pas* over the years and had since made a study of the topic.

He went around the room, making the proper introductions and always referring to Leigh as his fiancée, Miss Cutler—a title he enjoyed repeating perhaps more than he should. They'd decided to keep her name true—the more their stories clung to the truth, the better. Each time she was introduced to someone, Leigh responded with an upper-class air that rivaled any ballroom in London during the Season.

"A pleasure to meet you," she'd say. She'd then curtsy

with such ease that even the most astute observer would assume she'd been meeting nobility ever since learning how to curtsy at a finishing school.

Her ease and grace helped him relax; she played the part to perfection, and without the slightest hint of the anxiety she'd spoken of before.

After additional introductions and mingling, the party withdrew to the dining room. Once more, Leigh's arm was through his. The gentle weight of her hand felt assuring, but more than that, it felt natural, as if it belonged there. As if the two of them should always be walking side by side, whether through the streets of London, along rolling country roads, or through the corridors of a grand estate such as Woodland Park. It did not feel *normal*, however; the slight pressure from her hand sent his heart racing, pumping as if he were a horse attempting to win a steeplechase.

At the table, they were seated side by side. He looked over the china, the crystal, the silver, and concluded that it was all as expected. No additional forks or spoons or plates to unsettle Leigh. His gaze slid to her in admiration. She still appeared entirely at ease, as if she belonged at the table as much as anyone, notwithstanding the guests' varied births and stations.

I could learn from her, he thought. More times than he could count, he'd felt less than others, and he had for as long as he could remember. First as a poor Dublin boy, then in London, where the Irish were viewed with disdain, and later as a successful novelist who hid his true identity. In many ways, Mattias was a man who never truly belonged in any world. Not in Ireland—if he ever had—and certainly not in the high-end of English society, either.

After the soup course, footmen entered to take away the dishes. Leigh's conversation with the wife of William

Greggory, another candidate for the patronage, so diverted them that neither Leigh nor Mattias noticed the footmen until one of them spoke.

"Leigh Cutler, is that you? What are you doing here?"

Mattias and Leigh both froze in their seats. For his part, Mattias held his breath and waited. Had he imagined the footman's words? The whole of the situation was unbelievable. He half expected to wake up and discover he'd dreamt it all. Leigh was stunned into immobility as well.

"Excuse me, young man," Mr. Campton said, addressing the young footman. "How dare you address one of my guests in such a rude manner?"

Mattias glanced surreptitiously at Leigh, wondering if perhaps all would be well after all. But she didn't look hopeful. Instead, her face had drained of color—her skin was positively alabaster.

"Apologies, m'lord," the young man said with a bow. "Seeing her—that is, Miss Cutler—caught me unawares. I'll not say another word." He stepped back to stand against the wall with the other footmen. The livery certainly had disguised him at first, but on further examination, Mattias recognized the young man as the one who'd spoken to him and Leigh in the dining hall of the Old Grey Inn.

Jack. No wonder Leigh looked ready to faint or flee.

Mr. Campton faced the table again, his attention now on Mattias and Leigh. "Is this true, Mr. Blackmore? Does your fiancée know this young man, and so well that he uses her given name?"

His wife scoffed. "Certainly not. She's engaged to marry Mr. Blackmore. How would she possibly be familiar with an inconsequential footman?" She narrowed her eyes and studied Jack. "Are you new to Woodland Park? I don't recognize you."

As the attention of everyone at the table turned to Jack,

his face reddened. He panicked as he spoke to Mrs. Campton, though he looked at Leigh the entire time. "I was hired for the evening, m'lady, to help with the increased duties of the dinner. I—my—that is—I am employed at the Old Grey Inn in Kellettshire." He tipped his head toward Leigh slightly. "That's how I know Lei—that is, Miss Cutler. She works there too."

He went quiet, but he'd already said too much.

Mr. and Mrs. Campton studied the pair. Mrs. Campton, sitting straight as a rail, posed a question to Leigh.

"Is this true, Miss Cutler?" She gestured toward Jack. "Do you know this young man from some inn? Are you not, in fact, Miss Cutler, fiancée to Mr. Blackmore?"

"I—"

"Surely a man such as Mr. Blackmore wouldn't find a prospective wife working in service," Mrs. Campton added.

Mattias's chest felt as if an iron band restricted it, so tight each breath felt oppressive. He sensed more than saw Leigh shudder slightly, but there was no mistaking the single bright tear falling down her cheek. Let the *ton* think he was the uncouth, low-born man he truly was; he couldn't allow Leigh to suffer in such a manner a moment longer.

"She is not a lowly worker," he said, then silently berated himself. Working in service was nothing to be ashamed of. His mother had earned an honest wage there. But he needed Campton and the others around the table to accept her, not judge her. "The owners of the inn are her family. She stands to inherit the place one day." He knew nothing of the sort, though the odds were quite good, seeing as the Forsters had no children of their own.

Jack spoke next, entirely out of turn, from his post on the wall. "But, Leigh, you aren't engaged. You just met the man, and I must say, Mr. Campton, something is awry; this man's named McGrady."

A collective gasp seemed to suck the air out of the room. Campton pierced Mattias with a stare. "Mr. Blackmore?"

"Yes?" Mattias felt perspiration trickle down the back of his neck as if he were a criminal awaiting a sentence from a judge.

"Is this true? Did you only recently meet Miss Cutler, and is she merely a servant at a country inn?"

"Strictly speaking, yes, but—"

"And you have the audacity to pretend she is your affianced?"

"It's not quite like—" Mattias began.

Campton motioned for Jack to approach him. "What do you know of this young woman?"

The boy looked positively terrified. When he answered, he addressed Leigh, not Campton. "Mrs. Forster said you were trying to earn money to get away," Jack said.

Mattias glared daggers at him, wanting Jack to hold his tongue.

The young man, however, went on. "Did he pay ye, Leigh, to be on his arm tonight?"

A ripple of shock went around the table. One woman actually clutched the necklace of pearls at her throat—all acting as if Jack had declared Leigh to be little better than a common woman of the streets. Mattias racked his mind for what he could do or say to remove the humiliation so clearly washing over Leigh.

He couldn't deny the accusations. He *did* meet Leigh recently—within the preceding week. She *did* want to leave the inn. She *did* need money to do so. And he *did* offer to provide that money in exchange for her appearance tonight. The bare facts were all true, yet they sounded vulgar when said in so many words.

"Pardon me," Leigh said suddenly. She pushed away

from the table, scooting her chair back. "I'll take my leave so as to not spoil any more of your evening." With that, she hurried out of the dining room.

Mattias had scarcely comprehended her words before she was gone. The quick tapping of her heels on the tile floor echoed into the dining room from the corridor. The sound propelled him to push away from the table and stand as well. He was about to destroy any prospect he had of securing the patronage and would likely cause a scandal in the society pages. Harold would be apoplectic.

Bartholomew Nelson, reporter for the *London Star*, sat on the other side of the table, his attention rapt. Career or not, Mattias couldn't sit there and do nothing, no matter how scandalously the man decided to report on the evening's events. All eyes around the table were trained on Mattias; he felt their gaze like a weight. If a cat had been sitting on the sideboard, it, too, would be staring at him.

"It's true," he said. "Though not in the uncivilized manner that Jack here has implied. Miss Cutler is my friend, not my fiancée."

But what if she were my betrothed? Oh, that she were.

Mattias addressed all seated around the table. "Miss Cutler is a young woman of impeccable character. She works hard at an inn owned by her aunt and uncle. She is an orphan of respectable parents, and it was an honor to escort her to dinner this evening."

Campton folded his arms. "She is a common servant?"

"Yes, but—"

"And you paid for her company this evening? Do I understand that part correctly?"

How would Mattias answer truthfully without making the situation worse? Yes, he'd offered to pay the debts Leigh had that held her to the inn and a life of servitude. Yes, she was born to a humble situation—as he was. There was nothing unsavory in what he was paying for.

He looked directly at his host. "I apologize for not being forthright, Mr. Campton. I am not currently engaged to marry *any* woman. That information is an invention of another, and I was told that perpetuating the belief tonight was necessary." He was doing his utmost not to drag Harold into the papers too. "Miss Cutler, you must understand, is a woman of integrity. I find nothing shameful in any person making an honest living, no matter how humble their circumstances. That is precisely what Miss Cutler does every day."

In the hushed surprise hanging over the table, Mattias placed his serviette beside his plate. "If you'll excuse me, I must see to Miss Cutler. Mr. Campton, Mrs. Campton, thank you for your most generous invitation. Good night."

He left the room as quickly as he could, then ran down the corridor. When he left the main building, he raced toward the stables, guessing that was where Leigh was headed.

Dear, wonderful Leigh. Leigh, who understood his love of nature and thought of it in magical terms as he did.

Who'd loved his work before she knew him. Who wanted to be his friend for who he was, not for any status or money he could provide. Who simply wanted to have a life of her own choosing, not one fate or the Forsters selected for her.

Leigh, who deserved to be loved and cherished and given every luxury instead of having to work for her keep, wearing others' cast-off clothing, scrubbing laundry, preparing meals, washing dishes, and more, until her hands were chapped and callused.

As he approached the stables, a shadow moved. "Leigh?"

The figure stopped and turned, then hurried inside. He increased his pace. Once he entered, he looked around the dimly lit building trying to find her. He found her saddling one of the inn's horses that had been pulling the coach he'd rented from the inn.

"Leigh," he said, breathing heavily as he came to her.

She tightened the buckle. Her face was streaked with tears, wet tracks shiny in the lamplight. "Take the other horse back after dinner. It can pull the coach just fine alone."

"Leigh—"

She shook her head sharply, cutting him off. "If you need hitching tack, borrow some, and I'll make arrangements for it to be returned." With the back of her glove, she swiped at her wet face. She reached up to grip the saddle and secured one foot in a stirrup. She hopped three times, and then—to Mattias's surprise—went up and was suddenly sitting atop the horse, the reins resting comfortably in her hands.

"Good night, Mr. McGrady. I'm so sorry I ruined . . ." Her voice caught as she tried to finish. "Ruined everything."

"You didn't," Mattias said. "Leigh, please—"

She nudged the horse in its flanks, which propelled it forward. Mattias jumped out of its way, and just like that, she and the horse were gone into the night, returning to the Old Grey Inn.

Should he follow on the other horse? She didn't wish to speak with him. Perhaps waiting until morning to do so would be wise. Should he return to the dinner? No, he couldn't. Not because of any embarrassment, considerable as that was. He cared only for Leigh's well-being. She'd been humiliated, thanks to the charade he'd invented. His plan, such as it was, might ruin her.

He had to make things right for her, whatever that meant. Not only from guilt, though he felt enough of that to fill several lifetimes, but also from love. Yes, he was finally recognizing that the regard he had for Leigh Cutler went far beyond friendship and light banter. She drew him to her, summoning his soul to hers like a fairy to a rune in one of his stories. Like the fairy, he felt that if Leigh left his life, he'd cease to exist.

Leigh gave him joy and life in a way he'd known only in stories—including his own. He'd given many characters the love he once hoped to find. Now that he'd found love, he might lose it.

Yes, he loved Leigh Cutler, as much as any man could with as brief an acquaintance as theirs was. She knew parts of his soul no other living person did. He hoped to spend the rest of his mortal life getting to know everything about her.

But would she have him? Would she assume that any attempt on his part was only to repair the damage from the evening and ease his guilty conscience? Or would she believe he truly wanted to be with her long into the future? Or she might reject him because she didn't love him in return.

Whether she'd accept or reject him had no bearing on his primary object: clear her name.

Though the trajectory of his career would likely drop like a falling star into the water after tonight, he'd survive. He was a young man with a strong constitution. More importantly, he knew how to read and write. He could work in a variety of jobs to feed and shelter himself. Many opportunities existed for him as a man that simply did not for a woman. A woman like Leigh.

He simply could not bear to have Leigh become considered a common woman of the streets because he'd given her money for pretending to be his fiancée. If she never forgave him for ruining her reputation, so be it.

But he would *not* be the cause of her downfall. Somehow he would make everything right for her. He'd find a way.

Eleven

NEVER IN ALL OF Leigh's life did she work as hard as she did over the days following the debacle at Woodland Park. She cleaned the linens and added bluing until they were as bright as new. She slaved away in the kitchen, peeling and chopping for the meals, then baking bread and sweets. She washed more dishes than she knew the place had. When her hands grew chapped and cracked from all the water, she set to cleaning the fireplaces in guest rooms, washing windows, and even sanding floors.

She did all of this with one aim in mind: avoid further humiliation by crossing paths with Mattias or guests who'd read about it in the society papers. The one time she ventured into town was to fetch a cut of meat from the butcher. During that short trip, she saw and heard plenty of tittering and whispers as locals gossiped amongst themselves.

Uncle had asked if she'd indeed sold herself like a common woman as Aunt stood beside him wearing a thin, victorious smile. Aunt was so pleased with herself that Leigh felt quite sure she'd sent Jack to Woodland Park specifically to be Leigh's undoing. He'd apologized many times, which told her that he'd been naïvely following orders, happy to do a new kind of work for one night of good pay. Leigh did not believe for one moment that Aunt Edyth sent away one of her few workers out of the goodness of her heart.

To preserve the reputation of the inn, or so Uncle said, he began handling all matters at the front desk. Mattias began taking breakfast, tea, and supper all in his room, thank heavens.

One day, while Leigh served guests in the dining area, Uncle called her to the front desk.

"Room nineteen needs new linens right away," he told her.

"Right away," she echoed with a nod. After fetching a basket for the linens, she headed for the stairs. She hadn't gone two steps before Uncle spoke again.

"In about an hour, room seventeen will need fresh linens, too."

Mattias's room. He's leaving. Her feet stopped, and she looked over her shoulder. Uncle smirked. He knew his words would cut her to the quick. How could she continue to endure this life?

At the top of the stairs, she peered around the corner. When she was assured that Mattias's door was closed, she walked lightly past it to room nineteen. She stripped the bed in silence but accidentally bumped the bed's wood frame, which scraped the floor slightly. She braced herself. Did Mattias hear that?

"Mrs. Forster?" Mattias called. He'd definitely heard it.

A moan of hinges, followed by footsteps on the wood floor, said he'd opened his door and stepped into the hall. Leigh froze and held her breath. Did he know which direction the sound had come from? Thank the heavens she hadn't been in the hall.

Creaks on the stairs were followed by, "You called, Mr. McGrady?" as Aunt came upstairs. Her voice had a note of forced cheerfulness, one Leigh knew all too well. Aunt Edyth had no regard for Mattias except insofar as he provided income. The moment he left the inn was the last she'd show any esteem.

"Could I—rather, is Miss Cutler about? I have a matter to discuss with her."

The following silence stretched like honey taffy until Leigh felt ready to burst with curiosity. What did he want to say after five days? She'd spent days fleeing the very thought of Mattias, certain he despised her for ruining his career. Did she want to hear anything he had to say? More to the point, would Aunt permit the conversation?

"My niece is quite busy, I'm afraid." Aunt Edyth's voice was so sweet it dripped like syrup.

Conflicting waves of emotion warred inside Leigh: relief that perhaps she wouldn't have to face Mattias fighting on one side, and the deep desire to see him again, to speak to him again, warring on the other. She wanted more than that—she wanted to walk with him again, spend hours with him every day. With Mattias, she could be her true self. He was a confidant and more—he was something no one else could ever be. Not a brother, for brothers didn't evoke a flutter in one's middle, a yearning to be wrapped his arms, or to be held and loved.

Tearful, she pressed her face into the armful of sheets. *Foolish girl.* She could ill afford to think such things. She knew her place. *Best to stay in it.*

"But I'm leaving soon. Within the hour."

"Are you, now?"

Which would be worse: to never see him again and always wonder what he would've said, or to see him and face his ire over having his career in shambles? No, Mattias wouldn't treat her with anger. He'd run out of the banquet to catch her, an act that had likely cost his reputation—if anything of it had been salvageable.

"Alas, she's unavailable."

"In that case . . ." His voice trailed off. Leigh couldn't help but lean closer to the hall to listen. "Will you send her my regards?"

"Is that all?"

"Yes, thank you."

Lightheaded, Leigh waited for Mattias's door to close so she could slip past unseen, but she didn't hear his door close. Perhaps she'd missed hearing the groan of hinges and the click of the lock. She eased nearer to the threshold to have a better vantage, to no avail. She felt trapped. All of her feelings for Mattias flooded back, and with them the dream of leaving the inn for a life she could choose for herself.

She refused to ponder whether that life would include him. Her whims and fancies had brought her nothing but sore hands and a broken heart. The inn would always be her life—a miserable one now that everyone in town assumed she was a wanton woman. She willed away all tears and straightened her spine.

A creak sounded in the hall. Mattias had likely shifted his weight, perhaps to lean against the doorframe. She could picture him as she'd last seen him, in fine clothes, trousers tucked into his shining black boots, his white cravat and coat with tails—but with a little growth of his whiskers added to the picture, just like the morning they'd gone berry picking.

Oh, to have one more walk with him. Her heart physically ached.

Footfalls sounded. Was he walking down the hall toward her? Back into his room? Toward the stairs? In her emotional state, she couldn't be sure. She clung to the sheets and waited. After more footsteps and few murmured words from Mattias, spoken too quietly for her to make out, his door finally closed with a click. A thud marked the locking of the door.

She didn't trust herself to reach the laundry area or the kitchen without tears betraying her. The linens could wait; her heart could not. After silently dropping the linens on the bed, she quickly tiptoed past Mattias's room, avoiding the old board in the center with the loose nail, then went down to the landing. In a few moments, she'd be safely inside the priest hole, where she could weep for her broken heart. Then she'd leave her sorrows inside, hidden behind the panel, and she'd never speak of them again. Her fingers fumbled on the panel as the urgency grew to get in before the tears burst through.

At last the panel gave way, and she climbed through. As soon as she closed the panel, however, something felt different in the air, almost as if she could smell Mattias's soap—the scents of sage and sandalwood hung in the air. Of course, Mattias *wasn't* in here, in her shelter from the world. She knew firsthand that he was in his room.

Would that he were here. An ache returned to her chest with a longing for what she'd glimpsed as a future but could never have. How long would such phantom memories plague her?

On the next step, her foot landed on something other than stone. A crinkle sounded like paper. Had she been so careless as to leave a notebook where she'd step on it? Leigh bent down expecting to retrieve the notebook and return it to the shelf.

Instead, her fingers found a sheaf of paper bound with a leather tie. What was it, and who put it there? Had someone found and violated her private sanctuary? Fighting alarm, she moved to the wall where the most sunlight came through the cracks from outside, looking about the place to ensure she was, indeed, alone. Finding no one there eased her worry and allowed curiosity to rise within her like bubbles in a newly opened bottle of wine.

She pulled back the corner of the leather wrap enough to see the writing on the top of the first page. She held it in a shaft of sunlight and read a short note.

If I were a faster writer, I could have given this to you days ago. I pray it's not too late.

A partial explanation for the days of silence. Intrigued, she turned to the next page.

For Leigh

The Fairy Princess

A Fairy Tale by Mattias McGrady—Simon Blackmore

A thrill shot through her. Had he truly written a story for her? He must have placed it in the priest hole when Aunt Edyth refused to let him speak with her. *This* was what he wanted to tell her—or give her.

Her fingers burned holding the pages. She'd admired his work ever since she'd discovered his first book. She'd imagined what Blackmore would be like in person. Now she knew firsthand what he was like, though the knowledge was tempered with the reality that Mattias was even more than she'd imagined. He was not only a great storyteller who conjured beautiful words and images, but he was also a good man who was genuine, kind, compassionate. Handsome. So handsome.

She knew the real Simon Blackmore but could not be with him. Worse, she'd likely ruined him. How could anyone want to be with someone who'd taken away their livelihood?

Perhaps she should set the story aside unread. Then someday, when her heart wasn't so tender, she'd read it. Or she'd toss it into the rubbish bin without pain. Of one thing she was certain: she'd never show it to anyone. One could easily sell an unpublished work by Blackmore, especially one that revealed his true name. The pages in her hands could buy her freedom.

The thought flitted into and then out of her head in the span of a blink, so quickly did she dismiss it. No matter if she ended up living on the streets begging for food, she'd never betray him.

He must know that, for he'd entrusted her with a story that included both names.

Unsure of what to expect, she untied the leather strap and began to read. A few sentences into the tale, the silken words of Simon Blackmore soothed her troubled soul and transported her, and she knew she'd find refuge in the pages again and again. For a time, she lived in that magical place, one that usually existed only between sleep and wakefulness, where fairies lived and magic was possible.

While in the realm of his creation, she read of a wealthy yet lonely man searching for peace but knowing not where to find it. She read of a young fairy cursed by greedy relatives to work as a human servant and deny her true powers. Together, the man and the fairy formed an unbreakable bond of love, which freed them both.

For the man, it broke the chains of wealth he'd been trapped in, freeing him to love, be loved, and never again be lonely. For the fairy, the bond strengthened her magic until she burst free from her life of toil. Liberated, they flew into the horizon together toward a sunrise and all that such new beginnings promised.

The parallels were patently clear, yet she wasn't entirely sure what Mattias meant.

She'd grown to care deeply for him—love him—but did the story mean he cared for her in the same way? Or was this a fanciful yet friendly way to say goodbye? Was it only a way to thank her for helping him be less lonely for a time?

Leigh had inferred that because the story's hero loved the fairy, Mattias must love her. But what if no literal meaning was intended? Sure she'd go mad if she kept wondering, she picked up the stack of pages and tapped the bottom edge to straighten them.

Only then did she notice a small pocket in the back of the leather case with a paper peeking out. She set the story pages to one side and slipped the paper out of the pocket.

The page was folded in thirds and sealed with wax. She turned it over and leaned toward the sunlight again to read the ink on the other side: *Miss Leigh Cutler.*

Her middle tumbled over itself in anxious anticipation as she cracked the wax and unfolded the page. A single glance made her mouth hang open, agape, in shock.

At the top of the paper was a second smaller one attached with a dab of wax. It was a banknote promising Miss Leigh Cutler the amount of a thousand pounds, signed by Mattias McGrady. Below that was a short, handwritten note.

Even a fairy needs wings to fly to freedom. Let this be yours. —M

The sum was more than she could comprehend. Perhaps a resident of Woodland Park could imagine what such wealth could buy, but she certainly could not. What she *did* know was that it was plenty to pay any lingering debts to Aunt and Uncle tenfold and still have enough to leave the inn and start a new life.

The only thing she could wish for beyond that would be tempting the fates, and only a foolish person did that. She would earnestly try to be content with the "fairy wings" that Mattias's money provided her and to not long for the man who'd given them to her.

He was about to leave the inn. Within the hour, he'd said. How long had she been reading? Had she missed him already?

A pressing need to see Mattias one more time—to *thank* him for his extraordinary gifts of the story *and* the money—came over her like a spell. She slipped the story and banknote between two notebooks on the shelf and hurried up the little staircase to the secret panel. She didn't wait to listen for passersby; she hadn't time. Mattias's trunk might already be loaded onto a wagon. She stepped out of the priest hole and quickly pressed the panel closed.

"Leigh?"

Getting caught exiting the priest hole startled her so much, she yelped and whirled around. There, sitting halfway up the stairs from the landing, sat Mattias.

"I was hoping you were in there."

She tried to speak, but all thoughts and words fled her mind. She looked at the panel, at Mattias, and back again, then felt herself flushing hot from her neck to her forehead.

"Did you . . . read . . ."

She nodded and managed, "Yes." Tears sprang to her eyes. "Thank you for . . . just . . . thank you."

Mattias looked disheveled in a way she hadn't known could be masculine and strong. His hair was even more unkempt than the day he got the urgent letter. His shirt was rumpled, and his vest unbuttoned. He hadn't yet shaved, which made him that much more handsome. He reached out, and she happily surrendered her hands to his kind grasp. He descended to the landing. "I understand if you'd rather I leave."

Before she could insist otherwise, he shook his head and continued. "The gift is yours to use as you please, with no qualifications or requirements."

"It's so much," Leigh said, shaking her head. "I could never repay—"

"One does not repay a gift."

"But you owe me nothing," she said quietly. "I accompanied you to the banquet willingly, and it was under very cruel pretense that I was discovered. It seems my aunt sent Jack to expose us and humiliate you before your colleagues and cost you the patronage. If anyone has need of making amends, it is I."

"Leigh, I didn't give it to you from guilt. I gave it to you because . . ." He swallowed as if summoning courage then looked deeply into her eyes. "I love you."

Warm chills went up her arms and down her back. "You—do?"

"So very much. I could not bear to think that you'd suffer because of me. For pretending to—"

"To love you?" Happy tears slipped down her cheeks. She shook her head. "I didn't have to pretend that, Mattias."

Hope and love seemed to light him from inside. He drew nearer, and her heart sped up. "Then, perhaps . . . would you be amenable to considering . . ."

Leigh could hardly contain her curiosity, for she knew that smile. "What?"

The clinking dishes floated up to them from the dining room. Aunt called for her, but Leigh cared nothing about whether Edyth would be cross with her. Instead, she tugged him to follow her into the priest hole. With the panel clicked shut and the sun setting, Mattias was but a dim outline standing before her on the top stair.

Leigh reached for his hands in the darkness. They were warm and strong. "You were asking if I'd be amenable to . . . ?"

"Would you—that is, would you consider—" His flustered words bolstered her courage.

"Consider what, Mattias?" She drew closer and could smell sage, sandalwood, and leather.

He ran his thumbs along the tops of her hands and chuckled at his stammering. She could picture him as clearly as if they were standing by the Ogre's Hump at noon day, complete with his crooked smile. "What if you were in actual fact my fiancée?"

Was she dreaming? She couldn't have imagined such a splendid ending to her own story. If Simon Blackmore himself had written such a thing, even she might have thought it a bit *too* perfect to be believable.

"What about my reputation? And your books? If I take your gift, how will you live?" Even a man of means couldn't silence the rumors already circulating the country thanks to Bartholomew Nelson's article about the dinner in the *London Star*.

"All that matters is the truth," Mattias said. "I know who you are. And you know me in ways no one else does, including my publisher." He reached forward and smoothed one side of her hair, then cradled her cheek in his hand. She leaned into his touch, which warmed her from the inside out. "I assure you, you are far superior to Harold."

They both laughed.

"So would you," he continued. "That is . . . goodness, for someone who makes his living with words, I'm a terrible example of elocutionary excellence."

"Yes," Leigh said.

"Yes . . . I'm—"

"Yes, I want to be your fiancée—and your wife." Leigh leaned even closer.

He did too. She could feel his breath on her cheek. "You do?"

"Definitely, no matter how unladylike that makes me. Though I suppose hiding in a secret room with a beau isn't precisely ladylike."

"Truly, etiquette is something I've never cared much for." Mattias made a pleased sound, then put his arms around her and held her. Enveloped in his embrace, she felt safer than she ever had, even in the priest hole, for Mattias was full of love and warmth and reality; he wasn't merely a fantastical escape.

He went down one step so he stood lower than she did, making them almost the same height. Then he leaned in and kissed her.

In the hidden sanctuary, her heart opened. Life expanded before her, broader and brighter than she'd ever hoped for. With Mattias at her side, with or without money, she'd be happy, and she felt certain she'd make him happy too.

"Shall we tell my relations I am no longer in their employ?" she whispered, their faces still close.

Mattias snorted lightly. "No longer their prisoner, more like. But yes, let's tell them, then leave this place behind. We'll marry and create an entirely new life together."

Leigh wrapped her arms around his neck, and they held each other tight. She breathed in his scent, letting it fill her. "It sounds like a fairy tale."

Annette Lyon is a *USA Today* bestselling author, a 6-time Best of State medalist for fiction in Utah, and a Whitney Award winner. She's had success as a professional editor and in newspaper, magazine, and technical writing, but her first love has always been fiction.

She's a cum laude graduate from BYU with a degree in English and is the author of over a dozen books, including the Whitney Award-winning *Band of Sisters*, a chocolate cookbook, and a grammar guide. She co-founded and was served as the original editor of the *Timeless Romance Anthology* series and continues to be a regular contributor to the collections.

She has received five publication awards from the League of Utah Writers, including the Silver Quill, and she's one of the four coauthors of the *Newport Ladies Book Club* series. Annette is represented by Heather Karpas at ICM Partners.

Find Annette online:
Website: https://annettelyon.wordpress.com/
Blog: http://blog.AnnetteLyon.com
Twitter: @AnnetteLyon
Facebook: AnnetteLyon
Instagram: @annette.lyon
Pinterest: AnnetteLyon

The Coachman's Choice

Deborah M. Hathaway

*For my family and friends—
you are my "home"*

One

Clovelly, Devonshire—Thursday, April 13, 1815

IT WAS SAID THAT nothing could rival the view from the Golden Mermaid Inn. Guests claimed they could see the blue-green sea stretching for miles on a clear day, as well as the heavy clouds of approaching storms hours beforehand.

Shoals of pilchards migrating round the peninsula were impossible to miss from the upper windows, and—rumor had it—even mermaids could be spotted from the edge of the inn's property.

Of course, Mary Thorne had never seen a mermaid herself, nor did she agree with the guests' opinions. The view was, indeed, spectacular. But it wasn't the view *from* the inn she preferred.

It was the view *of* the inn.

Her footsteps slowed. Three and twenty years of living at the Golden Mermaid still had not lessened her anxious anticipation upon rounding the bend in the road from Clovelly and coming upon the first image of her family's inn, the inn she would one day run.

Ivy—growing greener now that April had arrived—crept across the front of the inn's white walls. Carefully trimmed bushes lined the stone path to the wooden front door, and above it, the carved wooden sign portraying a mermaid fin dipping into a wave rocked back and forth in the wind. The thatched roof of the inn shone golden in the afternoon light, and the windows were hooded by the heavy, dry straw, like Papa's thick brows, which had once shadowed his brown eyes.

Mary and her mother prided themselves in caring for the Golden Mermaid, ensuring the outside promised what would be enjoyed on the inside: warm food, clean rooms, and a charitable reception.

Papa had taught them to do that.

Mary pulled out the small, gold pocket watch that had once belonged to him.

"There is no one he'd rather give possession of it than to you, my dear," Mama had said.

The narrow hands on the watch verged at the edge of five o'clock, and a soft jingling on the wind slipped past Mary's ears from behind, drawing her mind from her twisting heart.

Right on time. As usual.

Glancing over her shoulder, she searched for any sign of the approaching stagecoach. The dirt road was empty, though fraught with divots caused by carriages and puddles of mud still lingering from last night's rainstorm.

Even without any visible sign of the coach, everything pointed to the contraption pulling around the bend in minutes—the time ticking away on her watch, the growing rattles of spinning wheels, the hooves pounding against the earth like thunder rolling across the sky.

And, of course, the fact that it was Thursday.

He always drove the coach on Thursdays, and *he* was never late.

Just as she suspected, a moment later, the carriage finally rounded the bend behind her, and her ears perked like a hound on the hunt.

Her brow furrowed. No, not like a hound on the hunt. She was nothing like a hound on the hunt. She wasn't on the hunt at all. In fact, she was on the *opposite* of a hunt. She was . . . she was on the run, that was it. She was on the run from anything that would distract her from her responsibilities.

Not that a passing stagecoach would be a distraction nor the coachman directing it either. Mama and Papa had always warned her about those men—their desire for mischief with women, their only duty being to ensure they arrived at their next destination on time.

Her parents were right, of course. Mary had been wounded before by, well, never mind by whom. She'd moved on, she'd learned her lesson, and she'd made a solemn promise to never associate with a coachman again.

The coach rattled closer, but she kept her gaze forward. She didn't have the time to even glance at the contraption, let alone the driver. She needed to get back to the inn and her many duties.

Although, she would have to stand aside to ensure she was far away from the coach to be safe. And if she had to stop anyway . . .

She slowed her steps, moving farther off the lane as her eyes trailed along the puddle-pocked road, slid up the powerful bodies of the horses, then landed squarely on the intolerably handsome coachman.

Mr. Robert Northcott.

He watched her in return, his typical, overly confident smile already spread across his lips. He'd taken residence at the inn every Thursday over the last two months, enough for

Mary to know that his smile was always accompanied with some sort of trouble—playful words, winks, and grins.

Of course, she was too busy to deal with the uncommitted flirtations of a wanderer. Even one who was nearer her age and far younger than most coachmen. And far more attractive.

Thank heavens for his inflexible schedule, otherwise, she was sure he'd stop and speak with her. Incorrigible man.

But when their eyes locked, Mary's traitor-of-a-heart leapt in her chest. With a nod of her head, she extended a simple greeting, if only to prove to herself how indifferently she felt about him.

Then, just like that, the moment was gone, the stagecoach had passed, and Mr. Northcott—

"Oh!" she gasped, jerking her face and body to the side too late as the carriage tore through a deep puddle, spraying mud into the air and across the front of her.

In a daze, she stood still, holding her arms out from her sides as muddy water dripped from her sleeves. With her mouth agape, she blinked, giving her head a little shake. Droplets fled from her now-stringy hair and slipped down the front of her dress.

"Unbelievable," she muttered.

Mr. Northcott continued to fly down the road, apparently unaware of what he'd just inflicted upon her.

Not that he would care. After all, coachmen were all the same.

Robert Northcott traveled the final distance to the Golden Mermaid and pulled his team to a stop at the back of the inn, the passengers filing away from the coach as the ostler and stable boys rushed forward. Robert climbed down the side of the coach, planted his heavy boots on the ground, and arched his back with a groan and a satisfying stretch of his arms overhead. A few of his bones cracked as they settled back into place.

The journeys were getting longer. Not necessarily the distance but his ability to withstand the shifts of no sleep and short stops, constantly riding from post to post and inn to inn.

"Fine journey, sir?"

Robert glanced to the ostler, Mr. Berry, who worked with nimble movements to remove the carriage gear from the horses.

"Mostly," Robert responded, stroking the sweaty, matted hair of the black horse nearest him—a gelding known as Onyx.

"Fair weather?" Mr. Berry asked next, his common accent thick.

"Fortunately. Not a cloud in sight the entire journey." Robert firmly patted the horse—the only way he could express his gratitude to the creatures who pulled him and his passengers from county to county.

Mr. Berry removed the first horse, the stable boy racing the exhausted animal to a nearby stall and returning swiftly for the next.

"We must've taken all the rain from ye," Mr. Berry continued. "T'only just let up this mornin'."

Despite carrying on the conversation, the man's work never faltered. Robert wasn't surprised. Mr. Berry was as quick an ostler as he'd ever seen. He could change a horse in nearly under three minutes' time and never appeared anxious while doing so.

Another horse was led away as Robert continued stroking Onyx. Though none of the horses belonged to him, and they were changed every journey, he felt a certain kinship with them all. They worked together as a team with Robert at the head. He did his best not to push the horses to their limit, but what could be done when he, himself, was so beholden to a schedule? A schedule that, if not kept, could lead him to lose his position as a coachman forever.

As the ostler handed over Onyx to the stable boy, Robert winced at the sweaty markings spread across the animal's body from the tack. "Give them all a good rubbing down for me, will you?" he asked. "They rode well for me this journey."

"We will, sir." Mr. Berry nodded without missing a beat. He tacked up the four new horses in quick succession then looked past Robert's shoulder. "Nearly ready for ye, sir."

Robert glanced back to see the next coachman approaching from the inn. The man readjusted his gloves and stifled a yawn, grey circles framing his eyes.

Robert knew the man's exhaustion all too well. The dread of beginning a route was almost worse than the journey itself.

With an understanding nod, Robert passed him by and headed for the back door of the Golden Mermaid. Now was not the time to dread. Now was the time to put off the strain of his work and rest. To sit back by a warm fire and eat a hearty meal. To revel in his lack of attachments and responsibilities. To visit with other guests and converse with someone other than the coach's guard.

And to finally have the chance to speak with Miss Thorne again. She was always the one to help his loneliness subside the fastest.

"Mr. Northcott, may I have a word?"

Had his thoughts caused her sudden appearance?

With an instant smile, Robert turned to greet the woman. "What excellent timing, Miss Thorne. I was just . . ." He paused, taking in the sight of her. Typically, he did so in a slow manner, admiring her from head to toe—though never too improperly. Just enough to unsettle her under his gaze.

This time, however, *he* was ruffled. Brown stains tainted her dress, and her hair no longer hung in pretty ringlets at her temples, merely dripping straight in a stringy, wet mess. He'd never seen her in such disarray. It was rather . . . endearing.

"Miss Thorne, what on earth has happened to you?"

She gaped, propping her hands on her hips. Partially dried mud stained the tops of her fingers in long, dark streaks. "As if you do not know."

He pulled back, only vaguely aware of the coach and its new driver leaving the busy innyard. "I'm sure I do not know," he said. "If I was required to make an assumption, however, I would say you became involved in a disagreement with a mud puddle"—he leaned forward, lowering his voice—"and the mud puddle won."

Her lips pressed so firmly together, he could hardly see them anymore. Ah, he had missed this all week. Teasing Miss Thorne until she couldn't help but smile back. It was only a matter of time before her eyes twinkled with delight.

"How can you make light of this situation when it was you who caused it?" She watched him pointedly.

"You mean to imply that *I* did this?" He pulled back and gestured to her muddied brow.

With an impatient sigh, she nodded.

Finally, Robert's conscience was pricked. "I am terribly sorry, Miss Thorne. Truly, I had no idea." He reached for his handkerchief, extending it to her, then paused. "Oh dear. This will hardly help with the extent of washing you need. I ought to fetch you a towel, or perhaps even a bedsheet."

"How humorous you are, Mr. Northcott." She snatched his handkerchief from his hand and used it to wipe away the mud from around her eyes, though she only proved to smear it further.

He nearly snickered. "You resemble . . ." His words slowed at her ferocious scowl.

She really *was* upset. Perhaps telling her she reminded him of a very miserable badger he'd once chased as a boy was not the best of ideas. He cleared his throat. He did not wait all week to have Miss Thorne truly upset with him. Where was the enjoyment in that?

He sobered and stared deep into her eyes. "Miss Thorne, truly, I do apologize for having done this to you. I had not even the slightest notion I did. Believe me, I would have avoided you altogether had I known splashing you was even possible. I do hope you will forgive me."

She eyed him warily, clearly summing up his apology. After lowering his handkerchief, she raised her chin and attempted a dignified look.

She still looked like a badger.

"Thank you, Mr. Northcott. Your apology is accepted." She then took to wringing out her muddied, blond hair with the handkerchief, brown water dripping onto the dirt.

Her furrowed brow eased, and he was no longer able to resist. "I must say, I cannot regret what happened to you completely. I've always wondered how you would appear if you had darker hair." He stared, pretending to contemplate her appearance for a moment. "Now I can decidedly say that you were born with the color of hair that suits you best."

He flashed a grin, and she shook her head. "Will you never change, Mr. Northcott?"

He would have been discouraged by her words had he not seen the minor twitching of her lip which hinted at a greater smile to come.

He tipped his head toward her. "If I were a gambling man, I'd bet I could change more swiftly if you'd finally agree to sit beside me during dinner."

He knew her response before she even gave it. It was the same she'd given him once a week for two months.

"I'm terribly sorry, but I've a duty to my guests, as you well know."

"Do you not consider me one of your guests?"

She brushed her stringy hair away from her brow. "You certainly cause more trouble than any of them."

"Trouble? I'm always on my best behavior."

She huffed out a derisive laugh, though her scowl had disappeared altogether.

Success.

"If you've been on your best behavior," she said, "I'd hate to see you at your worst."

He chuckled, but a voice from behind cut his joviality short.

"Mary?"

Robert and Miss Thorne turned at once to the back of the inn where Mary's mother poked her head out of the open doorway.

"Will you help me, please?" she asked. Her scrutinizing gaze fell on Robert, and though he was fast approaching nine and twenty, he still squirmed like a guilty child under her calculating gaze.

Since the moment he'd left his route in Somerset and started driving the route that passed by the Golden Mermaid, he'd known Mrs. Thorne was a woman not to be crossed. Her stern gaze and no-nonsense approach to running her inn was admirable, though intimidating. Clearly, she did not approve of coachmen.

Or perhaps it was just Robert of whom she didn't approve.

"How do you do, Mr. Northcott?" she asked, not a hint of friendliness in her tone.

He nodded in greeting. "Looking forward to spending the night here, Mrs. Thorne, as usual."

She jerked her chin forward in what he could only assume was a nod then stifled a yawn and looked back to her daughter. "Mary?"

"I'm coming, Mama," Miss Thorne replied. She walked around Robert with swift steps.

"Miss Thorne?" he called out in a soft voice so her mother could not hear. "What of my request?"

With a slight lift of her lips, she nodded her head. "We shall see, Mr. Northcott." Then she scurried toward her mother.

Robert watched after her swaying skirts before realizing Mrs. Thorne was watching *him*. Swiftly, he cleared his throat and looked away, pretending to focus on the lint on his sleeve until Mrs. Thorne returned indoors with her daughter.

Robert would do well to tread carefully around the Thornes. One wrong move and he was certain he'd be prevented from speaking with Miss Thorne at all.

His work as a coachman didn't allow for attachments, and he was more than fine with that. He'd realize his goal of acquiring a route through London first, then he'd see where else life would take him. But for now, he wasn't ready to give up the harmless fun that he had flirting with the woman. Nor was he ready for responsibility.

At least, not yet.

Two

Thursday, April 20, 1815—One Week Later

MARY'S LONE FOOTSTEPS ECHOED down the empty corridor, reverberating against the deep-brown walls of the inn. At night, the darkness upstairs was impenetrable without a candle. But now, in the late afternoon, with slivers of light slipping beneath closed doors, an ethereal glow filled the air.

She loved this time of day, checking the rooms just before dinner. The new guests were below in the dining area, the old guests having already left on the outgoing coach. It was the one rare moment when all was still upstairs, when Mary could amble down the corridor and have a moment of peace amidst the tumult of the day, even though she was still hard at work.

Most of all, she enjoyed these moments because memories of her papa wrapped even more tenderly round her heart.

Pausing at the first door on her right, she gave a gentle knock, waiting the customary moment before entering the empty room. She knew exactly which accommodations had been vacated by the departing guests, but she hated the thought of intruding on anyone's privacy.

She swept her gaze about the room, ensuring she was, indeed, alone before going about her work.

Despite the maids being tasked with seeing to the rooms, Mary still made daily rounds to ensure all was in order and to take a swift inventory of what was needed from the servants. Floors washed of muddy footprints. Furnishings straightened. Linens removed and exchanged. Waning candles switched for new ones. Though most inns did not bother with such details, Papa had always insisted upon going above and beyond.

Show them we care, and the guests will return, he'd say.

Of course he was right.

Satisfied with the state of the room, Mary moved to the next and to the next, every step bringing back the memory of her time as a child doing the very same with Papa. She could almost imagine his tall figure leading her from room to room, her small hand wrapped in his long fingers, the aromatic smell of his pipe swirling around them.

She had eventually grown out of accompanying him during all of his tasks, but she never grew too old to miss his company.

Her heart grew heavy, weighed down by the memory that always followed any thought of Papa—when he lay on his bed, his skin as white as his sheets.

"We all have heartaches and trials, Mary," Papa had whispered as Mama cried at his opposite side. "And it is all right to have days filled with sorrow and pain. But these moments will pass. You will be happy again. The sun always shines behind heavy clouds. You must look hard for the light or simply wait for the storms to pass, for they always do."

Mary had spent five years attempting to overcome his death. The only thing pushing her to feel joy now was knowing Papa wished her to do so.

With a deep breath, she continued down the corridor,

skipping the rooms she knew guests were already occupying for the evening and moving on to the others.

After the fourth room had been checked, she turned to face the next, stopping abruptly when she realized whose accommodations she'd now reached—the room he always occupied every Thursday night.

Surely Mr. Northcott would be seated at the dining table already, awaiting a hearty meal after his long journey. Still, it was better to be safe. With swift footing, she scurried past the room on her tiptoes, not stopping until she reached the next vacant room, entering silently.

She had almost believed him last Thursday when he had said he wished to sit beside her at dinner. He must not have been too heartbroken when she'd avoided him though, for he'd spent the entirety of the meal flirting instead with another guest's eligible daughter.

Typical. The only person a coachman was concerned with was himself. And the only *thing* he was concerned with was reaching his destination on time, and even that was so he was compensated. Although, these men always did their best to ensure women believed the opposite was true, that money was not important.

Her brow furrowed as she absentmindedly eyed the room, memories entering her mind of another coachman, one who had promised her the world.

Charles Bolton had failed on that promise, leaving Clovelly and abandoning his hometown, his family, and Mary, all for a coachman's route and higher pay in London. She could imagine him now, flirting with all the women on his route without a care in the world, just like Mr. Northcott.

A swallow's happy twittering nearby caught her attention, and she snapped out of her thoughts long enough to notice the window partly open. It wouldn't do to have another bird fly into a room. The last time that had happened, the cleanup had lasted for nearly an hour.

Moving to the open window, she clasped the top of the frame and pushed down firmly, but it didn't budge. She grunted, trying again, but no amount of pushing or wriggling urged the stubborn frame from its place.

A creak sounded behind her, then soft footsteps came to an abrupt halt. "Miss Thorne?"

Dread pushed the breath from her lungs, and she closed her eyes in dismay. Blast Mr. Northcott for finding her in there. Blast Charles Bolton and his miserable memory that drove her to distraction.

And blast herself for not closing the door behind her to keep from being found.

Slowly, she turned around, drawing in measured breaths to avoid the appearance of being overexerted from attempting to shut the window. "Mr. Northcott." She brushed a strand of hair from her brow. "What are you doing in here?"

He remained in the doorway. "I could ask you the very same question." His smile revealed just how pleasantly surprised he was to have come upon her.

"Have I not the right to inspect the rooms we are to lease?" she asked.

"Of course. Only, I wonder why you're examining a room that is already occupied."

"This room isn't . . ." Her words faded away on their own as her logic finally returned. She spun her eyes about the room, only then noticing the bedsheets properly changed, the floor perfectly cleaned, and a portmanteau beside the bed. "This . . . this is your room?"

"It is."

"But what about the room you typically occupy?"

He took a few steps closer. She eyed the doorway that

now appeared three miles away due to his broad shoulders blocking most of her view.

"Another guest wished for the view of the sea," he explained. "Since I've seen it so often, I saw no harm in giving it up to her for an evening."

"I see," she said, refusing to believe he did so to be gallant. His actions were no doubt to deceive the woman into thinking he was a selfless individual.

She eyed the door again. This situation was hardly appropriate. Should another guest walk past them or, heaven forbid, Mama...

"Well, I do apologize, Mr. Northcott, for entering your bedchamber." She swallowed. "I never would have had I known you were staying here."

"That is a shame." He flashed a grin.

Appalling man. "I will leave you now to your privacy."

Before she could move, he stepped forward, motioning to the window. "Were you attempting to close this?"

She nodded, turning around to focus on the bubbled glass of one of the panes that warped the view of the garden below. "We've had experiences in the past with swallows flying into rooms."

"Then you must allow me to assist you, as I am the one to have opened it."

Of course he would be the culprit. He was always causing her trouble. Like when he'd arrived the first time and requested of her—rather, *insisted*—that he occupy the same room each time he stayed at the inn.

Never mind that he paid extra for the privilege.

She turned to face him. Intent on instructing him on the ways of a polite guest, her mouth dropped open, but she froze as she was met with the view of his bright yellow waistcoat and loosened cravat right before her eyes. When had he drawn so close to her?

She took a step back, bumping against the small window ledge as she peered up at him. His dark brown eyes shimmered with their usual teasing light, as if Mr. Northcott was more than aware of her tripping heart.

Taking a deep breath, she raised her chin. "Yes, closing the window is the least you could do."

He raised a knowing brow. "Indeed?"

Heat dragged its discomfiting fingers up her throat and settled heavily in her cheeks. How had she not caught the double meaning that could be taken from her words?

Because she was not a despicable coachman, that's how.

She propped her hands on her hips. "Clearly that is not what I intended to say, Mr. Northcott."

His grin only grew. Reaching forward, both his arms at either side of her, he leaned toward her.

She pulled back as much as the window ledge allowed. "What are you about?" she asked, indignation firing within her—not only because of his sheer audacity but because of her quickening pulse.

The scent of leather and a musty cologne slipped past her nose, and as he moved his arms down, brushing against her sleeves, chills erupted across her skin.

But she would not allow her logic to be compromised. "Step back, sir," she stated firmly. "I do not appreciate your advances, nor will I stand for them." Nor could she physically stand for much longer. For some reason, her knees had begun to quake.

Mr. Northcott smiled, filling her chest with something she couldn't quite put her finger on. No doubt annoyance.

"I was merely assisting you with the window, Miss Thorne." A thud sounded behind her, and he pulled his arms back from her sides without a touch.

Silence hung around them, the sound of the sea and

passing carriage wheels now muted from the closed window—the window he'd shut. How utterly humiliating.

"Heavens." He took a step back. "What did you imagine I was doing?"

Mary swallowed, face still burning. Mr. Northcott's expression revealed his lack of innocence in the matter, but still, her embarrassment would not yield.

"My apologies," she mumbled. "Thank you for your help. It would not budge for me."

"Nonsense. I'm sure you loosened it with all of your grunting earlier."

She looked up at him in time to see his wink, and suddenly, she was fighting off a smile. How did he always know what to say to elicit such a response from her? Even when they'd first met and his compliments had revealed his ridiculous flirtations, she'd still been unable to keep from smiling.

"At any rate," Mr. Northcott continued, "I'd do anything for you, Miss Thorne."

Mary froze. Those words. How she despised those words. They echoed round her mind and brought back the frequent moments Charles Bolton had said the very same to her.

I'd do anything for you, Miss Thorne.

The similarity was no coincidence. It was evidence. Evidence that Mr. Northcott and Charles were one and the same. Concerned only about themselves. Wanting only money and flirting. No responsibility, no commitment.

Never mind how they made a woman feel as though she could never be *enough*.

Thank heavens she was wiser than six years before. Thank heavens she would never fall for a coachman again.

"Miss Thorne?"

Blinking, she came out of her reverie.

"Are you well?" he asked.

With a curt nod, she spun on her heel. "I have never been better, Mr. Northcott. Good day." Without awaiting a response, she marched from the room.

Friday, April 28, 1815—One Week Later

A WEEK HAD PASSED since Mary had been discovered in Mr. Northcott's room, yet she still couldn't bear the thought of facing him.

Early Friday morning, she peered out the front door of her home behind the inn. Papa had built the two-bedroom house years ago to provide Mama with privacy. Though the chambers and small sitting room were attached to one of the inn's corridors, Mary preferred leaving through the front entrance, if only to step outside for a moment of fresh air. This morning would be no different, she'd make sure of it—just like she'd ensure there was no chance of happening upon Mr. Northcott.

She swept her eyes across the grounds, taking a hesitant step forward. This was silly. If she knew one thing about coachmen, it was their stringent rule to leave and arrive at the precise moment they were scheduled to. According to the coach's route, Mr. Northcott would've left exactly five minutes ago. Mary really had no need to worry.

After a few slightly confident steps across the grounds, her attention was drawn to a horse's shrill whinny cutting through the air from the stables, followed by a man's shouting and more neighs from the horse.

Mary shifted directions at once, making for the stables. As she approached the innyard entrance, however, she stopped.

The coach was still there. Why was it still there?

Swiftly, she swept her gaze about the innyard, but there was no sign of Mr. Northcott.

The horse's whinny stole her attention again, and her eyes drew to the large, black horse rearing on its hind legs.

Onyx. He was the most high-spirited horse they housed.

Mr. Berry stood before the animal, pulling him back down with a firm tug on the reins. "Whoa!" he shouted, red-faced. A vein pulsed straight down the center of his forehead. "Easy, boy!"

The horse didn't listen, attempting to rear again. He tossed his head up and down, stomping his hooves on the straw-covered cobblestones. The clacking sound filled the air before Onyx sent another shrill whinny through the innyard.

Despite her chest tightening at the sight, Mary's heart reached out to the animal. He had to be exhausted, even after the rest he'd received. One evening wasn't long enough to recover from the coachmen running him and all the other horses into the ground.

Of course, the *owners* of the coaches, routes, and horses were mostly to blame. Mr. Drake—the man who controlled the route through Clovelly—had promised to purchase more horses for years but had never actually followed through.

"James!" Mr. Berry called over his shoulder. "Fetch another lead!"

James, the stable boy, disappeared into the row of stalls.

"Easy!" the ostler continued shouting.

Two stable hands stood back without any offer of aid, their eyes wide with terror. Had they really only one able man competent enough to care for the horse?

She knew better than to think she could help the man or the animal, but perhaps she could fetch someone who could.

"He doesn't need another lead."

The calm voice spoken at the side of the coach sent a jolt through Mary's stomach. With a soft gasp, she darted behind a nearby stall to hide from the coachman.

"He needs help," Mr. Northcott continued, his voice reaching Mary in her hiding place.

Slowly, she peered around the light wood of the stall. From her vantage point, she could see the interaction perfectly.

"I know that, sir," Mr. Berry said. "That's what I be tryin' to do for 'im. But 'e be angry, sir. Too angry."

The horse flung his head in the air again as if to prove the man's words.

"He's not angry," Mr. Northcott said with level words. "He's anxious." He reached forward, his hand grasping the lead above Mr. Berry's fingers and taking control of the horse.

"He always be like this, sir," Mr. Berry said, backing away with a wary look. "He never calms down 'til he's had 'is fit."

Mary leaned farther out of the stall. She needn't worry about being seen. Mr. Northcott wasn't looking at anyone but the horse.

"Whoa," he said, his voice deep and low. "Whoa, there." The horse continued with his rant, but Mr. Northcott was unyielding. He allowed the horse another rear then tightened the slack on the lead with a firm hand, drawing Onyx closer toward him. "Easy, easy," he soothed.

After a few more tosses of his head and another attempt

at rearing, the gelding finally stood on all fours. He stomped his feet on the ground, snorting with exhaustion.

"Whoa, boy." Mr. Northcott placed a calm hand on the horse's forehead. The horse attempted to rear again before he allowed Mr. Northcott's soothing touch, and the creature responded with a low, anxious nicker.

Mary fixed her gaze on the man, unable to look away. She'd heard of Mr. Northcott's horsemanship as much as she'd heard of his punctuality—and his ability to make grown women swoon, but that was neither here nor there. Never had she expected this calmness to exude from such a person before. Never had she expected such patience and control.

"Good man," he said, stroking the horse's nose then neck.

"Sir?" Mr. Berry spoke in a hushed whisper, his wide eyes on the horse and coachman. "I don't mean to rush ye, but ye already be late."

"I know."

Mary nearly fell over. Mr. Northcott *knew* he was late?

He stood, calmly patting the horse, his expression easy and stance comfortable. She could only imagine the passengers waiting at the front of the inn, wondering where their ever-so-prompt coachman was.

"It is better to have the horses at ease before we leave," Mr. Northcott said. "I wouldn't risk them being in more danger of injuring themselves than they already are."

He couldn't care so greatly about this horse that he'd risk losing money or even possibly his route . . . could he?

"Are there any other horses that can be used?" Mr. Northcott asked next.

"No, sir. We 'ave only eight for the coaches."

Mary could almost feel Mr. Northcott's disapproving frown directed at her. "There ought to be at least a few more to be kept for matters such as these."

"Aye, sir. The Thornes be pushin' the owner of the coaches to purchase more, but 'e hasn't budged for years."

There. At least Mr. Northcott now knew she and Mama were doing what they could to help the horses.

"Of course," Mr. Northcott grumbled with a heavy sigh. "Well, as wary as I am to have this one on the team, I suppose we haven't any other option."

"No, sir. At least 'e seems to 'ave lost 'is anger enough now."

Mr. Northcott was silent for a moment before responding in a soft voice. "As I said before, he wasn't angry or acting out of aggression. He is anxious. Perhaps he even feels the pressure of pulling the coach again."

Mr. Berry's expression shifted to one of thoughtfulness as he stared at the horse.

"Have you access to any chamomile?" Mr. Northcott asked.

"The 'erb, sir?"

"Yes."

"Aye, sir." He scrunched his brow together. "Ye be wantin' some tea right now?"

"No, it's for the horse."

Mr. Berry's expression crumpled with incredulity. "Tea for the horse?"

"No," Mr. Northcott said, smiling. "Although that is one way to administer it. Chamomile does wonders for anxious horses. Perhaps you could put a small handful of dried chamomile flowers in his feed just once a day when he is here. It will act as a mild sedative to help him rest while not running, then perhaps his mind will be more at ease when his turn comes to run again."

A strange warmth settled inside Mary's chest, as if she'd just taken a sip of hot chamomile tea herself.

"Well, I be willin' to try it, sir," Mr. Berry said.

Mr. Northcott nodded then gradually handed the lead to the ostler. "Move slowly. I'd hate to rile him up again."

"But the time, sir."

"I'm well aware of the time. It matters not if it assures the safety of the horse and the passengers, were he to become anxious again."

Mr. Berry nodded, carefully taking control of the horse and leading him toward the coach. But he stopped midway as he met Mary's gaze. "Anything I can do for ye, Miss Thorne?"

The warmth in her chest fled as quickly as light at sunset. He'd spotted her, which meant . . .

Her eyes darted to Mr. Northcott. Sure enough, he'd turned to face her as well. How had they managed to find her? She peered at the stall she'd taken shelter behind, realizing she had become so engrossed with what was happening that she'd removed herself from her hiding place altogether and now stood directly in front of the men in the entryway to the innyard.

Blast.

―――

Robert had to hide his smile. Miss Thorne's face was as red as the cherry tart the inn had served with dinner the evening before. How long had she been standing there, observing their interactions with Onyx?

"No, thank you, Mr. Berry." She glanced at Robert then looked away. "I only heard the commotion with the horse and came to see that all was well."

"Yes, ma'am. Mr. Northcott 'ere was able to 'elp."

She didn't look at Robert again. With a simple nod, she turned to leave.

Robert hesitated. The woman had been avoiding him

ever since he'd found her in his room—which had been, indeed, a delightful surprise. But her embarrassment had to have fled by now, hadn't it? Or was she avoiding him for another reason?

He didn't really wish to become involved in any potential female dramatics, but then Miss Thorne was different than most females. She didn't chase after him.

With a quick glance to the ostler who was still struggling to move slowly, Robert said, "I'll return in just a moment," then he left the innyard behind. "Miss Thorne?"

She continued walking across the dirt grounds, though he was fairly certain she'd heard him loud and clear.

"Miss Thorne, a moment?"

She forged ahead.

With a hidden smile, he stopped, folded his arms, and called after her one more time. "So you're still avoiding me, are you?"

She stopped, turning to face him. "Whyever would you say that?"

"Because you *have* been avoiding me."

She fidgeted with her fingers, her eyes shifting down. "I have not. I've merely been busy."

"Too busy to speak with me or notice me, yet not too busy to watch me from the shadows of a horse's stall?"

Her blush deepened. Instead of admitting to anything, however, she motioned to the innyard. "How . . . How did you know? About the chamomile, I mean."

Robert could only imagine his awaiting passengers tapping their feet impatiently and grumbling about his delay. It was fine. They could wait. Mr. Berry was no doubt still working on tacking up Onyx. Probably.

"I learned it as a stable boy. The stable master of the estate where I was employed knew a great deal about horses, and I listened and learned from him as best I could."

And that stable master was as close to a father figure as Robert ever had. Indeed, Robert owed the man everything, for he had been the one to turn Robert on to the path he was on now.

"So you're a stable boy turned coachman?" Miss Thorne asked.

From where were these questions coming? For the two months they'd known each other, Miss Thorne had never asked him about his past.

"I am," he replied. "With plenty of hard work in between."

"And this life appeals to you, the life of a coachman?"

He tipped his head to the side, taking in her averted gaze. Was she fishing for something? "What is not to enjoy about the freedom I experience?" Apart from being beholden to timetables and passengers' requests and horses' exhaustion, of course. In truth, the coachman's life was not glamorous, nor was it easy. Still, he'd worked far too hard to quit now. He was so close to obtaining his goal. Working a route in London would be just the thing to help him earn more of an income, and then he'd . . . he'd . . .

Well, he didn't know what he would do after that. But he'd worry about all of that just as soon as he accomplished what he'd spent eight years of his life striving for.

Miss Thorne's lips set in a rigid line. Did she not approve of his answer?

"Well," she said, "I am anxious to see if your little remedy of chamomile works."

"You doubt that it will?"

She shrugged. "I've just never seen a coachman care for a horse before."

Robert winced, the words burning him as if he'd sat too close to a fire. He knew better than anyone how his livelihood depended on pushing these animals. Did she not realize he was trying to remedy that by attempting to improve Onyx's life with the chamomile?

If Miss Thorne knew of his guilt even an ounce . . . but she didn't. No one did. And that was fine by him. He'd gone his whole adult life without any attachments, and he'd be just fine continuing on his own. Attachments just made life messy. He could stave off the loneliness without them. Not that he was lonely, of course. He had his passengers, the coach's guard, the horses.

He didn't need the innkeeper's daughter.

"I suppose you're right, Miss Thorne." With a curt nod, he backed away. "I'll be off now."

"Yes, your passengers will be waiting."

He didn't respond, ignoring the edge to her tone and focusing instead on how he was to make up for the time he'd lost on the road. Let Miss Thorne think the worst of him. He hardly cared about her poor opinion of him. After all, punctuality was more important than anything—or anyone—else.

It was time he showed that.

 Four

Thursday, May 4, 1815—One Week Later

MARY KNEW SHE'D OFFENDED Mr. Northcott. What she *didn't* know was why she cared. For days she rehearsed their conversation in her mind, searching for an explanation as to why she felt remorse when she'd merely pointed out the truth—that most coachmen didn't care for the welfare of their teams of horses.

The fact of the matter was, however, that Mr. Northcott had already proven her wrong. He clearly cared for the animals, even if he drove them hard. No wonder he'd disliked being grouped into that category of heartless, thoughtless, unfeeling men.

Now all Mary had to do was accept the belief that he *was* different, at least in that small regard. Even more regrettably, she needed to apologize. After all, she couldn't have him taking his business elsewhere or the business of the passengers he brought to the Golden Mermaid. He could very well request to have his route extended to the inns beyond Clovelly. Even though she disliked most coachmen, Mr. Northcott had never done anything to injure her. At least not yet.

As the weather warmed and the first Thursday in May arrived, Mary entered the dining room earlier than usual. She swallowed her pride, and she prepped her mind once again with what she would say to Mr. Northcott. Before she could rehearse her words silently once more, Mama arrived right behind her.

"Will you be joining us for dinner tonight, Mary?"

"I believe so."

She was silent for a moment. "I thought you were still avoiding Mr. Northcott."

Mary blushed. Mama had never been one to mince words. *Why remain silent when one is capable of avoiding misunderstandings by simply speaking?* Mama would always say.

Mary hesitated. She hadn't told Mama about her time in Mr. Northcott's room, nor would she. She could only imagine the unnecessary warnings she'd receive from Mama after already instructing herself to never allow such a thing to occur again.

"I *was* avoiding him," she answered carefully.

"And did he give you any reason *to* avoid him?"

She knew at once to what Mama was referring. "No. No, nothing like that. I simply did not wish to bear his flirtatious remarks." Not to mention the embarrassment she felt over being caught in his room and assuming he was about to kiss her. And the anger she'd felt over his reminding her of Charles.

Mama nodded. "Coachmen can be unrelenting in their pursuit of women. Though you and I both know they are married to their positions." She gave Mary a knowing look, one that spoke of the past, of Charles Bolton and his cruelty in his treatment of her. Her parents had both disapproved of him from the start, but they'd allowed Mary to make her own decision regarding the man—poor as it may have been.

She'd learned to never disregard their advice again.

Mama reached up, placing a hand to Mary's cheek. "Take heart, my dear. We will one day see you happily settled, as I was with your father."

Mary had every reason to believe her mother. But with most men already having planned their futures, the likelihood of finding someone who would support her decision to remain at the inn—to one day *run* the inn—seemed slimmer and slimmer.

If Mama would ever allow her to run the inn, that is.

Mary's brow furrowed. Her parents had always intended to give her sole control of the Golden Mermaid when she was older and had proven herself capable. With Papa's early death and Mama's exhaustion setting in, Mary thought perhaps she'd receive that control earlier.

But Mama had not spoken of it seriously for years. Of course, she hadn't spoken much of anything the last few years. Would she be more willing to discuss the matter now, to rest from her weariness and allow Mary charge over the inn?

"Mama, have you given any more thought to . . ." Her words trailed off as Mama stifled a yawn, her eyes watering. Was that due to her yawn, or were they tears of sorrow?

"More thought to what, my dear?"

Mary shook her head. She couldn't put Mama through even more stress by mentioning anything that might upset her further. "Never mind. Shall we welcome the guests together?"

She led the way to the front door, focusing on the task at hand while keeping her eye out for Mr. Northcott. But her chance to apologize to him never came.

The Coachman's Choice

She didn't see him until after the meal had begun, when he'd quietly slipped in at the opposite end of the table. She'd attempted to get his attention multiple times, but his focus had been taken by the man speaking beside him for the majority of the meal. At first, she thought it was simply because he was distracted, but when the meal concluded and the coachman walked past her without so much as a smile, merely a polite nod void of any twinkling eyes, her chest sank.

He was behaving this way on purpose. Was this because of her doing the same to him the week before? Or was his coldness due to her harsh words?

She attempted to brush off the slight as easily as she could brush off the crumbs from the dining room table, but her eyes continued to stray toward him.

Well, if he wouldn't even give her the chance to apologize, perhaps she didn't need to. And she really ought to be grateful he was no longer paying attention to her. Now she could go about her business without delay.

With a lighter step, she resolved to move on.

Just like Mr. Northcott had moved on, apparently with two of her maids.

Her throat constricted, as if she'd swallowed the half-chicken they'd had for dinner before fully chewing the meat. Seated beside Mr. Northcott at the fire were Agnes and Caroline, the servants Mama had hired weeks ago to help around the inn. Mr. Northcott had his arms stretched out behind both their chairs that were situated closely to him. He said something with a flash of that grin that had been so often directed at her, and the girls laughed.

Mary's face burned. She couldn't believe the audacity of the girls, sitting down when there was work to be done. She would not stand for this. With clenched fists, she marched toward them. "Agnes, Caroline."

The girls gasped, standing at once to face Mary. "Ma'am," they said in unison.

"You are neglecting your duties."

Mr. Northcott—still lounging back like a lazy hound in the summer sun—shook his head. "Not necessarily, Miss Thorne. They were looking after your guest here. I was only fortunate the two of them were so willing to oblige."

He winked at the girls, whose lips both pulled in to hide their grins.

"Mm, yes. I'm sure they were." Mary propped her hands on her hips and faced the maids. "If you two would like to keep your stations here, I suggest you run along and be about your *real* duties."

The girls' smiles faded at once, and they nodded before scurrying away with quick steps. Mary's gaze dropped, pulled down by the weight of guilt and regret. She needn't have been so harsh with them. Threatening their way of living was too much. Besides, she'd been older than they when she'd fallen for the cunning ways of a coachman.

"Do you really think that was necessary, Miss Thorne?"

Her eyes flew to Mr. Northcott. His smile had faded away, his disapproving gaze resting on her from where he still sat.

She blinked. No matter that she agreed with his assessment of her treatment of the girls. That didn't give him the right to judge her for it.

Her pride bristled, becoming as pointed as the pine trees on the road to Clovelly. "You have some nerve to say such a thing, Mr. Northcott, when you were the one to pull them from their work."

"We were merely having a carefree conversation."

How she ever thought this man deserved an apology was beyond her. She'd been absolutely correct in her assumption of him. He may care for horses, but he had no thought for anyone else.

"They are more than welcome to carry on such a conversation outside of the hours for which we pay them to work. I trust you'll not encourage them to shirk their duties again."

With his arms still draped over the backs of the now-vacant chairs, he smirked. "I'll do my best."

"That is not enough. Do I have your word, Mr. Northcott?" she pressed, enunciating each word as one would speak to a child she was instructing.

"Do you wish for me to no longer converse at all, or would you prefer my flirting to be solely directed at you, simply to assuage your jealousy?"

Her mouth popped open. "My jealousy? What a ridiculous thing to say."

Finally, Mr. Northcott stood to his full height. "Is it ridiculous?"

Mary did not typically think of herself as petite or short. In fact, she was taller than most women with whom she was acquainted. But standing in front of Mr. Northcott within such proximity to his broad shoulders and wide stance, she felt as if she'd be swallowed up in his figure alone.

She wouldn't let him know that though. She raised her chin, hoping it gave her another inch or so. "Of course it is ridiculous. I am not jealous. I am frustrated."

"If you insist."

She narrowed her eyes. "Why do you doubt me?"

"I don't."

"Yes, you do. I can see the disbelief written as clear as day across your face."

His lip twitched. "Perhaps I doubt you because I can see your jealousy over my flirting with others written as clear as day across *your* face."

"I . . . I . . ." Why did she sputter like a teapot running out of steam?

His smile grew. "Worry not. I will no longer pay such attention to your maids, if only to leave more time for the both of us to become better acquainted."

She pulled in her brows. She didn't want him to *not* flirt with the maids just so he *would* flirt with her. Before she could think, her words let loose. "Why do men believe flirting is the only way to know a woman better? We enjoy being flattered as much as the next person, but such conversation frankly becomes exhausting. Are you lacking in intelligence so greatly that you can think of no other way to speak to us?"

He stared mutely.

She should have stopped, but the carriage had already left the yard. "You would do well to remember that we are more than simple, delicate creatures ready to hear compliments and affectionate words alone, Mr. Northcott. We deserve more. We deserve better."

Silence followed her speech. His eyes narrowed just a fraction, as if he attempted to comprehend her words.

Heavens. She must have sounded excessively arrogant. She should have held her tongue. Backing away, she ducked her head to hide her growing blush. "I shall read your silence as your agreement to no longer interfere with me or the help here at the inn."

He nodded, resuming his seated position in silence.

"Thank you. Goodnight, Mr. Northcott."

Without awaiting a response, she fled from the dining room. Well, it appeared as if her point had finally been taken.

And now she only had two things on her mind—apologizing to the maids for snapping at them . . . and trying to figure out why she had done so in the first place.

Five

Friday, May 5, 1815—The Next Morning

ROBERT AWOKE THE NEXT morning with a stiff neck. He'd never had such a horrible night's sleep. If only he could blame it on the bed or the room, but the Golden Mermaid had always had the best—and cleanest—accommodations along his route. He was grateful to be back in his familiar room this week. The straw in the mattress was evenly distributed, the fresh scent of the newly picked flowers filled the space, and the area was quiet, apart from the soft sounds of the other guests moving about their rooms.

No, the inn was not at fault for his restless night. His troubled mind was. Still lying on his pillow, he turned to the window with a cricked neck. The morning sun glinted against the windowpanes. It couldn't be much later than six o'clock, still an hour before he would be required to take over his coaching duties.

What was he to do until then when sleep was futile and lying in bed was unproductive? He could spend some time with the horses perhaps. Or walk about Clovelly. Either way, he certainly wouldn't be seeking out the maids that morning.

His insides twisted like a strung rag. Miss Thorne had overreacted the night before. He'd meant no harm. He never did while flirting with maids, landladies, or female passengers alike. Furthermore, he'd never heard a complaint from any of them until Miss Thorne's last night.

There was no doubt her words were born from jealousy. Even still, they'd shaken his very core, enough to cause him to forget about her hurtful words about his treatment of horses the week before.

He'd always considered himself respectful of women. He'd certainly never pressed them in any physical manner. But was it possible, perhaps, that he'd allowed his flirtations to get out of hand? After all, the only conversations he now held with women were of the flattering sort.

With no rest from his agitated thoughts or pained neck, Robert rolled out of bed with a groan. It was going to be a wretch to drive along his route this way. Heaven help him.

He rubbed his tense muscles with one hand as he crossed the room to the window. A little fresh air would do him good, and the sound of the sea, unhindered by glass or rolling carriages, always helped when his mind was troubled.

He slid the glass open with ease. This window was far easier to open and close than the one with which he'd helped Miss Thorne.

He paused, his brow furrowing. All he'd done in that past moment was flirt too. Was Miss Thorne right? Was he lacking in intelligence because he could think of nothing else to do besides compliment women?

"Wretched, irresponsible, loathsome men."

His ears perked at the feminine voice floating toward him from the window. There was no mistaking Miss Thorne's grumbling. But where was she? He scoured the grounds visible from his room, her voice rising toward him again.

"Never staying here again, that's for certain," she continued.

Finally, he spotted her alone at the base of the inn, kneeling over a patch of dirt amidst a few rosebushes. Was she *gardening*?

He opened his mouth, ready to deliver his favorite flirtatious remark—"I certainly am enjoying the view, Miss Thorne." But when her words echoed in his mind, he paused.

You would do well to remember that we are more than simple, delicate creatures ready to hear compliments and affectionate words alone, Mr. Northcott.

Slowly, he closed the window to avoid any chance of her discovering him watching her. In silence he dressed, gathered his belongings, and headed down the stairs. The inn was quiet, except for the clinking of cutlery in the dining area as the help readied the morning meals.

Instead of going out the back door of the inn, Robert maneuvered his way to the front entrance, telling himself he was doing so simply to catch the view of the sea from the side of the house. Yet, as he rounded the inn, his eyes were instead taken by Miss Thorne, whose head was still buried beneath the rosebush, her arm extended far into the greenery.

"Blasted . . . wretched—"

"Miss Thorne?"

She gasped, her head swinging up into the bushes. Robert winced. Perhaps he should've alerted her of his presence in a better way.

"My apologies," he said, leaning forward to help, only to pull back when he realized there was nothing he *could* do to help.

Miss Thorne backed out of the bushes, peering up at him

from her hands and knees. "Mr. Northcott, what can I do for you?"

His instinct was to say something along the lines of, "You can tell me your secret to looking more beautiful every time I see you." But after last night...

"You can allow me to help you stand," he settled with instead. He shuffled his belongings—hat, outer coat, leather gloves, and portmanteau—to his other arm, then extended his free hand to her.

She peered at it with a wary eye then finally placed her dirt-riddled fingers into his palm and stood.

At her touch, a heat slid up his arm warmer than the summer sun. Their gazes met, and her blue eyes rounded. A few strands of her hair had been tugged loose by the branches, the wavy locks now curving down her smooth skin, cheeks as red as the roses beside them. She certainly was a striking woman. But he wouldn't risk saying such a thing.

Swiftly, she withdrew her hand and stood away from him. "Thank you, sir."

He nodded in silence. Had he tied his cravat too securely? That was the only explanation he could concoct as to why his throat suddenly felt too tight. He looked to the ground between them, only then noticing the pile of glass she'd accumulated near the rosebushes.

"What on earth caused that mess?" he asked.

Miss Thorne shook her head. "A few gentlemen met here last evening. They were in the private parlor before converging out of doors with their drinks until the early hours of the morning."

Robert grimaced. "I hope this is deducted from their amount owed."

"The three of them chose to leave earlier on a privately hired carriage before we could confront them. Though, rest assured, they're no longer welcome at the Golden Mermaid." Her voice was tense, as if she was at the end of her patience.

He wouldn't blame her if she was. He glanced around, amazed he hadn't heard the gentlemen with them being just outside his room. Chairs were overturned, burn marks were scattered across the table from the pipes' ashes, and glass was spread from one end of the cobblestoned sitting area to the next.

"What could possess anyone to mistreat someone's property in such a way is beyond me," he mumbled.

"Mm. If only it weren't typical of—" She cut her own words off and averted her gaze.

"Typical of whom, exactly?" he coaxed. "Of coachmen?"

She eyed him sidelong. "I was going to say men in general. Then I thought perhaps you'd had enough scolding after last night."

He paused. Was she teasing him?

Before he could decipher where this sudden change had come from, she turned away. "Are you in need of anything this morning, Mr. Northcott, before you depart? If not, I should like to continue with my task."

"No, by all means." He took a step back and motioned for her to continue.

As she crossed his path, the scent of roses followed her. He watched her every movement as she knelt beside the flower bed once more and removed another shard carefully from the dirt.

"May I ask why you are cleaning this rather than a gardener or another member of your household?"

She huffed, reaching for another piece. "Just because my mother owns the Mermaid does not mean I am incapable of tasks such as these." She pulled another piece of glass from the dirt. "At any rate, everyone else has their own duties to see to this morning."

"Yourself included, I take it."

"Yes, but I found a moment to spare. Besides, after you so shrewdly pointed out my cruelty to the maids last evening, I thought better than to burden them with this task."

Had it not been for the lightness of her tone, he would've sworn she was still upset with him. The tightness in his neck dissipated, and his thoughts cleared. Why was he just standing there when she was working?

Without hesitation, he righted a chair and draped his belongings over the arms of it. When he hunched down and began to create his own pile of glass pieces near the table, Miss Thorne's eyes seared into his back.

"What are you doing?"

"Helping you retrieve the glass."

"But, why? You did not create the mess."

"Neither did you."

"No, but I *do* work here. We both know you do not."

He retrieved a large piece of green glass from the crack in the cobbles where a broom could not reach. "No, but as you earlier pointed out your dislike for men as a whole, I would like to salvage your opinion of at least one of them."

Her cheeks colored red once again.

"Besides," he said, reaching for another piece of glass, "I'm fairly certain I brought the guilty men here on my coach." It wasn't difficult to surmise the fact. Three younger men. Reckless, uncaring, and boisterous. They certainly wouldn't have hesitated to create such destruction. "They requested driving the coach on the journey here," he said.

"And did you allow them to?"

Such a thing was not uncommon for coachmen to permit, especially for an extra price, but Robert rarely did so. It wasn't worth the risk. Hearing the judgment in Miss Thorne's voice, however, made him pause in his response.

"What do you think?" he asked, then he focused his eyes on her.

───~·~───

Mary had a mind to tell the coachman exactly what she thought of him and his whole *breed*. But then, doing so last night had only left her with that draining feeling of regret. And how could she say such things when he clearly cared for his horses' well-being and now crawled around on all fours to help the innkeeper's daughter pick up shards of glass so early in the morning?

"No," she finally answered. "No, I don't believe you'd ever intentionally endanger your horses or your passengers."

He remained stationary for a long moment, then smiled—not a flirtatious smirk but one of satisfaction. A smile so soft, she might've missed it had she not been looking straight at him.

"You are correct in your belief, Miss Thorne," he said, then he looked away and resumed his work.

Mary watched him for a moment, noting his strong brow and the angle of his jaw.

"So tell me, Miss Thorne. How long have you and your mother been running the inn together?"

Mary pulled her gaze away. How long had she been staring? "The Golden Mermaid has been in my family for generations." She ducked her head beneath a rose branch to retrieve a glass particularly far away. "Mama and I took control when my father died five years ago."

"Oh, I'm sorry to hear that." His eyes found hers. "That must have been a difficult time for you both."

She nodded but said nothing further. She didn't wish for pity. She'd had enough of that from all of Clovelly when Papa had succumbed to the fever. "And what of your parents or family?" she asked, desperate to change the subject. "Do you ever get to see them with your busy life as a coachman?"

"No, I have no family and never knew either of my parents."

Her heart sank. "Oh." Was that all she could say? She should apologize, express condolences, ask after them. But if he didn't know either of them, did that mean he was . . .

"I can see the question burning in your eyes," Mr. Northcott said. "No, I am not illegitimate. Merely a poor orphan boy who lost his parents to the same illness days apart when he was a babe."

He gave a simple smile, and Mary's cheeks pinched with heat. "I'm-I'm sorry."

"Are you apologizing for the loss of my parents or for assuming the worst of me again?"

She winced. "Both?"

He breathed a short laugh. "In that case, thank you, and your apology is accepted."

He returned his attention to the task, but Mary felt as if she needed to say something further, if only to change the subject. "So how did you become a coachman then?"

He ran his fingers through his brown hair then continued with the glass. "When I was very young, I was taken in by a farmer and his wife. Eventually, they could no longer care for me when their own family grew, so I moved on to work at a few different estates. I eventually ended up at Rudhek Manor in Cornwall, and as I mentioned before, I was taught by the stable master. I realized my dream of traveling across England with a team of horses, thanks to him." He straightened for a moment to look at her. "I really have been blessed."

Mary stared in awe, the glass pile by her side forgotten. He sounded—heaven forgive her for comparing the two—like Papa. His positivity, his outlook on life, was the very same.

"You are astonished by something I've said?" he asked.

She shook her head, unable to say a word.

Mr. Northcott gave her a questioning look then glanced to the ground around them. "Well, I believe we have gathered most of the larger pieces. If you so desire, I have been known to wield a broom to an acceptable degree."

"No," she stated at once, softening her words in an instant. "No, thank you. You've already done so much as it is. Besides, I'm certain you must make ready for the coach when it arrives."

He nodded, joining their piles of glass together then standing as she did. An awkward silence passed between them, and he looked out to the turquoise sea. Why was he not leaving? Why was *she* not leaving?

"Miss Thorne?"

She peered up at him. "Yes?"

"I have given a great deal of thought to what you said last night, and I'm inclined to agree with you."

Her mind raked through the words she'd said the night before. In what way did he agree with her? Had she not been overly harsh? Conceited even?

"At any rate," he continued, "I was simply hoping to apologize if I have ever offended you. Knowing you are not keen on . . . on the way I typically speak with you and other females, I wish to respect your wishes and hope we may begin our friendship anew."

Mary stared. Was this man truly in earnest? His stalwart gaze and missing smile certainly pointed in that direction. But then, how could she possibly be sure? She thought she'd known Charles Bolton, and that had turned out, well, less than noteworthy.

"I understand if you do not wish to though," he continued. His expression was contrite, void of any teasing at all.

And blast it all, if the barriers round Mary's heart didn't break into shards messier than the glass at her feet.

What could be the harm in agreeing to a friendship, really? If he strayed once, she'd be sure to let him know—and never speak with him again. Finally, she lowered her guard just enough to allow a sliver of light to pass beneath it. "I would be more than happy to begin our friendship anew, Mr. Northcott."

Relief crossed his face as his brow raised. "Excellent. Then I shall see you next Thursday, *my friend*."

She nodded in agreement as he retrieved his belongings from the chair. Replacing his hat, he tipped it to her then headed toward the stables.

My friend, he'd said. Mr. Northcott's friend. Who would have ever thought?

Six

Thursday, June 1, 1815—One Month Later

MARY HAD HAD LITTLE confidence Mr. Northcott would hold up his end of the bargain. To her utter surprise, however, over the last few weeks, he'd done more than that.

Not only did he stop flirting with Mary, but she was hard-pressed to discover him speaking words of flattery to any maid or guest at all. Of course, she was not naïve enough to think a coachman could change his ways so swiftly. He could very well be flirting with every woman in the county for all she knew.

Even though the thought made her stomach twist for reasons she couldn't decipher, she found herself caring less and less about what he may or may not be doing elsewhere as the weeks moved on, for she discovered a strange and surprising trust of and camaraderie with the man.

The first Thursday after they'd gathered the broken glass together, the two sat across from each other at the dining table, discussing comfortably every matter from Mary's experience growing up at the Golden Mermaid to Mr. Northcott's history working at the estate in Cornwall.

"I was treated well," Mr. Northcott had said. "The Summerfields provided a decent income, and living close to the sea was tremendous."

Mary had listened, deeply intrigued by his story. "And has traveling England been as grand as you imagined it to be?"

His smile had faltered. "Yes . . . and no. I do admit, it is a little exhausting at times. But I've a goal to achieve."

"And what goal is that?"

"Well, ever since I began my work as a coachman, I've wanted to obtain a route through London. I've been working hard for years now, and I believe it may soon be realized."

"How exciting," she'd responded, though her spirits had fallen instantly.

Thank heavens they were only friends. The reminder of how Mr. Northcott was similar to Charles Bolton—wishing for more money and for a London route, which provided better pay, tips, and customers—had just been further evidence that nothing more could happen between them.

Afterwards, Mr. Northcott had turned the attention on her. She then spent far longer than she'd meant to speaking of her love for the inn and how she looked forward to the day Mama entrusted her with total control of the Golden Mermaid.

"I've put in a great deal of thought as to how we can improve the quality of the inn and the lives of those who either work here or are guests here. Pushing for more coach horses to be purchased, leasing out some of the land to local farmers. I've heard of some inns even creating their own breweries for extra income."

She'd been more than flattered to note Mr. Northcott's impressed look. "Will your mother give you control soon, do you think?"

Mary had shrugged. "I've no idea. I know she has grown

weary of the work here. Her strength is not what it once was. And I believe I've earned her trust, but for now, I will simply continue to learn from her as best I can. And try to be patient."

Mr. Northcott had leaned back in his chair, swigging his drink. "Well, I know my opinion means very little, but this is by far the best inn at which I've ever stayed. The food, the cleanliness. I recommend it to every one of my passengers."

Mary had scrutinized him, fearing he was saying such things only out of flattery, but she could only find truth in his expression. She and her family had worked hard to make the Golden Mermaid a respite for the weary. To have it recognized and recommended as such inflated the pride in her heart like the billowing sails of a ship at sea.

From that point on, Mary had looked forward to their discussions every Thursday. Even when she'd opened up about how greatly she missed her father—and when Mr. Northcott had shared about wishing for parents of his own—their conversation had ended up as a positive experience, and their connection only continued to grow.

That was when Mary noticed the change.

The subtle glances in each other's directions, the lingering smiles, the way she looked forward to each Thursday as a child looked forward to the festivities of a saint's day.

Surely these were mere signs that their rapport was growing and nothing else. And surely—now that a month had passed since beginning their friendship—the fact that she was now staring at her reflection in her small mirror to ensure she looked presentable meant nothing either.

She wanted to appear approachable for *each* of her guests, obviously. Not just the one.

"Here you are."

Mary lowered her mirror to find Mama standing in the doorway, leaning against the frame with an easy smile. "I was wondering if I could speak with you for a moment. Before the new guests arrive."

Mary placed the mirror on her small dresser and nodded. "Of course. What is it?"

Mama entered the room more fully, taking a seat on Mary's bed and patting the wool blanket beside her. "Sit here, won't you?"

With a pursed brow, Mary did as she was told. What was going on? Mama never wished to speak in such a manner unless . . . unless she was concerned about something.

At the thought, Mary's stomach tossed. It was only a matter of time until they had this conversation. Mama was a shrewd observer, but surely even the most inattentive person could see the friendship—*friendship*, nothing more—forming between Mary and Mr. Northcott.

"What do you wish to speak about, Mama?" Mary asked, attempting a casual tone.

Mama was silent for a moment. "Well, I'd like to discuss you taking on more responsibilities here at the inn. All of the responsibilities, actually."

Mary's lips parted in surprise. That was the last thing she'd expected Mama to say and surely the most relieving. "Truly?"

"Yes. As you know, I am not growing any younger. I feel as if my energy fades more each day, and knowing you are prepared to take over the Mermaid will ease my mind."

Panic slipped into Mary's chest, the same breathless feeling as when Papa had grown ill. "Are you unwell, Mama?"

"Oh, no, my dear. You mustn't worry about my health. I assure you, I will be here for many, many years to come." She paused with a wink. "I am merely . . . tired."

The tightness around Mary's lungs eased as Mama continued. "You have more than proven yourself capable of managing the affairs of the inn by yourself, Mary. I'm certain you will improve the Mermaid in ways your father and I never could. I should like to give you that opportunity now. Of course, I will still be here to help in any possible way I can, should you need me."

Mary's mind seemed to fly about the room with how swiftly her thoughts churned. She did have plans—great plans. To implement them now would be a dream come true.

"However . . ." Mama said, her word cutting through Mary's thoughts.

"Yes?"

Mama hesitated. "You know your father and I have always planned to give you control here. We discussed it often before he died. But running an inn is difficult. We would never wish to push this life or these responsibilities on you if you do not want them."

Mary tipped her head to the side in confusion. "Mama, you know I have always wanted this. Always."

"I know." Mama looked straight ahead, peering out of the window with a pensive gaze. "But is it *still* what you want?"

Before Mary could reaffirm her desires, Mama continued.

"Three generations of Thornes have cared for this inn. Your father, grandfather, great-grandfather. Not one of them had difficulty finding a wife to help them manage it." She eyed Mary headlong. "As a woman, however, you know it may be complicated finding a husband willing to do the same."

Mary hated the fact that Mr. Northcott was the first man to pop into her mind at Mama's words. What on earth was wrong with her? That man was *not* an option. First and foremost, they were merely friends. And then there was the rather significant matter of him being a coachman with a goal of London driving—that was enough to warn her away from him forever.

"Mary," Mama continued, reaching for her hands and holding them in hers. "Should you not find a husband because of this inn, to subject you to a life of loneliness..." She trailed off, shaking her head. "I could never forgive myself if that occurred."

Mary nodded. "I understand." And she did. Clovelly was not ripe with options for a husband, and with the inn keeping her from traveling and finding a match elsewhere, her marrying for love was rather unlikely. "I'm so grateful for your thoughtfulness, Mama. But I assure you, I will not live a life of loneliness. I'll have you, our help, our guests. Our friends here in Clovelly." Not to mention a certain coachman passing by every Thursday. That is, until he left. She cleared her throat. "This is the life I wish to lead, to carry on our family's tradition. I always have, and I always will."

Finally, a smile curved Mama's lips. "Very well, my dear. Then carry on the family tradition, you shall." She patted Mary's face affectionately then stood. "Just one more thing. Mr. Northcott..."

Mary snapped to attention. "Yes?"

"I know if I can trust you with the inn, I can trust you to be cautious with the coachman." She delivered one final smile then left Mary alone to her thoughts.

She drew in a deep, calming breath. She hadn't expected Mama to mention Mr. Northcott, nor to give Mary control over the Golden Mermaid for years to come. Now that the time had finally arrived, she could hardly believe it, and having Mama's trust with it all was encouraging.

Overwhelmed and excited, the only thing she wished to do now was tell Mr. Northcott. That was still being cautious... was it not?

Seven

Thursday, June 1, 1815—Evening

MISS THORNE SEEMED BUSY that evening. Robert's eyes had followed her about the dining area as she'd greeted guests, instructed maids and servers, and moved in and out of the room at a rate he'd never seen before.

Typically, she would come and sit beside him after the meal, but Miss Thorne instead left the dining area, only to come back with her mother and a rather frazzled look. Still, her cheeks were rosy and her eyes were bright.

Instead of moping in the corner about his *friend* being preoccupied, he moved to the bar, asking for a small ale as he took a seat on a rickety stool two seats down from an older man accepting a tall drink of his own.

Taking a sip, Robert released a deep sigh. Despite the bustle behind him—the constant hum of chattering, the quick footsteps from the servers, the snapping of the fire at the far side of the room—the silence immediately around him was deafening. He didn't realize how used to Miss Thorne's conversation he had become. How he'd missed it while on his route. It appeared he would be missing it that evening too.

Stemming his regret, he tried to focus his mind elsewhere, but his thoughts inevitably returned to Miss Thorne. He couldn't believe the change that had occurred between them. It had taken him nearly a full month to curb his habit of flirting with her—well, flirting with *every* female.

He'd been behaving in such a way for years, ever since he'd first begun his profession, when he used to take the advice and opinions of coachmen as the only words to live by.

On one of his first routes, an older coachman had spoken to him with his typical jolly attitude. "Have a drink with us, son," he'd said. "Then enjoy the company of that young lady who's been making eyes at you all evening."

Robert had instantly protested both suggestions.

"There are no consequences for a coachman's actions while at an inn," the older man had said, clapping Robert on his back. "It's the one freedom we are awarded, so you'd best enjoy it."

The man hadn't been lying entirely. The life of a coachman did have its benefits, though Robert never adhered to taking advantage of a woman. Except, apparently, his flirtations. But now that he was kicking that habitual behavior to the side of the road, his life was already looking up. His loneliness had lessened to a degree, at least on Thursdays, and this was due to his friendship with Miss Thorne.

As his thoughts once more strayed to the woman, he glanced over his shoulder, discovering her eyes already on him. His heart tripped. Of course, that was only due to his surprise in seeing her, not because she headed toward him with a happy grin.

"Mr. Northcott," she greeted as she reached his side. "I trust your travels were well?"

He smiled. This was the way she greeted him every Thursday. "As always, Miss Thorne. You seem rather lively this evening."

She pumped her head up and down in quick succession. "I've had a wonderful day."

"Indeed?"

"Yes. You see, my mother—"

"Mary?"

Miss Thorne stopped, looking over her shoulder to where her mother motioned for her. Mrs. Thorne had still been rather standoffish toward Robert, but considerably less since he'd decided to befriend Miss Thorne instead of trivializing her.

Honestly, he couldn't blame Mrs. Thorne one bit for being wary.

"One moment, Mama," Miss Thorne said, then she turned back to Robert with an apologetic smile. "I fear I am excessively busy this evening. But I should still like to speak. Are you free later? Unless you wish to retire early..."

He shook his head at once. "I'd love to speak with you. Especially now you've intrigued me with ending your words prematurely." Her eyes sparkled. What did it remind him of? He couldn't quite put his finger on it.

"Then let us meet later tonight." And with that, she was gone once again.

Robert watched after her as she left the room with Mrs. Thorne, an airiness filling his chest as anticipation raised his spirits.

"She be a true beauty, that one."

Robert pulled his gaze from the empty doorway, focusing instead on the man who'd spoken, seated nearby at the bar. Robert stared, the man motioning to where Miss Thorne had just departed.

"Miss Thorne," he clarified. "She be a fine woman."

Robert nodded in silence, shifting uncomfortably in his seat. The man could pass for Miss Thorne's grandfather, what with his age. Robert straightened in his stool and faced the bar, intent on finishing his drink swiftly to leave the man as soon as possible.

"Name's Grigg. John Grigg," the man continued in between sips of his drink. He looked at Robert for only a moment before staring straight ahead at the wall behind the bar. "I knew Miss Thorne there since she be a new babe. I nearly watched her parents grow up too."

"I see," Robert replied.

"Her father was a good man, rest his soul," Mr. Grigg continued, clearly so taken with his memories he still didn't look at Robert. "He'd share a pint with me every night I'd come in 'ere."

"That must have been nice," Robert replied, not wishing to be rude but having no idea what else to say.

For some reason, Mr. Grigg unsettled him. Perhaps it was the man's slurred, drunken speech or his bloodshot eyes. Or because he was speaking without pause and would therefore give Robert no chance of escaping to be with Miss Thorne.

"He and Mrs. Thorne raised Mary to be quite a special girl," he continued.

"Yes, indeed they did." Robert finished the last of his drink—*finally*—then pushed away from the bar to end the conversation. He could spend the rest of the evening recouping in his room until Miss Thorne was ready to speak with him. "She and I have become good friends over the last few months. But if you will—"

The man swiveled toward Robert with rounded eyes, his focus so intent, Robert ended his words prematurely.

"Friends?" Mr. Grigg questioned, then his laughter barked out across the dining area.

Robert pulled back, noting the stares from others. "Why

do you laugh?" he asked in a lowered tone, hoping to encourage Mr. Grigg to do the same.

Mr. Grigg wiped away the moisture from his eyes. His chuckling continued, though fortunately softer. "Oh, ye be mad, man. Ye can't be no friends with 'er."

Robert narrowed his eyes. "What do you mean, sir?"

Another swig, another eye at Robert. "I mean that no one can be simply *friends* with a woman li'e that. Only a matter of time 'fore she turns ye into somethin' more."

A thick tightness circled round Robert's chest. Something more? No, there would never be anything more between him and Miss Thorne. They had opposing lives, opposing desires, opposing goals. He was not ready for the responsibility attachments led to. He needed to obtain his London route.

"It be like I always say with me own wife, Eunice," Mr. Grigg continued. "I was more 'an 'appy stayin' friends. Then she captured me and carried me away to a marriage with babies and family life." He gave Robert a sidelong glance, his glass on his lips. "Mark me words, son. 'Tis only a matter of time 'fore Miss Thorne be doin' the same to ye."

He finished his drink in a last gulp then placed the glass on the bar. "Speakin' o' me wife, I best be gettin' 'ome to 'er. Good day to ye, sir." He tipped his hat to Robert then left the room.

Robert, however, remained on his stool, staring at the empty glass Mr. Grigg had left behind. He was mad, that man. Didn't know what he was talking about, clearly.

Robert didn't need the responsibility that came with attachments. Nor did he need any distractions from reaching the goals he had strived for nearly his whole life. Yes, he and Miss Thorne were nothing more than friends. Robert *wished* to be nothing more than friends.

But then, what if Miss Thorne didn't wish for the same?

Eight

Thursday, June 1, 1815—Later That Evening

MARY DIDN'T FINISH HER work until the sun was nigh on setting into the sea. With Mama only just now sitting down with a few guests in the dining area, Mary knew she had only a few moments to herself before more tasks would begin, so she took the opportunity to slip away, searching the rest of the dining area and bar for any sign of Mr. Northcott.

She pulled her lips to one side. Where was he? Surely he wouldn't have retired already, what with their plan to meet. Perhaps he was merely out of doors.

Sure enough, as she approached the small tables situated at the side of the inn—where just weeks ago they'd gathered broken glass—she found him seated alone. The other tables nearby were filled with guests and their happy laughter and drinking, but Mr. Northcott stared at the setting sun in silence. His eyebrows were pursed, lines of worry carved into his brow. Was he upset with how long it had taken her to meet with him? Or was something else bothering him?

She approached with a hesitant smile. "Mr. Northcott? I'm so sorry for the delay."

He turned toward her, his smile taut, as if he stretched his lips any wider, they'd snap. "It is no trouble, of course."

Mary hesitated. She'd been waiting hours to share with him the news of her mother transferring control of the Mermaid to her, but she didn't wish to share such news if *he* wasn't happy.

"Are you well?" she asked.

"Of course. You were going to tell me something earlier?"

Boisterous laughter came from two gentlemen seated at the table nearby. Mr. Northcott's eyes once more trailed to the sea, and Mary hesitated.

Perhaps he was simply uncomfortable due to the proximity of the others? "It's quite busy now, isn't it?" She glanced around. "I wouldn't mind a walk along the sea, if you are up to it."

"I wouldn't wish to keep you from your duties."

"You won't be, I assure you." Did the creases in his brow grow deeper? "Unless you do not wish to?" she questioned.

For a moment, she thought he'd refuse, his eyes still averted. Finally, however, he nodded, pushing away from the table and motioning for her to precede him.

They walked in silence, the grassy pathway from the inn morphing into sand, giving way to the large expanse of the beach. All the while, Mr. Northcott remained a hearty distance from her side. He must be upset with her for taking so long, despite what he'd said. There really was no other reason for him to be so uncomfortable.

"I must apologize again for how long it took for me to meet with you," she tried again. "But I assure you, I have good reason."

"Oh?"

Why would he not look at her? "Yes. You see, my mother has given me more control over the inn."

Finally, he met her gaze, genuine delight raising his eyebrows, erasing the crevices from before. "That is wonderful news. I'm so pleased for you."

Was she beaming too greatly? It certainly felt like she was.

"Does this mean you will be allowed to implement the plans you've had for the inn?" he asked.

"I believe so. The first, of course, will be to convince Mr. Drake to purchase more horses for his route. I'll offer him more stalls in the stable or perhaps more money. Then I shall discuss with Mama the different ways we may increase our income. I've a few ideas that will surely improve our number of guests. And . . ." She paused, realizing she was rambling. She looked at Mr. Northcott apologetically, but he appeared nothing if not interested in her words.

"Of course," she began again, a little slower, "my plans for the future of the inn need not hinder the progression of our own friendship. I hope we may still speak Thursday nights, if not later than we typically have done."

"Our friendship?" he murmured under his breath. A half-smile cracked the tightness of his lips, and he gave a soft chuckle. "No, indeed. Our friendship will remain the same as it has always been."

The shadow lifted from his eyes, but Mary had no idea as to why.

Together, they approached the languid waves lapping at the shore. The water reflected the sky to perfection, lighting the world with shades of orange, pink, and purple. The sun, shaded only partially by clouds on the horizon, glowed white in a perfect, still circle.

They stopped just outside of the waves' reach and stared in silence at the view.

"You certainly live in a beautiful place, Miss Thorne," Mr. Northcott said in a soft tone.

"Indeed I do."

She tore her gaze from the spectacular sight to watch him instead. The lines in his brow were now completely missing, and the creamy orange light seemed to soften his features as the corners of his lips curled into a semi-smile.

She'd always enjoyed his smile.

"Have you ever wished to live elsewhere?" he asked her next.

Instantly, she shook her head. "Oh, no. I would never be happier anywhere other than Clovelly." She shrugged. "I can understand your desire to travel, to see remarkable sites. But this place . . . well, it is my home. I'm sure you can understand that."

"Actually, I cannot. I do not believe I have ever felt such a way about anywhere before."

How often could she lodge her foot in her mouth around him? Of course this orphaned coachman would not know what a home was.

"Surely the whole of England is your home then, what with your travels," she suggested, clearly grasping at anything she could.

"I suppose." His expression was unreadable as he stared at the recurring waves. "But more often than not, I feel as if I am a ship at sea with no anchor. Floating about alone wherever the wind takes me, no place to call home. It's . . . lonely."

Mary's heart reached out to him. She couldn't imagine living such a life—with no family to call hers or place to call home. And yet . . .

"I can understand, to a degree far less than you, that same feeling of loneliness," she said. "Ever since Papa died, I have very few people to speak with on a personal level. Mama does not often share a great deal, and the guests filter in and out of the inn so swiftly, I couldn't befriend them if I tried." She looked at him from the corner of her eye. "I suppose that is why I wished to befriend a certain coachman—and have not regretted it since."

He raised his brow in mock surprise. "Is that so? And here I thought you despised all of us."

"I might have once," she said with a hidden smile. "But now I find one of them at least moderately tolerable."

He chuckled, holding his hands behind his back and staring out at the water. The sun was gone now, leaving behind a pink glow to the wispy clouds covering the sky.

"I never believed a person with a home and a family could feel loneliness," he said, his tone soft. "But I suppose such a feeling cannot be escaped by anyone."

She nodded. "I'm sorry you've felt it to such a large degree though."

Their eyes met, understanding passing between them before something seemed to shift in his eyes.

Swiftly, he turned away. "Yes, well, fortunately I have grown used to such a feeling. It isn't all bad, you know. I'm pleased with my way of life. I'm more than happy."

Robert needed to stop talking. Now. If he shared his feelings any more, he and Miss Thorne would undoubtedly draw closer. Beyond friendship. Beyond—

No. No, he would not allow Mr. Grigg's unsettling words to affect him. Miss Thorne herself had said that she wished to keep their friendship the same, so that is what he would believe.

He had meant what he'd said to her too. He *was* happy.

He didn't need a home, or a wife, or children of his own. All he needed were no responsibilities, an open road, a team of horses, and a route through London. That was what he'd always wanted, and that's what he would always want.

But then... what if his life could be *better*?

His eyes moved of their own accord to Miss Thorne. Her blonde ringlets glowed in the waning sunlight as she stared at the greying sea.

He couldn't deny the woman's beauty, nor her intelligence and charm. And when she turned to meet his gaze, he finally realized what her blue eyes reminded him of. The sea, when the waters were calm and the sun sparkled across the azure surface.

If Robert possessed an ounce of intelligence, he would have looked away right then. But his eyes remained on hers, and hers on his. His heart thudded so forcefully against his chest, it began to ache. Or was that ache due to something—*someone*—else?

What had that foolish Mr. Grigg done, burrowing his maddening words beneath Robert's defenses, leaving him unprotected and senseless?

He tried to look away, but her eyes, her goodness, had captured him, and a warmth sparked at the base of his heart, spreading ribbons of heat throughout his person. He'd never felt anything like this before. And yet, there was something familiar about this warmth. It felt as if he sat on the beach, soaking in the heat of the sun. Or as if he'd breathed in the scent of a hearty bowl of homemade stew.

Or as if... as if he was... home.

Swiftly, he closed his eyes. He didn't know what having a home was like, and he never would.

He took a step away from her. "We ought to return before the light disappears altogether."

"Yes, of course."

Her words sounded as if she'd remained unaffected by their stares, which left him with only an ounce of comfort. At least she was not giving in to ridiculous notions born from the words of an even more ridiculous man.

Being around Miss Thorne, around the Golden Mermaid Inn . . . this would not do if he wished to keep his attachments to a minimum.

This would not do at all.

Nine

Thursday, June 8, 1815—One Week Later

AS THE DAYS PROGRESSED, Mary found it increasingly more difficult to accomplish the numerous tasks of the inn. Updating ledgers, maintaining lists of costs and requirements, greeting guests, hiring help.

Of course, she would be more capable of keeping up with matters were it not for her mind being entirely too focused on Mr. Northcott.

Sitting in the office days later, she pulled her pen up from the logbook, her eyes glazing over as memories overtook her.

There had been something different in the way he'd looked at her that evening on the beach. It wasn't typical admiration or that he was simply listening to her. There had been a connection of sorts between them, one she could not deny. But then, such a thing was futile to dwell on. After all, he was a coachman wishing for London.

Still, the following Thursday, Mary was just as anxious to see Mr. Northcott again. After swiftly ensuring dinner was on time, the ledgers had been filled, and the new guests had settled in, Mary moved at once to the dining area.

She found Mr. Northcott's hunched over form near the fireplace, his head hanging down as he rested his forearms on his knees.

"Mr. Northcott," she greeted with a friendly—from a *friend*—smile. "I trust your travels were well."

"Yes, thank you." He didn't look back at her, his voice ragged.

The journey must *not* have been well.

She moved around to face him, but she couldn't see his expression with how low he hung his head. "Are you well? You sound as if you are in need of refreshment. Perhaps I could fetch some lemonade or . . ."

He shook his head. "No, I am well."

She hesitated. Did he wish to be left alone? Or was he simply hungry? "Is something upsetting you?"

With a heavy sigh, he finally looked up at her. His eyes were bloodshot, the weary lines had returned to his brow, and his jaw was filled with days' old scruff.

"Are you aware, Miss Thorne, that just because we are friends, we are not always required to speak of our feelings?"

Mary pulled back at his biting response. Regret flickered across his face, but he said nothing more.

A few discomfited glances were given from the guests around them, and she blushed. Clearly the man was upset about something. But then, she was merely trying to help him.

Embarrassed and hurt, Mary raised her chin. "And are you aware, Mr. Northcott, that just because we are friends, you do not have the right to be so unkind?"

His eyes darted between hers, his jaw twitching, then he stood and stomped from the room.

Mary watched him go, anger furrowing her brow. That

man. He was insufferable, utterly confusing, and . . . and a typical *coachman*.

And she was done thinking of him.

~ ~ ~

When Mary came in that evening from checking the inn, Mama was asleep by the fire, upright in a chair. The book she'd been reading lay open on her lap, the pages fanned out like a bird mid-flight.

Mary could only imagine how exhausted the poor woman must be. Mary was tired herself, though she was more than happy to finally take on the brunt of the work to allow Mama to rest.

She tiptoed across the small front room, eying the view of the inn from the window while attempting to unbutton the back of her full apron. Blasted contraption. She'd mended the buttonholes a bit too securely, and now the buttons stubbornly remained in place whenever she attempted to remove them.

She hoped to prove a better innkeeper than she did a seamstress.

After another moment of fiddling, however, the still-attached apron was forgotten as she caught sight of a man's figure disappearing into the stables. She chewed the inside of her cheek and narrowed her eyes. Those shoulders had looked suspiciously like . . .

She shook her head. No, it wouldn't have been Mr. Northcott. He'd disappeared after their exchange and hadn't come down from his room since. But then, who else would be in the stables so late at night? Mr. Berry had a slighter frame, and the man had stridden far too confidently to be an intruder.

With a defeated sigh, she made for the front door. She

simply had to discover who the late-night visitor was. Such was her duty after all. Never mind that Mama would scold her for going out alone at night.

She stepped into the chilly air, holding her lantern aloft. The sea's cool air rustled her skirts and apron, so she picked up her pace until she reached the innyard.

His voice came from the stalls on the right side. It was soft and muffled, so much so that she could not make out a single word he said. She inched forward step-by-step, hiding her lantern's light behind the opposite wall until she spotted him leaning his forehead against Onyx's. His tone was soft as he spoke and stroked the horse's neck. His own lantern hung on a nail nearby, casting soft shadows across the ground.

"I'm sorry, boy," he said.

Mary grimaced. She should not be there, interrupting this man in his vulnerable state. Even *if* he'd been unkind earlier, this was no way to retaliate.

With a gentle step back, she attempted to leave before she heard anything further, but her boot rustled against a pile of hay. She looked down at her feet, cursing her lack of care. When she looked back up, Mr. Northcott's eyes were already on her.

He cleared his throat, his eyes still red, as if he'd had too much to drink . . . or as if he'd been crying.

"Miss Thorne?"

"Forgive me," she breathed. "I was simply here to ensure all was well with the horses. I did not mean to intrude."

At least the latter part was true.

He watched her in silence for a moment, the anger from before no longer apparent in his dark brown eyes. He turned back to the horse after a simple nod.

Did he expect her to leave now without another word? Perhaps she should. And yet, her feet refused to cooperate, the haunted look in his eyes defusing the anger she'd felt over their previous encounter entirely.

"Mr. Northcott," she said carefully, "I know you told me earlier that you do not wish to speak of your feelings. I will not make the mistake again to suggest that you do so. But I hope you know that I am willing to listen if ever you require it."

~~~

Robert closed his eyes, willing himself to gain control of his emotions. He longed to tell Miss Thorne to remain nearby so he could speak with her, apologize, share with her why this was the worst week of his life.

But it was better to keep such things to himself. He didn't wish to flaunt how horrible of a person he was, as was evident by what had happened on his route that week—and what he'd said to Miss Thorne that evening.

He remained silent, unresponsive to her words as he stroked Onyx's black hair. But when Miss Thorne's footsteps began to retreat through the hay, a panic rose within him at the notion of being alone again, especially with his own thoughts.

"I'm sorry," he blurted over his shoulder before he could think better of it. Relief filled him as her footsteps stopped. "I'm sorry for how I spoke to you earlier this evening. It was uncalled for, especially given your kindness."

He tried to focus on the calm horse before him, but his stomach churned at her following silence. He wished to face her, but surely one look would unravel his resolve to keep the rest of his thoughts to himself.

"I only wished to help you," she finally said.

He nodded, struggling to swallow the disgust he felt for himself. "I know. But I'm afraid nothing can help me at the moment."

Another beat of silence, then she spoke again. "I do not know about you, but speaking always helps me."

Robert closed his eyes. The last thing he wished to do was speak about what had occurred. But if he was being honest with himself, he couldn't very well feel any worse than he already did.

"I received news this week that I secured a route through London."

"Oh?" She cleared her throat. "But that's wonderful news, Mr. Northcott."

Her words twisted at his heart. "It should be."

"Why is it not?"

He sighed. "Because of what occurred directly after receiving said news."

She remained silent, clearly doing so to avoid another tongue-lashing from him.

"I was so distracted with the correspondence and my own excitement that I . . . I didn't realize I was pushing my team too hard." He ducked his head then turned to face her. He needed to see her reaction when he told her. "And one of the horses died in harness."

She flinched. The disappointment in her eyes was as clear as his own. "I'm so sorry," she breathed.

He shouldn't have been surprised by her reaction. Her compassion instead of judgments. She was too good of a person for him to have as a friend.

He turned away, facing Onyx again.

"How did it happen?" she asked. Her voice sounded closer, though he hadn't heard any footsteps.

"I was late leaving the inn at Barnstaple a few days ago, having just been told I had obtained the new route. To make up for my lost time, I pushed the horses harder than usual. One of them—an older gelding but still eager to prove himself—did not appear to be in good form, but I kept up their pace. Eventually, he... he tripped, righting himself just before the other horses could have dragged him forward." Flashes of the accident flew before Robert's eyes, and a knot tied in his throat. "I slowed them at once, but it was too late. The horse tripped again, dragging along the road until I managed to stop the other horses. And this time, he didn't get up."

As if he could understand Robert's words, Onyx tossed his head and backed away from the stall door, turning his back on Robert. Would Miss Thorne do the same?

When she put a soft hand to his back, he knew once again she was too kind to leave him.

"I'm so sorry," she whispered at the side of him. Her soft voice channeled the anxiousness from his body, and his shoulders relaxed.

The warmth from her hand seeped through the back of his waistcoat and shirt, and the chains binding his tongue fell to the ground, powerless against Miss Thorne's goodness.

"I have never been the cause of a horse's death before now," he said, staring at Onyx as the horse nibbled at the hay in the corner of his stall. "When I was being instructed on my first route, the coachman who had taught me drove the horses too hard. The accident was horrendous. Passengers thrown from the top of the coach as it teetered back and forth. The guard seriously injured. Two horses died. After that, I made a promise that I'd never do such a thing." He shook his head at himself. "I'm disgusted with myself."

Miss Thorne was silent for a long time. Removing her hand from his back, she hung her own lantern at the opposite side of his, casting a brighter glow around the both of them. Finally, she rested both arms against the stall door beside him.

"I do not like to admit when I am wrong," she said.

He glanced toward her, noting her slightly turned up nose and petite ears behind a few soft curls.

"I suppose that is my pride," she continued. "But it would be an injustice if I did not confess that I was wrong about *you*. I thought you were like all coachmen." She lowered her gaze. "Well, like one coachman in particular."

He studied her expression. One coachman? "Who?"

She pulled in her bottom lip, chewing on it before continuing. "Mr. Charles Bolton."

Robert raked through his memory for any recollection of the name, but nothing came to him. Was he supposed to know this man? And if not, why was this uneasiness creeping upon him like the shadow of evening, ready to pounce and cover him with darkness?

"Was he . . . a friend of yours?"

"Yes. And then he was my betrothed."

A jolt of shock cut through his middle. Miss Thorne, engaged? "I-I was not aware you had ever been engaged before."

"I don't speak of it often. Though years ago, it was all Clovelly talked about." Her voice was low and monotonous. "We grew up together, Charles and I. About six years ago, when I was but seventeen, we fell in love. He asked me to marry him, and I accepted."

Robert wasn't certain he'd ever felt jealousy before. Perhaps once when another coachman completed a route faster than him. But that was nothing compared to the heat now stirring in the center of his chest, circling round, harder and faster until his breathing labored. He cleared his throat, attempting to dispel the discomfort. "May I ask what occurred after that?"

She looked at Robert headlong, her eyes unwavering. "Then he fell out of love with me—and in love with the life of a coachman."

He stared, then suddenly everything cleared. No wonder

Miss Thorne loathed coachmen. No wonder she found them difficult to trust. No wonder she'd despised Robert's flirting. Everything must have been a firm trigger, igniting memories of her past with this other man.

"He'd heard he could make a good income as a coachman," Miss Thorne explained. "He took on a few routes on the premise that he would only do so long enough to provide for myself and the children we would one day have. But he would leave for weeks at a time, and his return journeys became fewer and farther between. I hadn't seen him for three months when I received a correspondence from him, alerting me that we could no longer wed. He'd grown too attached to his way of life and could not give it up. So he gave me up instead."

Robert's disgust for his own sex—and for coachmen in general—doubled. They really were a despicable bunch, himself included. But especially Charles Bolton. What a cad that man was. How could he have chosen the coachman's life over Miss Thorne?

He blanched, the sudden thought striking a chord of fear within him, but he swiftly shoved it aside. "I'm sorry. I can't even imagine having to go through something so awful. It really is no wonder you mistrust us as you do."

She gave a half-smile. "Thank you. But do you not see that it was my mistake? I harbored ill will, expecting the very worst of all of you for years, and I was miserable because of it. Only now can I be grateful for the mistake of falling in love with Charles. For now, I've been able to grow. To do better and be better." She looked up at him again with a softened expression. "All of that is to say, now that you've made one single, solitary mistake of being distracted and pushing the horses too hard, you can learn from it and never allow it to happen again."

He'd almost forgotten about the accident in light of her unexpected revelations. "I suppose you are right," he said with a half-smile. "And I should've known you would be teaching me a lesson—and a very good one at that."

She turned toward him with a smile of her own. "My father always said that attempting to teach an individual comes far easier when one shares one's own personal hardships first." They exchanged a smile, and she leaned toward him. "I only hope you'll learn what needs to be done sooner than I ever did. Then the next time you are in such a situation, you will know just what to do."

Robert's smile faltered, and he turned to face Onyx.

Next time? Did there have to be a *next time* with a horse dying right before his eyes?

A weight dropped onto his shoulders, nearly knocking him forward. He'd been thrilled to learn his goal was soon to be accomplished, that more money would be coming in and he'd be changing his route to London. But until this very moment, he didn't really have the chance to acknowledge just what this actually entailed.

How much longer could he do this? The late nights, the early mornings. The loneliness and stress. The death of horses on his hands. Leaving Miss Thorne, Clovelly, and Devonshire altogether.

Would he simply keel over himself one day, unable to continue his route like the horses?

"You are still troubled." Miss Thorne's words cut through the weight. "Perhaps I ought to fetch you some chamomile tea. It seems to have done wonders for Onyx here."

Robert pushed aside his thoughts. "I'm happy to hear it has helped him."

She clicked her tongue, and the horse instantly raised his head, moving toward Miss Thorne with his head over the stall door. She smiled, rubbing his forelock. "Oh, it has absolutely helped him. Mr. Berry tells me so every day."

She moved to pet his neck, and the horse responded with a gentle nudge to her stomach. She smiled. "You are happier, aren't you, boy? You tell Mr. Northcott here that you—"

Her words ended in a gasp when the horse sneezed, and she stepped back in surprise.

"Heavens," she breathed. Holding her arms out from her side, she peered down at the front of her apron. Across the entire bodice, white discharge spread thickly across the otherwise clean fabric.

Her eyes widened. "Oh . . . oh, I don't like this."

A smile cracked across Robert's lips.

"Oh, I don't like this at all."

He didn't blame her one ounce for her flaring nostrils and curved-down lips. Had he received the brunt of the horse's sneeze, he'd be disgusted too.

Fortune had it, he hadn't received any of it himself. "Thank heavens for your apron," he said, attempting to lighten the mood.

"The apron. Oh, I can remove the apron!"

She reached her hands round her back, leaning her head forward as she unbuttoned—or rather tried to unbutton—the apron. But after multiple failed attempts, she dropped her arms in exasperation. "Oh, blast these wretched buttons. I can't undo them."

With a grimace and another drop of her gaze to what the horse had bestowed upon her front, she shook her head. Then she turned pleading eyes on Robert.

"Would you mind very much . . ." She turned around, her back facing him, then motioned to the buttons securing her apron.

"Of course," he said at once. Anything to help her disgust from rising again, the poor woman. But as he drew near her, his hands paused just out of reach of the buttons. What was he doing, undressing a woman in the stables?

Don't be ridiculous, Robert, he scolded himself. He was hardly undressing her. It was simply her apron. And the buttons were only just below her shoulder bones. There was nothing untoward about this at all.

Except for their proximity. And the fact that it was late at night. And that they were alone in the innyard.

"Do you see the buttons?"

Her words jarred him back to the task at hand. "Yes." He needed to relax. He was helping a woman who was clearly in desperate need. That was all.

And those were the words he repeated to himself as his fingers finally made contact with the buttons.

The subtle scent of roses reached his nose, despite the strong smell of the hay and horses surrounding them. Her hair was pulled up to the crown of her head, and his eyes, instead of remaining on the apron, constantly found their way to the delicate arch of her neck and the short wisps that accentuated it.

He swallowed. Focusing harder on his task, he finally managed to free one of the buttons, but each time his fingers brushed against her dress, a tingling, numbing sensation filled his limbs, and he struggled even harder to make them obey his command.

"Did you manage it?" she asked, her voice hardly above a whisper.

"Nearly."

He glanced up. Her eyes were focused to the side of them, revealing her profile once again.

At the sight, his heart pattered against his chest like rain at the beginning of a storm. Then slowly, it grew in strength as his breathing shallowed.

After another moment of struggling—his eyes straying to

the shadows on her face—he finally managed to free her from her apron.

"There you are," he said, attempting nonchalance, though he feared his husky voice revealed far too much of what he was feeling.

Miss Thorne only took a small step away from him as she slipped the apron off and folded it slowly and neatly so the discharge was untouched. Then she looked up at him, and he was captured once more by her blue-eyed gaze.

"Thank you," she whispered.

He nodded in silence. The candlelight danced across her high cheekbones and lips.

Her lips. Pink and full. Flawless, just like the rest of her.

But he shouldn't be looking at her lips, nor the way they parted as if in an invitation for him to partake of their sweetness.

This was madness, thinking such thoughts, entertaining the idea of kissing this woman.

Yet, still, he didn't look away.

"Miss Thorne," he whispered, his voice huskier than even before.

She peered up at him. "Yes?"

But he could think of nothing to say. He *had* nothing else to say, other than voicing that his desire to kiss her, to feel her close, was greater than any longing he'd ever had before in his life.

A spare breeze moved through the stables, and the soft curl near her temple fluttered toward her eye. Was it as soft as it appeared? Could he . . . could he see for himself?

Slowly, he reached forward to brush aside the curl, gently grazing her skin in the process. For just a moment, she closed her eyes as if she relished his touch. Did she long for their physical connection as greatly as he did?

Instead of pulling his hand away as any sensible man

would, Robert kept it there, taking a step toward her to better reach her. His fingertips caressed the side of her face before he cradled her cheek in his palm.

She closed her eyes again, her shoulders shifting, as if she attempted to hide a shiver. And when she nestled into his touch, a soft sigh leaving her lips, he was finished. He wanted to kiss her, to hold her. He *needed* to.

But what did she want?

"Miss Thorne . . ."

She nodded before he could even finish his words. "Yes," she breathed. There was no question in her tone.

Yes.

Never had his heart beat so fiercely, but he welcomed it. For in the next moment, he leaned closer to her, inch by inch, until finally, their lips touched.

The contact was soft, gentle, nothing like he'd ever felt before. The physical desire he had for this woman was undeniable. But there was something deeper that he felt as their lips touched. Something that burned greater than the jealousy he'd felt before. Something lasting and overpowering.

He pulled back just enough to draw a solid breath then returned again, hoping, praying for understanding as to what he felt for this woman—and the courage to pursue it.

Mary had never felt this way from a kiss before. The way he held her face, so soft and gentle, she could hardly breathe. Her logic fled faster than she could comprehend, leaving behind only the soothing warmth of joy.

She leaned in, dropping her apron from her hands, and it rustled to the ground at their feet. Slowly, she slipped her hands around his back, feeling the ridges of his muscles through his waistcoat.

He responded, moving in closer. His unshaven face now rubbed against her chin, prickling it softly with his gentle kiss.

She didn't quite know what was happening or why in the world they were even kissing, but she did know that she never wanted it to end.

Which made his pulling away all the more disappointing.

He slowly released her face, trailing his fingertips past her jaw and down her shoulder and arm before dropping his hand to his side, all while he stared at her.

He blinked, appearing to come out of a daze. "Forgive me," he mumbled, taking a step back as his voice grew stronger. "We should not have done that."

She swallowed. He was right. They shouldn't have. And yet, she couldn't find it within herself to apologize in return.

He turned away from her, running his fingers through his hair then rubbing the back of his neck. "You are running an inn. And I'm a coachman."

His words were simple, but Mary knew at once what he was saying. She'd told herself to be careful. She'd told herself not to fall for another coachman, and what did she do? She'd kissed the man she knew would break her heart—just like Charles Bolton had.

Although this time, it was different. This time, the pain was more acute. This time, her love ran through her soul.

She may have known Charles for longer, but that allowed her to see even more that he had never helped her around the inn. He had never shared her care for horses. He had never encouraged her dreams of running the inn.

But Mr. Northcott had.

Tears burned in her eyes, but she refused to release them. Not when all of this was her fault.

"I'm sorry, Miss Thorne."

Had he seen her tears? She looked to the ground, forcing

a smile that felt as permanent as the sand on the beach during high tide. "Please, do not apologize. It was merely a kiss, that is all. It meant . . . it meant nothing, surely."

And yet, it had meant everything to her. Because for some reason she could not comprehend, she had allowed herself to believe for the smallest fraction of a moment that perhaps Mr. Northcott, the coachman, loved her—that perhaps he would *choose* her.

But of course he could not, and she did not blame him, for this was her own doing. She should've known better. She should've known she was not enough.

"Miss Thorne, allow me to explain . . ."

He trailed off when she shook her head. She could not even bear to look at him as she backed away from their place at the stall.

Her words were swift, coming one after another, as if to prove she was well. "No, there is no need, I assure you. You are as attached to the goals you've made as a coachman as greatly as I am attached to this inn. Now that you have your route in London, you . . . you will have the life of which you've always dreamt. Please, forget we even . . ." She shook her head, unable to finish her words.

She dared a glance at him, but she shouldn't have, for the regret in his eyes told her everything she needed to know.

"Goodnight, Mr. Northcott," she blurted, fearing he might attempt to apologize for their kiss again.

He said nothing as she retrieved her apron from the floor and walked away, though she felt his gaze on her until she disappeared around the corner of the stables and finally allowed her tears to spill down her cheeks.

Ten

Friday, June 9, 1815—The Next Morning

"Did you have a nice stay at the Mermaid, Northcott?"

Robert nodded in response to the coach guard's question, keeping his gaze trained on the team of horses running before them. "As always."

He used one hand to tighten his coat around his shoulders. Despite being nearly the middle of June, the temperature had dropped that morning—and with the sun being cloaked by clouds and Robert being exposed to the wind at the top of the coach, a chill rushed through his body.

The guard, Mr. Wilson, nudged Robert with his elbow. "No doubt due to the company of a few women, eh?" he teased, his voice loud to be heard above the racing coach and pounding hooves.

Robert grimaced. "No doubt." No doubt Mr. Wilson had never been more wrong about anything in his entire life.

"Well I cannot be jealous of you for too long," Mr. Wilson continued. "I'm scheduled to stop at the Red Lion where I'll be able to enjoy my own *company*." He chuckled.

The coach had been fairly full that morning, so the guard had opted to sit beside Robert until their next stop. Rather unfortunate for Robert's sake, as Mr. Wilson enjoyed the sound of his voice a little too much.

"Mind you," the man continued, "the food isn't as good, nor is the accommodation. But at least the Thorne women won't be at the inn to stop any fun that might be had."

Robert's thick, leather gloves tightened round the reins.

"If only we could find an inn that had it all, eh? Nice food. Comfortable lodging. Lack of vexing women. It would surely be the most popular in all of England."

Robert said nothing in return. He couldn't engage in this conversation again. That was all anyone ever seemed to speak with him about now—women. He didn't wish to speak about *women*. He wished to speak about, think about, and be with *one* woman.

But he shouldn't. That much was made clear when he'd lost all sense and kissed her the night before. He was no better than that Bolton fellow, stringing Miss Thorne along, all while knowing he'd choose his coaching position in London over her.

"Did you hear Jones was hired along the route? He'll be taking your place," Mr. Wilson said.

He didn't wait for a response from Robert to continue, so Robert didn't bother listening to his words in return. He took in the sights around him, the seemingly never-ending grassy fields, the distant patches of trees tucked into the crevices where short hills met longer valleys. Then he moved to the horses. He was able to ride with Onyx that morning. Any other day he would have been more than pleased to have such a horse as his lead, but now, the animal simply brought back painful memories—and the fear he'd drive another horse to its death.

Robert was not only regretting his actions last night but also his cowardice from this morning. He'd wanted to speak with Miss Thorne before he'd left, but his courage had failed, and he'd slipped silently from the inn for the last time.

Yes, his last time. He would soon be traveling to London, settling in, then adjusting to his new assignment. It was better this way. He couldn't bear seeing Miss Thorne and not *being* with Miss Thorne.

"No doubt he'll enjoy his route." Mr. Wilson's chattering had yet to cease, and it moseyed once again through Robert's mind. "You've seen the maids at the Red Lion, haven't you, Northcott? What am I saying? You've flirted with half of them."

His resulting laugh grated against Robert's patience. It mattered not if he'd flirted with half of them in the past. He'd lost such a desire weeks ago.

"Mind you," Mr. Wilson said, "you need to learn to share with the rest of us, I think."

"You're welcome to them, Wilson," came Robert's gruff reply.

"Now this is unheard of. Robert Northcott willing to share in his spoils of women? What could have happened to you?"

Robert gritted his teeth. If he didn't calm down soon, he'd be sorely tempted to push the guard to the back of the coach with the passengers. At the thought of those seated back-to-back behind him, his ears picked up their conversation rising just above the racket of the coach.

"To think we'll finally be back in Cornwall after so long, John. I simply cannot wait," spoke a feminine voice first.

"Indeed," responded the man—John—sitting directly behind Robert. "Although a fortnight is not so very long, I am more than anxious to see the children."

"Did you hear me, Northcott?"

Robert blinked as Mr. Wilson's voice cut through the conversation. "Pardon?"

"I was simply telling you that I have heard a rumor about you."

Could Mr. Wilson choose topics more unappealing to Robert? "Did you? I don't take to gossip much—"

"It was rather intriguing," Mr. Wilson interrupted. "I heard that you have fallen in love."

"Love?" Robert snapped to attention, his eyes swinging toward Mr. Wilson's in an instant.

Mr. Wilson guffawed. "I knew you would find such an idea humorous. I told Mr. Hobbes only yesterday that the idea of you falling for a landlady was absurd."

Robert looked away, staring absentmindedly at the horses pulling the coach with fervor.

Love.

His mind swirled, his thoughts creating chaos and confusion. But as he repeated the word over again in his mind, realization slipped into his heart like the sun pouring its light on the sea after a storm.

Love. It wasn't a rumor. He *had* fallen for Miss Thorne.

Such a thing should have been obvious, what with his reaction to their kiss last night, how he could not pull her image from his mind, how all he wished to do all day, every day, was speak with her, *be* with her.

"I told him," Mr. Wilson continued, preventing Robert from fully comprehending his realization, "there was no way on this green earth that you would sacrifice your freedom to become leg-shackled. That certainly is not the Northcott I know."

Months ago, Robert would have agreed with the man. He wouldn't have sacrificed anything for his freedom. But now, was that still the truth?

The voice of the female passenger from before drew his attention once again. "I think I shall wrap them all in a single embrace when I see them."

"As will I, my dear," John replied. "It will be more than wonderful to be home again."

Home.

The word echoed over and over in Robert's mind, now mingling with *love*, and his stomach hardened.

He wouldn't sacrifice anything for his freedom. But then what was that freedom he experienced? Merely having very little responsibility? As opposed to having a home, a family, love . . . and Miss Thorne. He'd known all along this woman had changed him. He'd known all along that she was the secret to his happiness.

Heavens above. What was he doing?

"I'm so pleased I took the wager and—"

Mr. Wilson's words ended as Robert pulled up the reins of the horses. The team whinnied as they slid on their hooves to stop as their master commanded, and Mr. Wilson lurched forward with a grunt, as did the other passengers.

"What in the devil—Northcott! What are you doing?"

Robert had a mind to shove the man from the coach. Frankly, it was none of the guard's business what he was doing. But as the other passengers began to complain from behind him and within the coach, he knew he needed to explain.

"I'm returning to the Golden Mermaid," he declared, maneuvering the team to turn around. They stomped and pranced, disappointed with having to slow their pace as they pulled the coach onto the grass before returning to the tight road.

Mr. Wilson eyed Robert as if he was mad. Perhaps he was. But that was better than being a coward. He'd been that way for too long, afraid of attachments and responsibility, afraid of change, afraid of giving up his lifelong goals as a coachman.

But he could not deny the clarity that had come moments ago, knowing Miss Thorne was worth it all.

"But-but why?" Mr. Wilson sputtered. "If you're this late, you can say farewell to any profit from this journey. And what about London?"

"What about London?"

"If they hear word of this, you'll surely lose your position there."

Robert said nothing, avoiding Mr. Wilson's gaze and ignoring the words of complaint he could still hear coming from the passengers. He could not care less about London, about money, or about anything else in this world. He only cared about Miss Thorne.

"Good heavens. It's true," Mr. Wilson said. "You've fallen for a woman, haven't you?"

Robert could deny it no longer. A half-smile cracked his lips. "Indeed I have."

Now to only pray she'd fallen for him as well.

Eleven

Friday, June 9, 1815—The Same Morning

STANDING AT THE MOUTH of the beach where the grass merged with sand, Mary stared at the waves rushing in. She'd stood there often, seeking peace and comfort. Solitude. A clear mind.

Mama had suggested for Mary to go there that morning after hearing her daughter's account. She'd held Mary as tears were shed, not giving a single accusatory remark, though Mary had not given herself the same courtesy.

She was a fool, and nothing could erase her regret and sorrow. She was better off working than standing in the sand, reminding herself of the last time she and Mr. Northcott had walked along the beach—remembering the warnings she had repeatedly given herself. The warnings she had repeatedly ignored.

As sorrowful as she was, she didn't regret the time she'd spent with Mr. Northcott, nor falling in love with him. He was a good man. And she couldn't blame him for choosing his passion in life when she was doing the very same at the inn. It was no wonder he left without a word. It was easier for both of them this way.

One day, she would be able to overcome her heartache. Just as soon as she could rid her mind of his memory, her lips of his kiss, and her ears of his voice.

"Miss Thorne?"

His voice.

No, Mr. Northcott was halfway to his next stop by now. And then he would be on his way to London. And she would be at the inn, working. Just as she ought to be doing right now.

She turned around, intent on heading for the inn, but as she focused her gaze forward, her feet froze.

It was him.

Her heart thumped in her ears, tears pricking her eyes as Mr. Northcott walked toward her.

What was he doing here? Why had he returned?

Hope blossomed within her, but she stamped it down in an instant. He no doubt had forgotten something. Or had merely returned to apologize again for their kiss. That was all.

She looked past his shoulder, noting for the first time her mother standing near the stables behind him, a soft smile on her lips.

This time, Mary's hope could not be diminished.

Mama turned and walked away then, and Mary's attention focused solely on Mr. Northcott, who continued striding toward her.

His great coat billowed behind him, the multiple shoulder capes increasing his large stature. He held his hat in his hand with his neckerchief loosened, though his deep-red waistcoat was still securely buttoned.

His eyes had yet to waver from hers, even when he stopped a few paces away. "Miss Thorne." He gave a short bow in greeting.

This was a dream, she was certain of it. "What are you doing here?"

He opened his mouth, clearly hesitating. "I spoke with your mother. She told me where I could find you."

That didn't exactly answer her question. "And may I ask why you needed to find me?"

He dropped his gaze, saying nothing further.

She waited, failing miserably as she fished for patience. "I don't wish to rush you, sir, but I do not imagine your passengers will be very pleased with your delay."

"The passengers are already on their way."

She tipped her head to the side. "How?"

"I bade the other coachman to continue with his route. Fortunately, for an extra price, he was willing to do so."

She could not bear this for much longer. Her chest was tight as she forced the hope within her to remain tamed. "I don't understand. Why did *you* not finish the route?"

Finally, he looked up at her, his gaze suddenly steady. "Because I am finished. Finished with having the life of a coachman. Finished with allowing fear to dictate my life. And finished being without you."

Mary's heart stuttered. This could not be true. It was too wonderful to be true.

Her mind spun as he took a step closer. "I have always been content with my ordinary life—no attachments, no responsibilities—for I had nothing else to compare it to. Until I met you. I quickly discovered how lonely I was, how empty my life was. I tried to convince myself that I still wanted the life of a coachman." He paused with a soft scoff. "How terribly wrong I was."

Mary listened, her head spinning. "But it was your dream being a coachman, obtaining a route through London. You've finally achieved it. How can you give that up?"

"Don't you see? Because it was an old dream. Have you never wondered why I desired to occupy the same room while staying here?"

She shook her head. "I thought it was because you wished for the view of the sea."

"That was part of it, yes. But mostly because my heart was longing for a home. You and your mother were the only ones to ever honor my request to occupy the same room at an inn. You allowed me that one constant in my life when I had none. And because of that, this inn has become more of a home than anything I've ever had. As a coachman, I had freedom, yes. But freedom from what? Having connections with others? A place to call home?" He paused, swallowing. "Being able to share a deep and abiding love with someone?"

Her breath caught in her throat. "Love?"

His expression softened, and as his eyes caressed her face softer than any touch, she knew the truth before he spoke another word. It was the same look he'd given her on the beach, and the same one from the stables.

"Yes, Miss Thorne. Love." He closed the distance between them, raising his hand to her cheek. The hint of leather—no doubt from his missing gloves—lingered beneath her nose. "I know our time together has been short, but it has been more than enough for me to know my feelings for you are true and abiding. You are loyal, kind, determined, and hardworking. You persevere through your trials with grace. And you have helped me become a better man. How could I not love you? How could I not *choose* you?"

Relief rushed over her, a weight raising from her shoulders so swiftly she thought she might float away. How long had she carried that burden of fearing she would never be enough for someone, that she would never be chosen? To have the man she loved more than anything in this world say such words to her was more than relieving. It was freeing.

It mattered not that she knew Charles Bolton for her entire life and Mr. Northcott for a mere few months. She knew her feelings were as real and steady as the sun rising on the sea.

"So now the question remains," he said, wiping a stray tear from her cheek that had managed to escape. "Will you choose me, Miss Thorne?"

"I believe you already know my answer, sir," she began, though she sobered at once. "But I must say first . . . I cannot leave my mother, nor can I give up our family's inn."

He held both of her hands in his. "Nor would I ever ask such a thing of you. I know how much the Golden Mermaid is a part of you. Far more than being a coachman was ever part of me."

"So, you would stay here with me?"

He smiled that charming grin she loved so much. "If you'll agree to hire me on, I will absolutely remain here. I'll begin work as a stable boy. No special treatment, even if I am to be your husband."

Her heart skipped a beat. Her husband. She could hardly believe it. With a smile of her own, she wrapped her arms around his neck, staring into his eyes. "In that case, Mr. Northcott, my answer is a firm and resounding yes."

Their chests rose and fell in unison as both of them were so overcome with emotion and joy they could no longer say a word. Beaming, Mr. Northcott leaned down, pressing his lips to hers. Instead of his kiss being marked with uncertainty, it held a promise of undaunted security. A promise of never-ending love.

After a moment, their smiles of happiness prevented their affection from continuing, and Mr. Northcott pulled back with a sparkle in his eye.

"So when shall I begin work as your new stable boy?"

She grinned. "I've a better job for you, I think."

"Oh?"

"Yes. You shall be the inn's primary tea-giver to the horses. Chamomile, to be exact."

He chuckled. Bringing her hand up to his lips, he kissed the back of it. "I accept the position most heartily."

He leaned down, delivering another soft, lingering kiss to her lips. As he pulled back once more, gratitude poured down upon her.

"Thank you," she whispered.

He studied her face. "For what, my love?"

"For coming back."

His features softened, and his brow raised. "You are my home, Miss Thorne. This is where I belong. And this is where I will stay. With you."

"Forever?"

He stared deep into her eyes. "Forever."

And there was no doubt in her heart that he meant it.

Epilogue

Thursday, June 17, 1819—Four Years Later

"Come along, Jane," Mary called out. "Your papa and baby George are waiting for us already."

The pattering of feet sounded against the wooden floor, and a three-year-old with a chubby face and distraught eyes rounded the corner. "My boots are too tight, Mama! I cannot put them on."

Mary smiled. "Here, let me help."

Jane plopped onto the ground, sticking her legs out in front of her with a pout. "They are too tight."

"Yes, I know, my dear." Mary's amused smile grew at Jane's repetition. "That is why I'm helping you."

She knelt on the ground, attempting to slip them around Jane's seemingly ever-growing feet, but the edges wouldn't budge. "Oh dear. They do appear to be a bit snug. You are just growing too fast. You'll be bigger than Papa soon."

She tapped Jane playfully on the nose, and Jane giggled. "Then I shall win every race we have!"

"Yes indeed."

"And then I shall be big enough to hold baby George all by myself!"

"All by yourself." Mary nodded, standing before helping Jane up to her bare feet. "We shall visit town after our picnic, yes? Until then, I suppose you'll simply have to walk barefoot in the sand."

Jane's eyes brightened, and she darted toward the door. "I love walking in the sand!"

"Your papa is just outside," Mary called after her. "Stay with him!"

"Yes, Mama!" Jane barely responded before leaving the inn through the back entrance.

"She certainly has a lot of energy."

Mary turned to the sound of her mother's voice. "She takes after her father," Mary returned.

She and Mama shared a smile as they watched Jane bound toward Robert outside.

"Will you join us for our picnic today?"

Mama shook her head. "Thank you, but perhaps next time. You four need time to yourselves, I think."

They stood in silence for a moment as Jane ran circles around a chuckling Robert, a smiling George in his arms.

"Your father would have loved Robert."

Mary nodded. How she wished the two could have met one another. "I believe the very same."

They exchanged a smile, Mama's eyes wrinkling at the edges as she continued to watch her granddaughter. Mary had noticed the change that had come over Mama over the years, ever since Mary and Robert had married. Yes, her wrinkles had become more pronounced, and the grey in her temples stood out like thick strokes of paint. But once the grandchildren had been born, her smile had also grown, and the peace in her eyes had replaced the sorrow left there from Papa's death.

It gave Mary comfort to no end knowing Mama was in a happier place. She truly was a blessing to Mary and her little family. Not only did she still help with the inn, but she also took it upon herself to watch the children whenever Robert and Mary were both occupied.

"Mama? Come along, Mama!"

Mary blinked, coming out of her reverie as Jane called from outside.

"You had better hurry before she loses her patience altogether," Mama said with a chuckle. "A trait she has inherited from you, I think."

Mary smiled, kissing her mother on the cheek. "Be sure to let me know if you need anything."

Mama nodded. "I will."

After another smile and a wave goodbye, Mary left the inn behind to join her family who awaited her outside.

Robert smiled, greeting his wife with a kiss. "Ready?"

She nodded, taking his free hand in hers as they headed toward the beach. Jane sprinted past them without hesitation, despite her lack of footwear.

"She's outgrown her boots again, I see," Robert said.

"Yes, she has. We can't seem to keep up with her."

George cooed, and Robert responded by bouncing the eight-month-old in his arms. "This little chap will be growing just as swiftly, I think."

George beamed his four-toothed grin at the movement, and Robert couldn't help but return it with a smile of his own. Robert loved having a home. He loved living in Clovelly. And he loved being an innkeeper, a son-in-law, and a father.

But nothing compared to how he loved being Mary's husband.

Each day, she brought excitement and joy to his life. And each day, he wondered what he did to deserve such happiness.

The first week they had married, the two of them had visited Mr. Drake directly, convincing him to finally purchase more horses for the Clovelly stagecoach route. Afterwards, they'd worked together—with the help and support of Mary's mother—to improve the livelihood of the animals they already housed, as well as any other improvements they could concoct for the inn.

He'd found such a measure of joy and satisfaction in their work, in being part of a family and having a home, that Robert often wondered how he'd ever considered living life differently.

What he did know, however, was that he would be eternally grateful for the chance he had to lead such a rich and fulfilling life with the woman who held his heart.

Mary spent the afternoon with her family, eating the food they'd brought with them before digging holes across the beach, burying Jane's toes in the sand, and watching Robert run with his daughter from the incoming tide.

When the sun grew a little too warm, Mary waved her family closer.

"That was wonderful, Mama!" Jane said, seawater dripping from her and Robert's hair. "Can we do it again tomorrow?"

"We shall see, my dear," Mary said. She shared a smile with Robert, and the four of them gathered their belongings.

"Shall we take a visit to the horses while we dry off?" Robert suggested.

"Oh yes!" Jane exclaimed.

Robert reached for George then took Jane's hand in his, leading them up the small incline back to the inn. Mary followed, pausing just a moment to ensure they'd left nothing on the sand.

When she turned forward again, she couldn't help but admire the sight before her. Robert looked over his shoulder to ensure she followed, an easy smile on his face, and a contented sigh left her lips.

Mary had always heard that nothing could rival the view from the Golden Mermaid Inn. Guests could see the blue-green sea stretch for miles on a clear day and the clouds of approaching storms hours beforehand.

Shoals of pilchards migrating round the peninsula were impossible to miss, and even mermaids could be spotted from the edge of the inn's property.

Mary still had never seen a mermaid, and she still did not agree with the guests' opinions. It wasn't the view *from* the inn she preferred, nor was it the view *of* the inn any longer.

Now, it was the image of Robert, a toddler's hand in his, a babe in his other arm, and his eyes looking back at her—eyes filled with a love of which she'd always dreamt. A love that would last forever.

And that was a view that could not be rivalled, indeed.

Deborah M. Hathaway graduated from Utah State University with a BA in English and an emphasis in Creative Writing. As a young girl, she devoured Jane Austen's novels while watching and re-watching every adaptation of Pride & Prejudice she could, entirely captured by all things Regency and romance.

Throughout her childhood, she wrote many short stories, poems, and essays, but it was not until after her marriage that she was finally able to complete her first romance novel, attributing the completion to her courtship with and love of her charming English husband.

Deborah finds her inspiration for her novels in her everyday experiences with her husband and children and during her travels to the United Kingdom, where she draws on the beauty of the country in such places as Ireland, Yorkshire, and her beloved Cornwall.

Visit Deborah's website here: www.deborahmhathaway.com
Instagram: @authordeborahmhathaway

www.ingramcontent.com/pod-product-compliance
Lightning Source LLC
LaVergne TN
LVHW021801060526
838201LV00058B/3199